In the
Warrior's
Bed

In the Warrior's Bed

MARY WINE

BRAVA

Kensington Publishing Corp.

www.kensingtonbooks.com

BRAVA BOOKS are published by

Kensington Publishing Corp.
119 West 40th Street
New York, NY 10018

All Kensington titles, imprints, and distributed lines are available at special quantity discounts for bulk purchases for sales promotion, premiums, fund-raising, educational, or institutional use.

Special book excerpts or customized printings can also be created to fit specific needs. For details, write or phone the office of the Kensington Special Sales Manager: Kensington Publishing Corp., 119 West 40th Street, New York, NY 10018, Attn: Special Sales Department. Phone: 1-800-221-2647.

Brava and the B logo Reg. U.S. Pat. & TM Off.

ISBN-13: 978-0-7582-3465-0
ISBN-10: 0-7582-3465-1

First Kensington Trade Paperback Printing: February 2010

10 9 8 7 6 5 4 3 2 1

Printed in the United States of America

This book is dedicated to the one and only Mama Zini. For years of mentoring
and partnering in crime, my dear friend, Frieda, who can size up any living soul and dress
them to the height of fashion, no matter the year. May you always know how talented you
are and how much you mean to those you touch.
Beware the spoon!!!

Chapter One

"Father writes that the king has given him leave from court."

Bronwyn McQuade flinched. In spite of years of steeling her feelings against her father's disdain, she still dreaded his return. Her sire was a hard man, and that was thinking kindly about him. Erik McQuade was laird and he enjoyed making sure that every man, woman, and child born on his land knew that bettering the clan was the most important duty they were charged with.

As his daughter, she felt the bite of his expectations more than most.

"I hope he has a safe journey home."

Her brother snorted. Keir McQuade failed to mask his personal feelings completely, too. The parchment in his grasp crinkled when his fingers tightened on it. Born third, Keir was often relegated by their sire to the more mundane tasks of running the estate while their older brothers stood at their father's side. Keir didn't seem to mind, though. He had a keen mind and raiding alongside his father wasn't the only thing that captured his attention. Their older brothers, Liam and Sodac, lived for night marauding—a fact that endeared them to their father. Keir shook his head before refolding the letter and storing it inside his writing desk.

"At least Jamie no' sent him home with snow on the road." A shadow darkened her brother's face. "No' that I'd blame our monarch for it."

Bronwyn didn't reply. She held her tongue with the aid of years of practice. Her father had no patience for any spirit in his only daughter. In truth, the man had little stomach for the sight of her at all. A girl child was of no use to Laird McQuade. Quite the opposite, and she'd grown up listening to her father lament the fact that someday he'd be pressed to dower her.

There was little chance of that happening, though.

Bronwyn sighed. She didn't love anyone and still her father's distaste for her chafed. There was no man wearing her father's colors who would dare flirt with her. Liam and Sodac helped ensure that by telling one and all that she was a shrew cursed with a demon temperament.

"Och now, sister, dinna look like that."

Bronwyn fluttered her eyelashes. "Look like what?"

Keir clicked his tongue. Raising a single finger, he pointed at her. "I know ye too well."

"But Father does not, so there is no reason to warn me. He'll see nothing but what he wants to see."

Her brother grunted. The sound reprimanded her by reminding her that she was not the only child their sire valued lowly. Keir was a huge man, his hands twice the size of her own. His lack of zeal for war earned him the cutting edge of his father's tongue. He was not a coward, simply a man who understood the value of finding other solutions that didn't include using a sword.

"Aye, ye have the right of it and still I see the hurt in yer eyes."

A soft smile lifted her lips. "My life is nae so hard as many have. Save yer pity for those that truly suffer."

She didn't want it. Nor need it. Holding her chin steady, Bronwyn pushed the floor pedal of the large loom she was working to switch the threads for the next pass of the shuttle. Rolled up on the finished end of the loom were several measures of the McQuade plaid. The loom itself was a prized possession. Modern and efficient, cloth could be woven as fine as any found in Edinburgh.

By a skilled hand, of course.

Trailing her fingers over the fabric nearest to the working edge, she smiled at how smooth it was. The heather, tan, and green stripes were perfectly repeated over and over throughout the length of fabric where they crossed, squares formed to perfection.

"Ye do fine work, Bronwyn."

Keir's voice was soft but she savored the approval she heard in the tone. Flashing her brother a smile, she pressed down on the opposite foot pedal.

"And ye are a master at managing the estate funds."

One of Keir's eyebrows rose. "I came to warn ye to take a ride afore ye canna anymore."

Her brother bowed before turning in a swirl of pleated McQuade kilt, the back ones falling longer than the front. A sturdy, thick belt was buckled around his waist to hold the wool against his lean frame. His shoulders were wide and thickly muscled, because while Keir might not lust for war, that did not mean he was any less skilled in the art of wielding a sword than any McQuade retainer.

But her brother's true worth was in his thinking. Keir had a keen mind when it came to investing. Their father had married three times in his effort to amass more wealth, but it was

Keir's careful handling of the family's gold that saw the Mc-Quade's fortunes increasing now. Her brother had seen the value in buying the loom she worked. They had wool aplenty from the sheep that grazed on their land. Four more of the large looms sat in the long room built alongside the great hall. Other McQuade women sat working them now, each one of them having earned the right to use the modern machines by spending years working the smaller looms that produced rougher fabric.

Being the laird's daughter did not mean she squandered the daylight hours away. Now that winter was creeping over the land, Bronwyn would work the loom almost every day. When she was not passing the shuttle back and forth between the threads, another woman would be. Not a single machine was allowed to be idle during daylight. In a single year, the looms had paid for themselves and Keir intended to see a profit by next spring.

That was her brother's way of proving his worth to their sire. She was not so confident that her father would see the part she played in turning coin for the family. Her feet and hands moved as her mind turned ideas over and over. She should have learned in twenty-three years to stop lamenting her sire's lack of affection for her. From her earliest memories he had told her often and bluntly that he had no use for a girl child. It was the harsh truth that many men agreed with him. Her mother was the one to pity. Her father's third wife, she had suffered every day until her death for birthing an un-wanted daughter.

But Bronwyn remembered her kindly. For the first seven years of her life there had been loving arms that held her. Soft kisses placed on her head and a mother that had delighted in sharing time with her daughter. Who knew? Perhaps it was the difference between men and women. The kitchens were forever full of new tales of lovers forsaking their lady loves once their bellies were full. Maybe men did not love. At least, it seemed they did not love women, anyway. Her father loved his land and money; that was a fact for certain. But Laird McQuade had never loved a woman as far as she knew.

Still, there was advantage to her struggle to please him. Her cloth was so fine no one could deny that her hands were skilled. Her entire life had been devoted to bettering herself, and the lack of interest from the men around her was more a blessing than burden. Her older siblings might label her ill-tempered but they could not call her slut. Some might say she was foolish to value her chastity when her sire planned to keep her unwed, but she still cradled the knowledge that she was pure close to her heart. Besides, her sire might change his mind and she had her own pride, too. Enough of it to make sure there was a soiled sheet to fly the morning after her vows, anyway. If that was a sin, so be it.

No one had a perfect life. Her heart rate increased as she considered her brother's words. Aye, she would take the opportunity to escape the castle before her father returned to flay her with his sharp words. Bronwyn stood and quit the weaving room. Hurrying up the stone stairs that led to the second story, she ducked into the small chamber that was hers. It was simple and modest, but private. Grabbing a good wool surcoat, she pulled a pair of gloves from a chest and turned back around. She cast a look both ways in the hallway before descending to the lower floor. The servants answered to her father and wouldn't protect her. The staff knew well who paid their wages.

The smell of supper filled the lower floor. Walking along the smooth stone, Bronwyn ducked into the kitchen. Set away from the main buildings of the castle, the kitchens were filled with the aromas of stewing meats and baking bread. Women worked on the long tables, kneading and shaping pastry. Some held long knives that they set to dicing vegetables brought up from the root cellars. Well into November, the vegetables, summer ones that had dried out in the root cellar over the months they had been stored, would need to simmer over the coals for hours to make them soft and palatable. The cook would stew them until it was time to sleep and then leave them in the huge iron kettles hanging in the fireplaces. These would form the base of tomorrow's meals.

She was not mistress of this house and her father had made it plain that she never would be. Most of the maids did not give her a second glance. They were not unkind, simply uninterested in being associated with her. Bronwyn could not blame them. Any new wife her father might bring home would detest her on sight simply because she represented a potential loss of income should she marry.

"Bronwyn . . ."

The voice was low. Turning, she found young Terri holding out a bundle. A kitchen cloth was tied around several lumps. The maid pressed it toward Bronwyn as her eyes cut quick glances about to see who was watching.

"Thank ye."

Tucking the bundle inside the loose surcoat, Bronwyn hurried away before Terri's kindness was noticed. The girl was sweet and one of her few friends. Bronwyn went to great lengths to make sure their liking for each other wasn't known by many. But Terri knew her and understood what wearing a surcoat in the middle of the day meant. The bundle clasped under her arm would have some sort of meal for her. Terri knew the kitchen and how to skim off scraps without being caught by anyone who would scold her.

Getting to the stables wasn't hard. Her dress was the same as any other. Good wool, grown, carded, spun and even woven at Red Stone Castle. There was no finery for her. The only silk gowns were locked away in the chests of her father's deceased wives. She did not have a mare of her own but the stable lads would not deny her a mount. No one was unkind to her. They simply did what they could within the rules the master of the estate set down.

Horses took feed and shelter. It took labor to tend to them properly. To have one simply for her own personal use was something that would turn her sire's face purple with rage if she ever asked him.

But she had never been one for wasting time.

Pulling a saddle from a rail, Bronwyn set it on top of a mare herself. Old Gilly, the stable master, noticed her but did not offer help. A smile graced her lips as she tugged the straps into position, checking to make sure they were not too tight across the belly of the horse. When she glanced toward Gilly, she received a single nod of approval from his silver-haired head.

The praise warmed her heart.

Old Gilly had taught her to ride. As well as every other aspect that went along with horses and their keeping. The man didn't seem to mind that she was a girl. Gilly was far more interested in whether or not she learned how to saddle a horse with a careful hand. Gaining approval from Gilly meant a great deal to her.

But that only fueled her quest to ride. She yearned for freedom, if only for one afternoon. The hills would offer her a feast of things to admire and savor. Fresh air filled with the scent of clover and cut hay. The clouds would offer her the renewing smell of water as they darkened with the promise of snow. She walked her mare out of the stall and swung up into the saddle with a happy smile on her lips. Once her father returned, she dare not take even a moment for herself lest she gain his notice.

But winter was closing its grasp on them now. Small white flurries danced in the air. They melted when they hit the ground but the swirling white flakes made for a magical scene as she rode out of Red Stone. Among the hills she was no longer the unwanted girl child. Here there was hope, the hope that life might hand her any number of things if she was simply willing to dare to dream.

Maybe the whispers of fairies weren't untrue at all. Bronwyn leaned close to the neck of her mare, urging the animal faster. The horse eagerly increased her pace as if she, too, understood that out here they both surrendered to no one.

Even if it was an illusion, Bronwyn enjoyed it all the same.

Sterling Castle, McJames land

"Cullen McJames, stop tossing my baby."

Anne glared at him as he softly patted the back of his new nephew. His brother's bride narrowed her eyes at him.

"Och now, why do ye look at me like that?"

"Because you have earned my suspicions. That is a baby, not a toy."

Cullen placed a kiss on top of Brendan McJames's head. The baby curled his small hand in his hair and yanked a handful of it toward his mouth. Cullen turned his head as the baby began gnawing on a hank of his shoulder-length hair.

"That's it, lad. Show yer uncle how strong ye are." Brodick McJames, earl of Alcaon, offered his brother a sheepish grin. But Cullen couldn't really work up any true temper. His brother was just too much in love and it made for an envious sight. That was the truth.

His English wife drew looks of longing from his brother that should have made him laugh but instead he found jealousy rising at the way the two longed for one another. Brodick lifted his son away, pride shimmering in his eyes. The baby squirmed, making smacking sounds with his lips. Anne sighed.

"He eats constantly." Her words lost a great deal of power when Cullen watched the way she cradled her son. Happiness illuminated her features as she turned to climb the stairs to her chamber. Anne would not let a wet nurse tend to her son. She'd turned her back on the English tradition, choosing to suckle her child. That made Cullen even more envious.

It shouldn't and still he couldn't dismiss the idea of it from his mind. A year ago, he'd have laughed good and hard at the idea of marriage and family. Now he watched his sister-in-law like a hungry man, enjoying the scent of a good meal.

Brodick straddled the bench next to him. With Anne gone, his brother's expression sobered. Cullen knew the look well. Inheriting the title of earl from their father had introduced both men to the weight of responsibility. The English queen was rumored to be on her death bed and Scotland was set to inherit the crown. The times were riddled with ambitious men all fighting to take as much English land as possible.

"I've news from the king." Brodick reached for a mug. "He's released McQuade and his sons from court."

Cullen scowled. Their neighbor would soon be raiding Mc-James land once more.

"That greedy bastard will be nibbling on our winter stocks the moment he returns."

"Aye, that's what I was thinking." Brodick held his tongue for a long moment.

Cullen stared at his brother. "What?"

Brodick merely raised an eyebrow.

"And what is that supposed to mean?"

Brodick shrugged. "Nothing."

Cullen snorted. "Well, it sure looks like something."

Brodick aimed a hard look at him. "Ye seem to be watching my family a lot. It looks like ye enjoy the sight of it, too."

"Is there something wrong with that? Would ye rather I brought a mistress home with me?"

Brodick shook his head. "I was thinking that there was something right about it."

"Get to yer point, brother, before I have to knock it out of ye."

"I was thinking that it is time to petition the king for a possible marriage between ye and Bronwyn McQuade."

Cullen stared at his brother. The teasing tone of their conversation died instantly. His brother might hold the title but the family was strong because they worked together to ensure that the McJames clan remained powerful.

Brodick ran a hand over his chin. "It's a sure thing that McQuade will no deal with either of us on the matter."

"Which leaves Jamie."

Their monarch might decide to grant them the match. If for no other reason than to rid himself of the headache McQuade caused with his endless ranting. Cullen's mother had been betrothed to the man but he'd lost her contract in a game of dice. McQuade still held a grudge against every McJames. His men raided and burned their farms every season. It was also a sure bet that some of his neighbors were thinking the same thing. Everyone knew McQuade had a single daughter and that she was of a good age for marriage. It wouldn't be the first time a laird's son took a wife based on the peace it might ensure over his lands.

"It would be a good match, I agree. I'll think upon it."

His brother nodded, not pressing the issue. Cullen rose and strode through the hall. His brother's faith in him weighed more on his shoulders than any well-rehearsed words might have. Brodick held his tongue because he trusted that Cullen would do right by the McJames people. As the son of the last laird it was his duty to place the welfare of the clan above his own wishes.

Even if that meant marrying a shrew.

Cullen didn't stop at the double doors that led to the inner yard. He kept walking, his legs covering the yard in a quick pace.

A loving family sounded good but not binding himself to a demon hellcat that would likely carve his eyes out if he fell asleep in her bed. Bronwyn McQuade was her father's daughter, born and reared to hate every drop of McJames blood flowing through his veins. Marrying for the good of the clan was one thing, but taking Bronwyn to his bed promised a life of misery. Even his brother had better hopes for his marriage and his bride had been English.

"I'll fetch yer Argyll." One of the younger lads that tended the horses was already running for his horse before Cullen realized he'd gained the stables.

With a grunt he shook his head. He was in a fine state, that was for sure. So deep in thought that he didn't know where his feet were taking him. The lad returned with Argyll, quite possibly the finest horse in Scotland. Reaching for his head, Cullen offered the beast a firm rub between the eyes. The animal snorted, stamping at the ground.

"Aye, I agree with ye."

Argyll liked to run and at the moment Cullen wanted to feel the slap of the Scottish wind against his face as well. Tugging on the saddle, he made sure it was solid before swinging up into it. Argyll shifted, snorting with his excitement. Cullen held the reins in a tight grasp, keeping the stallion still.

"Milord." The stable lad ran forward with a leather bag.

"Aye, lad, that's what I'm waiting for."

Cullen held Argyll steady as the lad tied the bag onto the rear of the saddle. It was the simplest of provisions. Oats, wine, and maybe some bread left from the midday meal. Leaving Sterling without it was a choice designed to see his belly rumbling by sundown. The boy finished his task and backed away from Argyll. Cullen flashed him a grin. He was a young lad but he had courage. McJames courage. Argyll was a powerful animal, one with the strength to kill the lad but he wasna afraid of the stallion.

Shrugging, Cullen felt the weight of his sword. It was strapped to his back, highland style. With a flick of the reins, he gave Argyll his freedom. The animal headed for the main gate, his hooves picking up speed as they neared the opening in the main wall that surrounded Sterling Castle.

Argyll charged forward, leaving the walls behind. The wind was brisk, hinting at winter. But the hills were still green and giving the stallion his head allowed Cullen to release his mental burden for a time. He pulled Argyll to a stop some time later. Looking down over the next valley, Cullen frowned.

He'd been here before. Summoned in the dark of night to defend the farmers below. There were three newly thatched roofs in sight, the reeds a brighter yellow than that of the others. It was a blunt reminder of the McQuade's lust for revenge. The man was nae content with plunder, his retainers always set the flame to the farms they attacked. The feud was near thirty-five years old now.

It seemed too simple to think that one wedding might wipe all that bitterness aside.

Kneeing Argyll forward, Cullen left the valley behind without a care for the sinking sun. He pressed onward and up the next ridge. Pulling up on the reins, he listened carefully. Only the wind whistled but he had to be sure. McQuade retainers would delight in hauling him back to their laird as a prize. Dismounting, he climbed the last few measures of the hill on foot. Staying low, he gazed down onto his enemy's land.

Wedding Bronwyn would only end the feud when her father was dead. Peering down into the valley below, he noted there was nothing but tall grass and heather swaying in the breeze. No one dared farm the land here because it was so often in the path of raids. A river ran through it and twisted among the rocks. It was good land and a testament to just how much the bitterness between the two neighbors cost. McQuade was so busy waging war, he was passing up the opportunity to have his land worked.

No marriage would dissolve that sort of hatred.

Not that the man would ever willingly give his only daughter over to a McJames. A sheepish grin worked over his lips. It was a pure shame that the lass didn't attend court. Wooing her might be fun. Asking the king for her dinna interest him but seducing her sounded like fun.

Of course, Jamie didn't allow hellcats in his court. That likely accounted for the fact that Bronwyn McQuade had never stepped foot in the presence of her king.

His thoughts faded as a rider entered the valley below him. Argyll snorted, shifting as the large horse lifted his nose to smell the air. Patting the thick neck of the animal, Cullen grinned. Gripping the saddle, Cullen swung back on top of Argyll. Getting caught on his feet was certainly no a good idea.

"What do ye smell, my friend? A pretty mare?"

Argyll stamped at the ground, taking a few steps before Cullen pulled him to a halt. He couldn't blame Argyll. No a bit. On top of that mare was a female that his own body approved of. Now, he'd always appreciated a pretty lass but this one was something more. He wasn't sure just what drew his attention so keenly. It wasna her face. She wasn't plain but neither was she a great beauty. He'd bedded a few lasses that were true beauties.

It was the way she rode the mare. Like she was as free as the flakes of snow floating in the air. His grip slacked and Argyll took advantage, moving down the slope toward the mare. The rider hadn't seen them yet. She was too absorbed in her moment of escape. Aye that was it, what drew his attention. She looked like she had no a care in the world and knew what a blessing it was to have nothing weighing down her shoulders.

His own burdens felt lighter just watching her.

A thick braid of hair bounced against her shoulders but her face was framed by strands that had been tugged free by her brisk ride.

It didn't seem to trouble her any. A tinkling of laughter was swept up to his ears by the wind. Argyll nickered, gaining another smell of the mare. The rider pulled up on her reins suddenly. She sat up tall in the saddle, soothing the neck of her mare with a steady hand. But the horse tossed her head and danced in a wide circle.

"There now, girl. What's yer worry?"

Her voice was as enticing as the sight of her. Cullen let Argyll close the distance a few more yards before he pulled up on the bridle. He was on McQuade land now. It was a sure bet that the lass would no be very happy when she noticed him. But he was curious to see what she did when she saw a Mc-James so close. He had no stomach for women who panicked; their screaming drove him near daft.

The mare smelled Argyll. The animal side-stepped and let out a loud snort. She slid off the saddle because she'd been perched on it side fashion but she didn't cower in fear. She grabbed the bridle and pulled the mare around to face her. It was impressive to watch because she was a small thing. The mare could hurt her but she kept sure command of the animal, refusing to allow it to rule her.

"Easy now." Her face rose from where she'd been looking at

her horse. Cullen watched her eyes widen as she stared at him. She shook her head as though she were trying to get the sight of him to vanish.

Argyll grunted, proving that he was all too real.

She was a fool.

Bronwyn felt her heart freeze, because the man was huge. The hilt of his sword reflected the last of the daylight. His stallion was a good two hands taller than her mare. It could run her down with no trouble at all. Worse yet, the man wore the kilt of the McJames clan. With her father and brothers raiding their land, he had no reason to treat her kindly. His body was cut with hard muscles, and where his shirt sleeves were rolled up, she saw the evidence that spoke of his firsthand knowledge and skill with that sword. She scanned the ridge above him quickly, fearing that the McJames had decided to repay her father's raids by doing a few themselves.

But there was no one in the fading light. Her teeth worried her lower lip as she returned her attention to him. She'd never considered that a McJames warrior might enjoy an afternoon ride the same as she.

"Good day to ye, lass." His voice was deep and edged with playfulness. He reached up and tugged on the corner of his knitted bonnet, a half smile curving his lips. His light-colored hair brushing his wide shoulders, a single thin braid ran down along the side of his face to keep it out of his eyes. He wore only a leather doublet over his shirt and the sleeves of the doublet were hanging behind him. There was a majestic quality to him. One that was mesmerizing. Her brother Keir was a very large man and she wasn't used to meeting men who measured up to his size. This one did. He radiated strength from his booted feet to his blond hair. There was nothing small or weak about him. In his presence she felt petite, something she was unaccustomed to. Almost as though she noticed that she was a woman and that her body was fashioned to fit against his male one.

"Good day."

She had no idea why she spoke to him. It was an impulse. A shiver raced down her back. Her eyes widened, heat stinging her cheeks, her mouth suddenly dry. A shudder shook her gently, surprising her. Beneath her doublet, her nipples tingled, the sensation unnerving.

His gaze touched on her face, witnessing the scarlet stain creeping across it. A flicker of heat entered his eyes. It was bold but something inside her enjoyed knowing that she sparked such a look in him.

"It's a fine day for riding."

His words were innocent of double meaning, but Bronwyn drew in a sharp breath because her mind imagined a far different sort of riding. Her own thoughts shocked her deeply. She'd never been so aware of just what a man might do with a woman when they were alone, and now was the poorest time for her body to be reacting to such things. It felt as though he could read her mind. At least the roguish smile he flashed her hinted that he could. His lips settled back into a firm line. She had to jerk her eyes away from them but that left her staring into his blue eyes. Hunger flickered there and her body approved. Her nipples drew tight, hitting her boned stays.

"Ye shouldna look at me like that, lass." He sounded like he was warning himself more than her, but her blush burned hotter because he was very correct.

"Nor should ye look at me as ye are."

A grin split his lips, flashing a hint of his teeth. "Ye have that right. But what am I to do when ye stand there so tempting? I'm merely a man."

And for some reason she felt more like a woman than she

ever had. Something hot and thick flowed through her veins. There was no thinking about anything. Her body was alive with sensations, touching off longings she'd thought deeply buried beneath the harsh reality of her father's loathing to see her wed.

"A man who is far from his home." Her gaze touched on his kilt for a moment, the blue, yellow, and orange of the Mc-James clan holding her attention. "I'm a McQuade."

"I figured that already, but its nae my clan that keeps us quarreling."

He let his horse close the distance again. The mare didn't move now, she stood quivering as the large stallion made a circle around her. The same flood of excitement swept through Bronwyn, keeping her mesmerized by the man moving around her. Bronwyn shook her head, trying to regain her wits.

"But I'm thinking that we just might be able to get along quite nicely." His eyes flickered with promise. "Ye and I."

"Ye should go. Ye're correct that it is my clansmen that seek trouble with the McJames. Ye shouldna give them a reason to begin a fight."

"And ye would nae see that happen? I'm pleasantly surprised."

His stallion was still moving in a circle around her. Bronwyn had to twist her neck to keep him in sight. Every time he went behind her, her body tightened, every muscle drawing taut with anticipation. Such a response defied everything that she knew.

"Surprised that I've no desire to see blood spilt? Being a Mc-James does not mean I am cruel at heart. What is yer name?" he asked.

Fear shot through her, ending her fascination with him. Being the laird's daughter meant she was a prize worth taking. Riding out alone so far had been a mistake she just might pay for with her body. Few would believe her if she told them her father wouldn't pay any ransom for her. Beyond money, there were men who would consider taking her virtue a fine way to strike back at her clan.

"I'll no tell ye that. McQuade is enough for ye to know."

"I disagree with ye. 'Tis much too formal only knowing your clan name. I want to know what ye were baptized."

"Yet ye'll have to be content for I shall nae tell ye my Christian name." He frowned but Bronwyn forced herself to be firm. This flirtation was dangerous. Her heart was racing but with more than fear. "If ye get caught on McQuade land, I'll no be able to help ye."

"Would that make ye sad, lass?"

"No." He was toying with her. "But it would ruin supper, what with all the gloating from the men that drove ye back onto McJames land. There would be talk of nothing else."

One golden eyebrow rose as the horse moved closer to her. He swung a leg over the saddle and jumped to the ground. Her belly quivered in the oddest fashion. But she had been correct about one thing—this man was huge.

"Are ye sure, lass? I might be willing to press me luck if I thought ye'd feel something for me."

"That's foolishness. Get on with ye. I willna tell ye my name. Ye're a stranger; I dinna feel anything beyond Christian good will toward ye."

"Is that so?"

"It is."

He flashed another grin at her, but this one was far more calculating and full of intent. "Afraid I might sneak into yer home and steal ye if I know whose daughter ye are?"

He came closer but kept a firm hand on the reins of his mount. Authority shone from his face now, clear, determined, and undeniable. This man was accustomed to leading. It was part of the fibers that made up his being. He would have the nerve to steal her if that was what he decided upon. There was plenty enough arrogance in him, for certain. She felt it in the pit of her belly. What made her eyelashes flutter to conceal her emotions was the excitement such knowledge unleashed in her.

"Enough teasing," she said. "Neither of us are children."

"Aye, I noticed that already."

Her face brightened once more. His eyes swept her and his expression tightened. Maybe she had never seen a man looking at her like that afore but her body seemed to understand exactly what the flicker of hunger meant. She stared at it, mesmerized.

"Tell me yer name, lass."

His voice was deep and quiet now. But there was no missing the determination edging it. She shook her head, not trusting her voice. It might betray the way her body shivered. She couldn't allow him to hear how much he affected her. This man was a hunter.

"I will not. Jesting about stealing a woman may be all well and good when ye're sipping yer whiskey, but it doesna make for good unions. We know nothing about each other."

"Ah . . . but if I tossed ye across my saddle, that would change. Once I took ye back to my home, we'd have plenty of time to learn about one another."

Shock raced through her but what alarmed her was the ripple of excitement that went hand in hand with that shock. He reached out, the back of his hand stroking down the surface of one cheek.

"Ye are blushing for me."

She jerked away from his touch, ashamed by how much she enjoyed it. Shamed by how much she wanted more than a mere stroke from his fingers. Shamed by how much of a woman he made her feel.

" 'Tis nothing."

He moved toward her again, closing the distance that she'd placed between them. "I disagree, lass. 'Tis something that I've a mind to understand better."

His persistence irritated her. "Are ye telling me that ye would ruin me for the sake of a moment's impulse? Stolen women are considered soiled when they return home. Is yer need to boast that important to ye?"

"What makes ye think I would return ye?" There was a hint of injured pride in his tone. "Maybe it's marriage I have on my mind."

She laughed at him. His lips twitched up and she knew that she'd caught him like a naughty boy pulling her braids.

"As if any man should marry for attraction alone. Ye'd be a fool and yer family would be sure to tell ye that the moment ye took a bride that came with nothing but lust."

"Ah, maybe, but still the idea is teasing me with possibilities . . ."

The stallion he held the reins to suddenly reared up, pawing at the air. Her mare jumped, dancing in a wide circle once more. As her horse turned, she stared at the line of her father's retainers cresting the ridge. Shouts drifted on the wind as they sighted her and her company. She lifted a foot to the stirrup and pushed hard but her body flew upward with the help of a solid hand on her bottom. He gripped one cheek, squeezing it boldly.

"Ye've got the nerve!"

He flashed her a grin that wasn't repentant one bit.

"Something for ye to remember me by since I dinna get the chance to steal a kiss from ye."

"I wouldna have let ye."

One golden eyebrow rose mockingly. "That's why I was planning on stealing it, lass."

Her mare was still agitated and dancing in a circle. Gripping the reins, she guided her horse back around to find all hints of playfulness gone from the McJames retainer's face. He frowned, his face taking on a fierce expression while he watched the McQuade clansmen begin racing down toward her. He gained his saddle in a motion that was fluid and strong. His thighs gripped the huge beast with confidence and the hilt of his sword rose above his right shoulder. The man was a warrior, no doubt about it.

A McJames one and that was a pity.

"It seems I'll have to wait to learn who ye are." But his expression changed when he looked at her once again. "Now that's something I'm going to regret."

Her own thoughts bothered her too much. "Go on with ye, else I'll think ye a fool."

"Ah, but ye will think of me and that is something I'll be treasuring, lass."

He reached for the corner of his bonnet once more. "Until we met again, sweet McQuade."

His gaze lingered on her mouth for a long moment before he turned his mount toward McJames land. He dug his knees into the large animal and it bore him up the hill. Stallion and rider looked as strong as a legend, the edges of his kilt bouncing with the motion of riding.

Mesmerizing . . .

He turned and shot her one last glance at the top of the ridge. She thought she saw him smile but really wasn't sure at such a distance. Her father's men swarmed around her, their rough language shattering the moment and allowing reality to rush over her.

"Are ye daft? Keeping company with a McJames?"

Her brother Liam spat before pointing a finger at her. "And Cullen McJames, no less."

Cullen McJames?

"It canna be . . ." Her words trailed off as she looked at the ridge. Another shiver shook her. This time it left goose bumps along her arms and legs. The McJames's laird's brother was a bold one and that was for sure. Keeping her name from him had been her saving grace.

"I never thought ye'd betray yer own clan."

Bronwyn snapped out of her own thoughts to stare at her brother. "I dinna betray anyone. I don't know the man. Dinna even know his name until ye spoke it. How could I know what the man looks like?"

"It dinna look that way to me."

Liam spat again as did several of the men riding with him. They glared at her, condemning her. Her pride bristled but there was never any reasoning with Liam and his men. They would follow him, whatever he said or did because he was the firstborn son and destined to become laird someday.

She was just an unwanted girl. But that fact wasn't enough to seal her lips today. Maybe it was the pure magnificence of the man she'd just met or the simple courtesy he'd shown her by tugging on the edge of his bonnet. She didn't know or care. Liam could choke on his suspicions.

"I was no meeting him."

Liam reached across the space between them, his hand connecting with her jaw in a hard blow.

"Save yer lies. I know what I saw with my own eyes."

He reached down and yanked the reins out of her grip. Liam turned and pulled her mare along with his horse toward the waiting line of her father's men. Their looks were every bit as harsh as the sting of Liam's hand. But the only thing she felt was her temper rising. Upon reflection, she noticed just how much stronger Cullen McJames had looked, and it had nothing to do with the width of the man's shoulders. It was in his smile and the way he didn't cast ugly accusations with his eyes.

Aye, it was the truth that she found him handsome. By far the most fetching man she'd ever laid eyes upon.

"Slut."

Her father didn't strike her. He tossed a goblet full of ale across her body. The hall of Red Stone was silent; no one even took a step as the laird condemned his daughter. No one would, either. Bronwyn gathered her strength because the laird ruled absolutely on McQuade land.

"This is the thanks I receive for sheltering ye since yer mother presented me with a daughter."

"I was not meeting him."

Her father pointed at her from his seat on the raised dais at one end of the room. She stood in front of him like a criminal facing her judge.

"Ye mean to try and tell me that Cullen McJames just happened to be riding down *onto my land* and it had never happened before?" There were a few snorts from Liam and Sodac. "That ye dinna have an arrangement, thinking that I was away at court."

"I do not lie. There is no arrangement between us."

Her father laughed. But it was not a kind sound. It was harsh and full of bitterness. "Then explain why his hand was on yer arse?" Liam grunted, helping to paint her guilty. Erik McQuade looked at her as though she were vermin. "How long have ye been letting him use ye, slut?"

"Never! I did not lay with him."

Bronwyn bristled under the harsh scrutiny being aimed at her. Even knowing her sire's lack of fondness for her, she would not have expected him to cast such filth upon her name. To soil herself was to bring shame on the entire clan. Besides, she knew full well how lowly he treated his own consorts. She had no desire to fall to such a state.

"Bronwyn does not lie, Father. I have never heard her speak falsely."

Erik McQuade glared at his youngest son. "How dare ye raise yer voice against mine."

Keir didn't flinch. He strode forward, uncaring of the hard looks aimed at him from the assembled retainers. He stopped in front of his father, giving the laird the briefest of nods in respect.

"I state a fact, Father. I have never heard Bronwyn lie. If she says she did not have a meeting with the younger McJames, I believe her. It is also a fact that I have never seen Bronwyn conducting herself like a lightskirt."

Her father erupted. He surged to his feet, roaring with outrage. He flung the empty goblet at her brother. It hit him square in the chest but Keir brushed it aside like a bothersome insect. He did not cower in the face of his sire's rage but stood straight and tall while their father turned purple.

"Why is fate set to curse me so?" McQuade shook his fist towards the heavens. "It saddles me with a useless daughter and a son who has the courage of Achilles but the temperament of a wife."

The laird stood up and swept the room. "We're returning to court." He pointed at Bronwyn. "Yer going with me. Until sunrise, someone get this slut out of my sight."

There was a scuff of boots against the stone floor as several retainers moved toward her. Keir turned in a tightly controlled motion, his kilt flaring out.

"No man touches her, save me." He turned back toward his father. "I disagree with ye."

Her father looked as though Keir had struck him. He sat back against the padded chair, shock whitening his face. His jaw worked but no words made it past his lips. Keir turned and hooked her upper arm in one hand. It was a kind grip that she willingly allowed to sweep her out of the hall.

"This will become worse before it is over, sister."

"I know."

And there was nothing to do about it. She felt like a leaf that had landed in a spring. The current was sweeping her along without any care for the rocks. There was only the single comfort of Keir willing to champion her. But their father would never forgive such a slight.

"Ye should not have done that, Keir."

Her brother grunted. "Honor is nae a thing that may be ignored when it is difficult to do what is right." Keir stopped and stared at her. His eyes were dark as night, inherited from his mother. She felt them looking straight into her soul, if such a thing were possible, but she did not look away.

Keir nodded. "Our father is blinded by hate."

Heavy distaste coated his words. Keir began walking and Bronwyn followed. She suddenly felt like a stranger in spite of knowing that she had grown up at Red Stone.

"Which is why ye should have remained silent."

"No." Keir didn't raise his voice but that dinna lessen the impact. His tone was solid steel.

"There's no need for ye to join me in father's disdain."

Keir shook his head. "I won't be his hound like Liam and Sodac. If he wants to dislike me for refusing to lick his boots, so be it. He'll never be able to say that I am not my own man."

Bronwyn felt a smile lifting the corners of her lips. She could not prevent it even with such dark things happening around them. But she winced when pain stabbed through her lips. Keir noticed and frowned as he looked at the mark their father had left on her face.

"I believe court is a good place for ye." Keir sounded pensive. His face was grave but he nodded. "Aye, I believe it is far past time that ye escaped this castle."

"But at what cost? I'll no help father accuse the McJames of wrongdoing."

Keir chuckled. "Ye know our sire too well, Bronwyn. I believe that is exactly what he plans to do by dragging ye to court."

Keir stopped talking. Bronwyn cast a suspicious look at her brother but he refused to comment further. A chill rippled over her skin. She couldn't shake the feeling of foreboding even when she stood in front of the small fire burning in her chamber. A sense of dread clung to her thoughts as she removed her surcoat. The wind whistled between the boards that made up the shutter for the windows. Once her boots were unlaced, she felt the chill of it on her toes. Her chamber had no floor coverings to help keep her feet warm. But one of the kitchen lasses had brought two buckets of water up. They sat near the fire, making her smile.

At least she would not have to smell of dried ale on the marrow.

Bronwyn undressed as close to the fire as possible to keep warm. Her doublet and wool skirt dropped to puddle around her ankles once she'd unhooked them. Stepping out of them, she stretched. Her chemise floated around her calves as she hurried to rinse her dress out. Once she finished, she hung it over a rough chair near the fire to dry. Working the lace free from her stays, she listened to the wind shake the shutter once more.

It was eerie. Icy fingers stroked across her heart as she crawled into bed with her bundle of kitchen scraps. She was grateful for the impulse that had seen her to the kitchens before her ride because it was a sure thing that no one would bring her supper.

It might have been enjoyable to share the meal with Cullen McJames . . .

Bronwyn frowned, but the image of her father's enemy rose in her memory until it was as if the man stood in her chamber. She recalled him clearly. She'd never met a man who drew her attention so keenly. For the moment, she didn't argue with her mind's impulse to replay their meeting. Alone with her thoughts, she might as well enjoy them.

Who knew what tomorrow would offer?

He was a fool.

Cullen actually amused himself with his own thoughts as he returned to the crest of the hill the next day. Late in the afternoon, he kneed Argyll up to the top of it so that he might peer down into the valley that belonged to the McQuades.

It was empty.

He should have expected such. And still he had ridden out once again, when there were plenty of other tasks needing his attention.

He wanted to see her again.

Cullen scoffed at himself. He dinna even know who she was. Only that she was a McQuade and her laird had likely chastised her greatly for being anywhere near him.

The sweetness of her face had kept him company most of the night. Something that he'd no been happy about. Not when the lass was so far beyond his reach.

Kneeing Argyll and pulling the reins to guide the stallion back toward Sterling, Cullen turned his back on the valley. He lacked the patience to chase his sweet-faced lass because what he really desired was to be able to touch her. A pulse of need laced his blood as he rode toward home. It was bitter because there was no way to feed it. She was the only lass that held his interest and she was a McQuade.

Fate was a siren at times. Tempting and taunting mortal man with the things he could not have. But the one thing that fate had not counted on was the will of a McJames. He had never been a man to settle for being told that he could not have what he wanted.

He'd learn her name and that was a promise.

Chapter Two

A fist pounded on her door at dawn. Bronwyn rubbed her eyes but sat up when the door opened. Her brother, Sodac, strode into the room without a shred of courtesy. She held the covers tight against her body.

"Father says to tell ye to dress and get to the stables. We're to leave as soon as the horses are ready."

He raked her with a look that was full of loathing.

"Keir will be staying here, by Father's command. Best ye think long and hard about what will happen to him if ye speak out against yer laird's words. A third son needs the good will of his family in this life."

She gasped and her brother smiled at her distress.

"I don't expect a woman to understand the way the world works. So choose yer words carefully, or better still keep yer mouth shut, Bronwyn. The McJames owe us and we will get our due any way we can."

Sodac left and Bronwyn shivered. She wasn't cold; no, she was horrified at the pure malevolence she'd just witnessed. Cullen's face surfaced from her dreams and seemed so vastly different from her brother's. There had not been malice in his eyes, only enjoyment of the moment.

Her stomach twisted as she crawled from the bed. Aye, there was a great difference between Cullen and Sodac. But Keir did need the goodwill of his family. With his sense of honor, her brother would hold his head high as he was cast aside. That left only her to protect him. She would not lie but there was nothing wrong with remaining silent. Her father had been at court for eight months, banished to the outer receiving area, not even allowed into the royal hall because he'd angered the king with his accusations against the McJames. Maybe she'd be fortunate and James Stuart would refuse to see her father.

She would hope for the best, anyway. There was no point in dwelling on the darker things that her father might shackle onto her. Red Stone promised to be a colder place now that he'd called her a slut openly. Even if no one believed that she was a lightskirt, they could not miss the lack of affection from her sire. The fact remained that he was laird and Liam set to follow him by tradition. It was even supported by the scriptures.

Nay, she would not think about the life that was awaiting her after she went to court. Nor would she banish the memory of her meeting with Cullen McJames from her thoughts. It was for certain that she would not be riding again soon, if at all. She would enjoy what she could. Besides, she had felt more in those moments than she had in a year. Cullen had stirred something in her that she had never felt before. There had been so much excitement jumping about inside her that just thinking about it made her heart pump faster.

Perhaps that was wickedness. But it felt too good to cast aside in favor of a father that called her slut.

The road to court was long, but it passed quickly as she tumbled her thoughts over and over in her mind. The cold glances of her father's retainers didn't even make her shudder. She was far too absorbed with thinking of a way to satisfy her father without damning Cullen McJames.

To be sure, she would never ride in that valley again.

A twinge of pain startled her, stunning her as it ripped at her heart. Surely it was impossible to lament never seeing the man again. She had to prevent another meeting because her father would use any contact to damn the younger brother of the McJames family. Besides, Cullen might set to strike at her father through her once he knew whom he'd met. He was a warrior as devoted to his clan as her brothers were to her father.

And still she felt it. A small rent in the fabric of her heart. It softly throbbed as she pictured his face once again.

Well, her memories would have to be enough. His family had even more reason to dislike her than her father had to hate him. Her father raided the McJames. Oh yes, she knew it. Cullen McJames would never believe that her father detested her almost as much as he hated the McJames.

A soft chuckle made it past her frozen lips. It truly was a comedy of errors that she found the man so fetching. Once Cullen McJames knew her name, he would curse her unto hell.

She should have let him steal that kiss.

The court of Scotland was filled with men who waited. Bronwyn looked at their pensive faces as she was led through the mass of richly attired men toward the main entrance to the great hall where the king sat. Armed guards kept the velvet-clad hordes from entering the hall without a summons from their monarch. Every set of eyes seemed to be judging her, calculating what she might do to further their cause. To be king suddenly looked like a burden too heavy for any mere man. The guards with their weapons and the press of people all seeking an audience felt thick enough to smother.

Her wool dress was plain. More than one set of female eyes looked surprised as they raked over her common dress. The women waiting to be admitted into the hall wore lavish gowns made of velvet and silk. There was the twinkle of gold and silver sewn right onto the expensive garments. Each gown was supported with undergarments that made the skirts wider and grander than her own dress. The women held their arms carefully arched, without resting their hands on the dresses. There were pearls and jewels. Large wigs and powder and paint on their faces.

Their stays were so long, they looked as though they didn't have any hips. The abundance of fabric reminded her of her father's bed with its rich tapestry curtains. Her father held up a parchment, and to her surprise, the guards allowed them to pass into the receiving hall. A ripple of whispers went through those waiting, but Bronwyn lost interest in them as a new sea of faces cast inquiring glances toward them.

At the end of the hall the king sat. Musicians played in the eves surrounding the hall. Some of his courtiers were dancing but she did not recognize the steps. Still, music was a delight to hear. At Red Stone it was rare because her father refused to offer coin for entertainment. In the spring there would be market fairs, and with the merchants came music. Even if her father's reasons for bringing her to court were distasteful, Bronwyn couldn't keep herself from enjoying the music.

The king suddenly stiffened.

"McQuade." His voice rose in a tone that silenced everyone who heard it. Her father seemed to be the only one who didn't hear the warning. He marched forward and bowed to his king.

James Stuart didn't look impressed.

"I gave ye leave to return home."

Her father yanked her forward. Bronwyn stumbled because she wasn't expecting her sire to touch her; he went for years without placing a finger on her.

"Aye, I returned home to discover that Cullen McJames has been using my daughter as his whore."

There was an instant uproar in the hall. The air felt stuck in her lungs. Bronwyn watched the sea of faces peering at her, their eyes narrowing, dark condemning sneers aimed at her over lace fans. Several of the men smiled at her, invitation clearly written on their faces. Sweat popped out on her forehead while her heart began to race. The king scowled at her.

"My private chambers, McQuade. Now."

The king was quite clearly displeased. He quit the room on fast steps, his guards keeping pace. Conversation rose in the hall as necks angled and stretched to get a clear look at her.

"Now ye'll understand the penalties for turning traitor on me, Daughter."

Her father hooked her arm and pulled her toward the back of the hall behind the throne. Heavy, ornately carved doors were held open by the royal guard. The moment they passed over the threshold, the doors were pushed shut behind them with a hard sound that made her flinch. The king was pacing, his servants meekly standing well behind him.

"Ye had better have a good explanation for that outburst, man. I've had my limit with yer schemes to paint the McJames clan black."

"I rode home and found Cullen McJames on my land."

The king stopped. He turned to face Erik McQuade. "Is that so?"

"It's a fact, he was meeting my daughter. The thieving mongrel. Both my sons witnessed it the very moment we set foot back onto our land."

The king looked at her, but her father pushed her behind him. "I brought her here so that ye might see the look of guilt on her face. I would never allow her to spew her filthy lies in yer presence."

"I'll be the judge of that." The king sat down in his ornate chair but he did not extend permission for his company to sit

in the chairs behind them. He considered each of her brothers, Liam and Sodac. They puffed up their chests, hunger for
vengeance brightening their eyes. They were the image of their
father. James looked at her last, his eyes considering her.

"What say you, Bronwyn McQuade?"

"I told ye, she's a lying whore . . ."

"And I told ye, Laird McQuade, that ye shall no tell me what
to do, man." James glared at her father. "I'm getting very tired
of hearing yer dislike for yer neighbors. More importantly, I
have had enough of listening to yer neighbors complain about
yer thieving. I've three sound petitions for ye to be clamped
into chains like a common thief, and it's a fact that ye're doing
nothing to sway my opinion in yer favor."

"Cullen McJames was with me daughter! He comes before
ye like the very image of a martyred saint but he's a blackguard
who has fouled me daughter and left her disgraced." Her father was shouting now and the guards behind the chair took
one large step forward. Her sire instantly bowed his head in
deference.

"Is that so, Bronwyn?"

She could not refuse to answer. Not to the king of Scotland.
But Keir's position weighed on her mind. She remained silent,
torn as to what words to use. How to state the truth and not
anger her sire, but it seemed impossible.

"Ye see? She's choking on her shame."

"I told ye that I've heard enough from ye." The king gestured
with his hand. "Remove him and his sons. The daughter stays."

"She's my child!"

"And my subject. I'll hear what she has to say, even if I must
toss ye out so that the girl can speak. The girl must have learned
manners from someone other than ye because she at least
knows better than to rage in my presence."

The king's voice cut through her father's blustering like a

knife. The guards behind him moved around the small dais with their swords drawn. The sharp tips pointed toward her father and brothers. All three glared at her, blaming her for the king's displeasure.

"Your Majesty, I pray ye allow my family to remain."

The guards froze, awaiting their monarch's response.

"No."

There was no more hesitation from the royal guard. Her family was sent back through the double doors without another word. When they closed again, the sound felt like a gunshot going through her.

"Now, answer my question. What is Cullen McJames to you?"

"A stranger."

The king sat back down. He fixed her with a stern look. "Yer father claims he caught ye with him."

"I was riding and he was at the top of the ridge. We did speak, that is all. I did not even know his name until my father told me."

"But it was on McQuade land?"

"The border. We were both on the edges of our land."

The king sighed, clearly frustrated. "How many men were with him?"

"None."

James Stuart snorted, a chuckle rising from his chest. A gleam flickered in his eye and he raked her from head to toe. "Did Cullen know who ye were?"

Heat spread across her face. "I refused to tell him. He was wearing the McJames plaid."

The king scoffed. "Cullen always wears his family colors. The man is pure Scot and proud of his family name. He's a brazen one, too, riding onto yer land with no one to guard his back."

He was . . .

The thought rose instantly from her memory of that meeting. The way Cullen had closed the distance between them, brash and unafraid of the possibility of being discovered. But the king was watching her intently. Bronwyn lowered her eyelashes to mask the excitement in her eyes.

"Did he touch ye?"

"Nay." She spoke too sharply for the presence of a king, but her pride was blistered from her father's words.

The king's eyes narrowed. "Are ye a maiden?"

Her eyes widened. The man might be her king but she had not expected such an intimate question from him. Her temper flared up because never once had she behaved in a way to bring suspicion onto herself.

"Indeed I am."

A slow smile covered the king's face. But it did not soothe her. Quite the opposite. Just as Cullen's grin had promised her something else, the king's pleasant look made her stomach tighten with anticipation.

"Has yer father betrothed ye to anyone?"

The question startled her. It shouldn't have, but she looked at the floor for a moment.

"Papa . . . I want a night blessing." A curtain behind the dais moved and a little girl emerged. Dressed in a fine linen chemise and nightcap that were worked with masterful blackwork embroidery, the wee girl was only waist high. Her cheeks still chubby and her eyes large in her face. The cuffs and collar of the chemise were edged in bobbin lace. Bronwyn stared at the hours of work employed to decorate a garment that was only for sleeping. The fabric itself was finer than any Bronwyn had ever seen.

Fit for a princess.

"Elizabeth, my rose, where is your nurse?"

The king transformed into a loving parent before her eyes. He scooped up the wee girl and she clasped her arms around his neck.

"Please, Papa. All good children get a blessing from their father at night. They told me so in my studies."

"Yer're a good wee lass to listen to yer tutors."

Bronwyn watched the way the king pressed a kiss on the top of the child's head. Bronwyn couldn't help staring. Never once had her own father kissed her so lovingly. The king noticed her watching and covered his emotions once again.

"This is my daughter, Elizabeth. Who should be abed." He patted her bottom before turning to place the little girl on her feet. One of the guards held out a hand for the child and Elizabeth took it easily. Clearly the little girl was not an uncommon visitor in the king's private receiving chamber.

"I see from yer face that yer own father has never been so kind to ye."

The king sat back down, looking pensive. Bronwyn held her tongue. James waved his hand.

"There is no point in denying it. I see the way ye stare at my daughter, as though ye've never considered that a father might show affection."

It was a hard truth and one that near choked her. "My father loves his sons very much, sire." It was no an uncommon thing. Henry the Eighth of England had gone through six wives in his quest for sons.

The king snorted. "How old are ye now?"

"Twenty-three."

The king shook his head. "No one seemed to know yer age exactly. Yer father has done a good job of hiding ye." James Stuart looked at the guards behind her.

"Bring her family back. Bronwyn, ye may wait in the outer hall. I've a few things to say to yer father."

She lowered herself and gratefully quit the room. If she wasn't near the king, she couldn't say things that would upset the harmony of Red Stone for Keir. It was the honest truth that she never wanted to look at another mare, much less ride one.

But that stung because it was the only escape she had. Despair gripped her and she was out of reasons to avoid tumbling into its grasp. The guards opened the doors for her and summoned her father back into the presence of the king. She breathed a sigh of relief when she heard those same doors seal behind her. But the feeling was short-lived. Staring at her was an ocean of eyes. The great hall was much quieter than it had been when they entered. Now women whispered behind their fans while they peered at her like something foul. A few smirks decorated the lips of the men, and more than one was even bold enough to wink at her.

She kept her chin level with the aid of years of practice. But she cringed when she heard one lady whisper . . .

"Soiled dove . . ."

"Ye're a hard man, McQuade."

James Stuart sat on his throne, making his position clear. For once McQuade didn't shout out a denial. In fact, the man was too quiet. The laird had never been meek and it made the king suspicious.

"I need to think. Ye'll stay at court until I give ye leave."

"It's winter."

The king snorted. "Indeed. I've eyes that work, man. Ye are the one who decided to travel. I sent ye home only to have ye on my doorstep once more. So ye may stay, since it appears that is what ye want."

James waved a hand. "Go. Ye have my permission to enter the great hall if ye bring yer daughter. If ye do not, ye'll stand in the outer reception room. Mark my words, man, ye had better be there when I summon ye."

McQuade opened his mouth but shut it when the royal guard pulled their swords partially free from their scabbards. He bowed low and quit the room. The sight of his daughter staring at the faces of James's Court quickened his step. Setting a brisk pace, he strode down the center of the crowed hall. Many that they passed tugged on their hats, while the women curtsied in respect for his position. Aye, he was the laird of a large clan. A man to be feared and respected. Truly, he didn't care how that respect came to him, only that it was presented in a timely manner.

He was the McQuade.

Her father's town home was closed up for the winter like so many of the noble houses. The servants looked shocked to see their laird returning so soon. They quickly removed cloths from the furniture that had been draped over the upholstery to keep it free of dust. Lamps were brought in to light the entry hall while a few maids hastily tucked their linen caps onto their heads.

"Take yerself out of my sight, Daughter."

Bronwyn had never been so happy to obey her father. He gestured to a younger maid. "Put her in the small room."

"Um . . . yes, my laird." The girl dropped an unbalanced curtsy. She looked confused by her instructions but didn't waste any time picking up a candle and leading the way towards the foot of the stairs.

Bronwyn followed the maid to the second floor. There was one more above it but the maid led her into a small room at the back of the hallway. The girl snuck several looks at her from beneath lowered eyelashes, because she had never set foot in the house, but all knew that her father had a daughter. In most noble families, she would have been placed at court to be dangled in front of powerful nobles. All in the hope that she would marry into a family with connections. Instead of that, her father had labeled her a lightskirt in the middle of the royal court of Scotland and now sent her to the *small* room.

Aye, she could see how that might confuse the staff. She didn't know what to think of it herself.

The chamber was very small and didn't even have a fireplace. One small window had a shutter that slid open and closed. The maid used the candle in her hand to light the wick of a lamp sitting on the single table in the room. With a silent nod the girl left.

The bed was rolled into a tight bundle to keep it clean. A chest sat under the window. Lifting the lid, Bronwyn found the bedding. Making the bed gave her hands something to do while her mind was still stunned.

Soiled . . .

Never had she believed that a single word might actually hurt. She'd heard it whispered over and over until it felt like it was being chanted at a deafening volume.

She was not soiled . . .

She ached to scream that truth from the rooftops, but who would believe her? Who, indeed, when her own father had stood in the great hall and called her slut?

Tears burned her eyes but she wiped them away with an angry hand. Her sire was not worthy of her heartache. She refused to grant him her tears. Finished dressing the bed, she turned to removing her clothing. The table was bare save for the lamp, all of the other things locked away when the laird left the house for the winter.

At least there was a door. Some homes did not have hallways yet. It was a newer fashion that allowed guests to get to their chambers without passing through the ones in front of it.

When she was stripped down to her chemise, she snuffed the candle. At least the room was so small that she dinna need to worry about finding the bed. With no fire it was cold. Her feet felt like ice on the wooden floor. Turning back around, she felt for her skirt and found it. Tossing the cartridge pleated wool garment over the top of the bed, she crawled beneath the blankets. Her skirt might help keep the chill away from her skin but there was no way to stop the ice that formed over her heart.

Soiled, she was not, but it was the truth that she wished she were so that her father might feel the same shame he'd heaped on her.

Erik McQuade eyed his sons.

"Ye think me too harsh."

Liam didn't look at him but Sodac did. Indecision flickered in his eyes.

"Land is the only thing that truly makes a man wealthy. Never allow it to slip out of yer grasp. Always marry for it. Money can be generated from yer tenants." He paused for a moment, making sure they were not overheard by any nosy servants. "Listen, my sons, the inheritance that ye shall have is better than the one I got from my own father. I've worked too hard to see any land leave the McQuade name. She is one woman, made to service the needs of men. The fact that she is my daughter doesna change that."

His sons nodded their agreement. Liam spoke quietly. "But was it necessary to blacken her name publicly?"

"Aye, it was. Now Jamie will no press me to see Bronwyn wed. The land that is her dowry was legally bound to her mother and any female offspring she had by royal power. It cannot be broken. Bronwyn must never marry or we lose that land. 'Tis no different than what I expect from each of ye. Strength and endurance. I've had too many offers for her this year."

McQuade snorted. "But she's a female and I wouldn't expect her to have the endurance to remain in her maiden's bed without help from me. Women are weak creatures. They will seek a lover in the dead of night when they're ripe for breeding. That's why I've made it plain that no man wearing McQuade colors is to even look at my daughter. If she births a daughter, that land will pass to the whelp, bastard or not."

His sons remained silent, but their faces told him they were no longer feeling the pinch of guilt. He had long ago killed any kind emotions stirred up by his daughter. He'd married her mother for the land she brought with her noble name only to discover that it was bound to her female descendants after her death. He'd consulted some of the best legal minds in the country and they all agreed that the will could not be broken. Even though it was rare, females descended from royal blood sometimes came with inheritances that were bound to their female offspring.

So Bronwyn could never marry. If she remained unwed, the land would become McQuade property. Calling her slut in the open court would see to the end of most of the offers for her hand.

"When I'm gone, it will fall to the pair of ye to see that she does not run off to wed."

Label it what ye would, McQuade land was increasing under his leadership. He'd married three times to ensure that. What was besmirching the reputation of one woman when one considered the gain to be had for the entire clan?

"Aye, father."

McQuade nodded approval toward his sons.

'Twas a done thing. He was laird and building the clan's holding was his duty. Someday the McQuade would be even more powerful than the stinking McJames. Bronwyn was simply one more link in the chain to achieving that goal.

Bronwyn kicked at the bedding. Cullen was riding toward her. She saw it clearly in her mind as she slept. He was so fetching, it couldn't be real. Her eyes were drawn to his face, hypnotized by the look of hunger in his eyes.

Heat brushed across her belly. It spread up towards her breast, gently covering both soft mounds until it found her nipples. The tender points drew taut. She kicked again, her head moving from side to side while her dream held her in its grip.

Coming closer . . .

No man had ever looked at her in such a way. It was wicked but enticing, too. There was a longing deep inside that made her want to move toward him and discover just what he did to satisfy his hunger. Her skin was flushed and warm now, her heart beating faster. One hand lifted toward his outstretched one without any thought . . .

Bronwyn jerked awake. She sat up, startled by the way her heart thumped inside her chest. It felt as if she'd been running. A fine sheen of perspiration coated her skin. Her chemise, twisted up around her hips with all her thrashing, felt rough against her sensitive skin. Even her nipples had hardened into twin points, stabbing against the undergarment. It was so shocking, she touched one hard nipple, wondering if she was still dreaming. Sensation shot into her body from that single touch. It was sweet but unsettling. The night air made her shiver so she lay back down and pulled the blanket and skirt up to her chin. She had to tuck her knees up so that her skirt covered all of her.

How could a dream be so real?

Better still, how could a man she had met but once make her body react so? And just when had fate decided to curse her? Before riding off for one last moment of freedom things had been simple. Now even her body wanted to add another difficulty to her heavy load. She didn't need lust for Cullen McJames, didn't need to burn for the touch of any man.

The tears she'd tried to deny returned. They eased down the side of her face as the wind rattled the shutter.

She wished she had never met Cullen McJames.

Chapter Three

Sterling

"I swear to God, if I never lay eyes on another royal messenger, I'll die a happy man." Cullen took a seat next to his brother at the head table at Sterling. Brodick had taken to eating at the high table only after bringing his son home. It was something he agreed with. The table had been the place where he and his own father broke bread together. It was not to be used but by a family. As unwed bachelors, he and his brother had supped with the men at the lower tables.

Brodick shot him a glare. "I agree with ye, Cullen. But it seems these messengers are looking for ye."

Cullen looked at the four men once more. They wore Jamie's colors but they were far better behaved than the last set to sit at a Sterling table. "Is that so?"

"It is." Brodick ripped a round of bread in half. He tore one in half again and handed a quarter of it to his wife. Anne sat with her son gurgling happily on one knee. Brendan was busy chewing on a knotted linen cloth but his eyes were bright and interested in everything going on around him.

"Well, Jamie can wait until I've eaten." Cullen reached into the center of the table to stab a piece of roast lamb with his dirk. The idea of running off to do the king's bidding wasn't sitting on his mind very well. Now that Brodick was wed with a family, it looked as though their king was turning his demands onto him.

Marrying was looking better and better, especially when he considered the snow threatening to fly outside. Jamie's court was a two-day ride from Sterling.

The face of his McQuade lass came to mind. He indulged his imagination for a moment as he chewed. But he chuckled as he considered what it would take to bring the girl to his bed. Since she was a McQuade, he'd have to steal her. Beneath his kilt, his cock throbbed softly, applauding that idea. The sensible part of his mind argued against it. If she were a McKorey or McAlister, tossing her across his saddle might serve since in time there might be happiness for both families.

But nay for a McQuade.

If he stole her, she'd never see her family again. That was a cruelty he'd rather not inflict on anyone, even for his own clan's gain. But he knew well that there were many men who did not share such a soft spot for the feelings of their stolen brides. In Scotland, weddings were often quick and shrouded in threats to get the bride to kneel in front of the altar.

"I hope the king does not call ye back to court, Cullen."

Anne's English accent jerked him away from thoughts of stealing a bride. What he needed to do was settle on a lass who would bring the clan something. As the laird's brother, he needed to marry a girl who came with a good dowry, or at least powerful connections.

Now, if she happened to be Bronwyn McQuade . . .

He shook his head to shake the idea loose. She'd been wearing a common wool dress. His own sister was clothed better and she had no affection for clothing at all. But the royal messengers suddenly drew a second glance from him. Most lasses did not venture out so far alone, not in a land where raiding was as common as kilts. Now, a laird's daughter might be so bold. With her father away at court, there was no one to tell her nay.

And she had refused to tell him her name . . .

"What does Bronwyn McQuade look like?"

The table went silent for a moment. His cousin, Druce, looked at Brodick and he shrugged.

Druce titled his head. "I don't suppose any of us really know. The rumors run from pitifully ugly to beauty worthy of a prince."

"Why do ye want to know?" Brodick asked the question quietly. Too quietly for Cullen's taste.

"I'm just thinking."

Druce grinned and it made Cullen want to fight. He could not explain it but the idea of any man poking fun at his McQuade lass sparked his temper.

"Since ye both seem to think I should marry her, I thought to ask what she looks like."

Druce chuckled. "Well, it's a fair bet ye won't get the chance to court her any too much."

Cullen glared at his cousin. "McKorey has a pair of sisters, too. Either would make a fine wife, bringing the McKoreys closer to the McJames."

"Aye, if ye've a taste for fashionable ladies. Those two are serving Queen Anne as maids of honor. Better brush up on yer dancing and posy reading if ye plan to wed one of them."

"Isn't it time ye took a bride, Druce? Ye aren't getting any younger." Cullen pointed at Druce. "I'm nae the only one who should think of securing a new connection for the McJames."

His cousin bristled and Brodick laughed. "Now that's a truth."

Druce grumbled but it was no more than the normal fun they all poked at one another. The only person at the table that didn't join in the banter was Anne's younger sister Bonnie. The girl was always quiet, her eyes watching as keen as a falcon's. At sixteen, she sat in her brother-in-law's house instead of her father's because she was wed by proxy to a violent man. The marriage had been arranged by Anne's father's noble wife in an attempt to force Anne to return to England before her son was born, so that Brodick might never know that Anne was not the noblewoman's daughter whom he had wed. Anne and Bonnie were the children of the Earl of Warwickshire's mistress, that the man loved full well. Even though the noblewoman was now dead, the proxy marriage stood firm in the eyes of the law. So Bonnie stayed on McJames land, well out of the reach of her husband.

Her attention was on him, and Cullen stared back at her. A tingle shot down his spine, but he was used to it now. Bonnie had the sight. Anne went to great lengths to conceal it, but there was no denying the way the girl looked straight into his soul. There were also only so many times that anyone might be right about the future. Bonnie had surpassed that the first two months she'd been at Sterling. But he understood why his sister-in-law tried to keep it hidden. There were men in the church who saw such sight as mark of the devil.

Bonnie spoke to him in a low tone. "You need to go to court."

The table went quiet. Bonnie bit into her lower lip when she noticed how much attention her words gained. But her blue eyes were still focused on him.

"Then I'll go."

He felt another ripple of sensation travel along his spine. Bonnie looked at the tabletop, severing their connection. Her meal sat half eaten but she rose to her feet and offered them all a curtsy before turning and leaving. His own appetite fled as the feeling wrapped tightly around him. His McQuade lass rose once more to capture his full attention. Her face so vivid in his mind, he was sure he could reach out and touch her cheek. There had to be over a thousand women wearing McQuade colors, but he was certain that she was Bronwyn. Not many could ride simply for pleasure. Her father had money or she would never have been out on such a fine horse. He felt it in his gut, and the tingle that had gone down his back turned into a burning desire to find her. Standing up, he looked at his brother and cousin.

"I'm going to court." He shot a look at Druce. "Maybe I'll come back with permission to wed Bronwyn McQuade."

His cousin snorted. "That wouldna do ye any good. I hear tell she's never been off her father's land."

Cullen tilted his head, considering his brother. "Well then, I suppose that's all the more reason for me to ask Jamie what he thinks of the idea. It's a fair bet I won't be gaining her father's blessing on the match."

Her father be damned. He was tired of the raids, and marrying his enemy's daughter was a tradition that went back longer than any other they knew.

Of course, he'd have to steal her, but turning the tables on McQuade sounded right fine to him.

Brodick lifted a hand and pointed at him. "We'll talk after ye have that permission from the king. I dinna need Jamie breathing fire on me because ye've decided to give McQuade a taste of raiding."

Druce looked disappointed but Cullen felt twice as much so. His brother aimed a harsh look at him. But it was nothing personal. Brodick was doing his best to make sure the McJames people prospered. He shared that ideal.

Which was why he was going to court.

And he was coming home with permission to wed Bronwyn McQuade.

Her father be damned.

* * *

Cullen wasn't planning on waiting. His mind was racing too fast to consider sleeping and starting for Jamie's court at dawn. It wasn't the first time he'd ridden out at night. His blood was hot, singing with the need to move.

He forced himself to take the time to inspect his sword. Pulling it from its leather scabbard, he eyed it critically. 'Twas a job that he never rushed. The weapon had served him well in many a battle. Making sure it was fit was a priority.

He did feel as though he was heading toward a conflict. His muscles were tight and his mind intently focused. He could practically hear his own heart beat.

After sheathing the sword, he shrugged into a leather doublet before hooking the sword to his back. The thick leather was dyed dark brown and quilted with small iron pieces between the leather and the wool lining. The doublet was designed to keep a blade from slicing into his body. Tonight it would also keep the winter chill off his skin. His kilt was belted firmly around his waist and his boots rose to just below his knees. Good leather lined with sheep's skin with the wool still attached. Tugging a knitted bonnet onto his head, he turned around and took his gauntlets up off the table.

Snuffing the candle, he walked into the hallway. A set of stairs allowed him to descend to the ground floor of the keep. Sterling had six towers in all with thick walls connecting each one together. Tin lanterns were always kept burning on the first floor of the keeps and every thirty feet along the walls. The tin shell had cuts in it to let the light out but the metal kept the fire hazard minimal. A lone figure stood near the door that let out onto the yard. A skirt telling him it was a female. A few more steps and he recognized young Bonnie.

That flare of sensation twisted in his gut again. She watched him, holding a square parcel that looked like a small pillow.

"You should take this with you." With only the lantern light, her voice took on a mystical quality. But the night often seemed alive with things the church told him not to listen to. He'd learned long ago to respect the night because a wise man kept all his senses open or he ended up dead.

"What is it?"

Bonnie shook her head and offered it to him. "You will need it after you leave court. Leave it wrapped until then."

The bundle was soft. Bonnie had wrapped it in soft wool and even sewn the edges tightly closed. She watched him grip it firmly. "Do not forget to place it in your riding bag, else you will forget it."

His brow furled as he tried to understand what the girl was hinting at. She shook her head but a small grin decorated her face.

"Och now, look at ye, teasing me when I've got a cold night of riding ahead."

Bonnie laughed, soft and delicately. "You are not cold because you feel the pull, too."

Cullen sobered. 'Tis a truth that I do, lass."

Bonnie lifted a hand, waving to him. "Safe journey, Cullen."

His horse was already waiting in the yard. Cullen stared at it, and his cousin. Druce tossed the reins toward him, keeping his own in a tight grip.

"When did I invite ye to join me?"

Druce mounted and flashed him a cocksure grin. "Ye dinna. 'Course I always said ye were a slow wit."

"And I always said ye talk too much."

Druce kneed his horse to follow when Cullen took to the road. Retainers followed them in a steady flow of horses and men. Druce's men following his cousin, and Cullen's men following him. His brother might be the earl, but Cullen was not without titles of his own. He remained at Sterling because they were stronger together. He really wasn't surprised to find Druce waiting for him. His father and Druce were brothers so his cousin had been raised with the same sense of family that he and Brodick shared. They were all McJames and that was what made them powerful. Druce had his own lands and title but he didn't hide on his estate wallowing in his station. The McJames were stronger because Druce refused to take his holding, and separate from the rest of the family. Cullen followed the same example. His land would always be McJames land.

And he was off to claim a bride who would benefit the clan. Of course, he was looking forward to it.

And that was a fact.

McQuade town house, Edinburgh

"Yer to attend court with us today."

Liam announced his father's wishes with a voice that lacked the normal tone of superiority she was accustomed to hearing from her sibling. It oddly sounded like her brother valued her this morning. Or pitied her. Having been ignored for a fortnight, she discovered that she enjoyed the lack of interest in her. Going back to court held no appeal, not with the slicing tongue sure to greet her there. As the days had dragged on, she'd hoped her father was satisfied with his vengeance.

Clearly he wasn't.

"That makes no sense to me." Bronwyn didn't care if Liam took exception to her words. Returning to the royal hall held no appeal for her. Better to let her father do as he would without her witnessing it. She could not change what blood flowed in her veins after all, and she didn't need to dislike herself.

"Be ready to leave within the hour."

It was on the tip of her tongue to refuse. But Liam remained, silently waiting for her to speak. The flicker of expectation in his eyes made her still the words before they got past her lips. At least she might keep him guessing at her true thoughts. A small thing but it was the only one in her control. Liam finally broke as the silence stretched out.

"Within the hour."

"So ye said already."

He grunted and stomped out of her doorway. A little wave of satisfaction washed through her. Her sibling was so easy to manipulate. Somehow she doubted that Liam would enjoy knowing that she felt that way. Which was why she enjoyed it so much.

But the feeling did not last.

Returning to court sent a wave of nausea through her. The half-eaten porridge in front of her lost its appeal instantly. Rising from her chair, she left the table in the small kitchen. Climbing back up the stairs to her room, she found a brush sitting on the table. A pitcher and washbasin had arrived as well. Linen and soap were placed neatly beside the basin.

She could thank the maid for such niceties. It was for certain that her father knew nothing of it, else she'd be fetching her own.

With a sigh she poured water into the basin. There was no point in being bitter. Life was not fair, and men were greedy. Her mother had taught her that. The Laird McQuade did not part with his gold, not even for a daughter. Done with washing her face, she enjoyed the feel of clean skin. The soap was plain with only a hint of rosemary for good luck, but it cleansed the dirt away, leaving her refreshed. Picking up the brush, she tended to her hair. When it was neat and braided once more, she reached for the door. She would not linger in the room. Her father might say many things about her, but Bronwyn Mc-

Quade was not a coward. She knew the truth of her own virtue, so she would hold her chin steady.

Cullen didn't waste time. He stopped at the McJames city house just long enough to wash the road dust from his body. The servants scurried to heat water and pull a clean doublet out of a chest for him. Neither he nor Brodick had any true liking for court so the staff dinna expect him, but they were always ready. A good wool doublet, made to his measurements, was kept on hand along with a shirt and clean kilt. It was constructed of smooth, russet wool and set with silver buttons. There were boots that didn't have the dirt from the road clinging to them A new bonnet, and pinned to the side was a broach with the McJames arms. He shaved his three days of beard off with the aid of a mirror.

When he entered the royal hall he remembered why he didn't care for court. Nobles watched him, their lips moving as they muttered some cutting remark to the man standing beside them. He didn't even bother to give them the benefit of the doubt, they were no saying anything kind. That was court, full of intrigue and suspicion. Gossip fueled the ambitions of most of the velvet-clad men. They looked like actors on the stage in their slashed silk hose and puffy pants that no real Scot needed. Most of the men had more jewels sewn to their court costumes than the woman wore in their jewelry.

He was quite content in his kilt and wool doublet. Pretty trimmings and shinny baubles were for women, not a man who often had to use a sword to defend his land. Some of the pants worn by the court men were so overstuffed, they had to stand in carefully posed positions. A few even had lace-edged handkerchiefs dangling from their gloved fingertips.

Fops. Half of them had boy lovers.

The ladies were just as repulsive to him. White powder covered their faces until one couldn't see what color their skin was. Thick red rouge colored their cheeks and lips. Some wore black "patches" on their skin in the shape of tiny stars or crescent moons. Their dresses were huge piles of lavish fabrics strapped to them over steel and wire so everything that he found pleasing about the female body was pushed into another shape. The only thing he did see was their breasts. The necklines of their court dresses were low and square cut. Their stiff corsets pushed their soft breasts up until the flesh looked hard and ready to burst from their bodices.

He far preferred Bronwyn as she'd looked riding . . .

The thought made him clench his teeth. No woman should be able to take command of his thoughts when he had not even tasted her kiss.

Yet . . .

He snorted in frustration. 'Twas becoming irritating, it was. There were other lasses who would make fine brides for him, too. Since he was at court, maybe he should take a look at some of them.

"Young McJames, I did no expect to see ye back this year." Alarik McKorey offered his hand in greeting. Neighbors on the southern side of McJames property, the man was a long-time ally against the McQuades. He also wore good Scottish wool without the elaborate trim and jewels. It was a welcome sight among the sea of presumptuous status seekers.

"I decided that both yer lovely sisters were too far away from me."

McKorey's sister Raelin peered over her lace fan at him. Her face wasn't painted, only a touch of color on her lips. It made for a refreshing sight that earned her a smile from his lips. Aye, here was a woman who would bring a good connection if he married her.

"Good day to ye, Raelin."

Her eyes narrowed in distaste before she gripped her sister's arm and tugged her away from him. Alarik shot them a hard look.

"What goes on here, Alarik? I dinna know I'd offended yer sisters." And it appeared that whatever his sin was, everyone around him knew it because there were whispers aplenty.

"I told them to reserve their judgment until yer side of the tale was voiced." Alarik offered him a hard look. "I know the McQuades have been a thorn in yer side too long."

"What are ye talking about, man? I've no done anything that I need my friends to make excuses for."

Alarik didn't answer. He looked past Cullen as another wave of whispers rippled across the courtiers. Turning around he gazed at the face he'd seen one too many times in his memory. A flare of satisfaction burned through him as he confirmed his suspicions. She stood next to McQuade, confirming that she was his daughter.

But her face was pale.

Cullen stared at the ashen shade and her bloodless lips. She held them tightly clamped together. Her chin trembled but only a tiny amount, so small he'd have missed it if he wasn't staring at her so intently. It was a stark contrast to the memory he held of her. His temper stirred as he watched the way her brothers looked at her; it was far from kind.

She wore no powder or paint. Only a good wool dress that buttoned up to her neck. There were creases where it had been folded back when it warmed up in the afternoons. At court such ware was misplaced almost as much as her somber expression. Even his own doublet had been pressed so that it didn't look like he'd appeared in front of his king fresh from the road.

The whispers in the room became louder as people noticed his attention on her. Bronwyn turned and found him. Her eyes widened when she saw him. Heat erupted throughout his body. It was instant and undeniable. The only thing that made it endurable was the small flicker he watched emerge in Bronwyn's eyes. The whispers in the hall increased, cutting through his fascination with her.

"Maybe the king will force them to wed . . ."

"She's soiled . . ."

"Why marry what he's already had . . ."

Cullen shot a look at Alarik. "What nonsense goes on here?"

McKorey leaned in closer. "McQuade accused ye of using his daughter."

Cullen's gaze shot back toward Bronwyn. His temper erupted but it was laced with desire so thick he wasn't sure what he felt. It took every shred of self-discipline he owned to remain standing still. Every fiber of his being wanted to close the distance so that he could hear Bronwyn tell him with her own lips what he'd done.

Like father . . . like child . . .

Did she really hate him enough to blacken her own reputation with such a lie? Her brothers would, he believed that without a doubt.

"Make way for the king!"

The whispers ceased abruptly. Cullen turned to find Jamie striding toward him. The courtiers all lowered themselves. When his king halted in front of him, he inclined his head in deference as well.

"Cullen McJames, my friend. I am pleased to see ye."

The tongues didn't start wagging until the king and Cullen McJames made it far enough down the carpet not to hear what was being said clearly.

Bronwyn did.

She set her mind to not caring but her pride refused to

obey her wishes. Pain slashed through her. Her father offered her no mercy. He stood steady as she was forced to endure the public display. He finally turned to look at her.

"Ye may return to the town house. I'll see ye sent home to Red Stone on the morrow."

May God forgive her, but even if the scriptures said she should ask for his blessing, every inch of her refused. She did not see a father before her, only the man who legally owned her. And he did. There was no one who would intervene, no one who would challenge his charge against her. The very clothing on her back was his by law.

"Yer greed knows no boundaries." Bronwyn lowered her voice so that only her sire and siblings heard her. There was a flare of outrage in her father's eyes, but she shot a look full of loathing back at him. "Deny it and label yourself a liar, sir. Ye blacken me falsely to avoid dowering me. I'm no so simple-minded as to not understand that."

A rare look of uncertainty entered Erik McQuade's eyes. "I'm laird and I'll do what's best for the clan. Yer place is to mind me. Dinna be laying any curse on my head, Daughter."

"Yer greed is yer curse and I dinna have anything to do with casting it on ye. 'Tis something ye have shackled to yerself."

With another scathing look, Bronwyn turned her back on her father. Heads turned as she walked proudly from the royal hall. She held her chin level and steady.

She was not soiled. All the gossip in the world would not change that.

Erik McQuade shivered. A chill swept over him like an icy winter wind. He looked at Sodac. "Go with her."

A prickle of fear shot through him, making his voice shake. Erik shook his head, attempting to dislodge the feeling. He pointed at Liam. "Follow her and make sure she stays in her room. Use a few men to ensure it."

Liam looked confused. "Sodac can deal with Bronwyn."

"I warned ye, boy. Don't assume that she's secure." He stopped when heads turned toward them. Waving his sons toward the doors he covered the distance in quick strides. Once they reached the outer entry room, he stopped in an empty alcove well away from the main entrance.

"As much as I detest the fact that I have a daughter, there is no getting past the fact that she is my child. Have her watched by my lad. I'd no put it past her to strike out on her own to try her hand at surviving among the middle class. One of those merchants will jump at the chance to wed the daughter of a laird. You can set the men to watching her, but it is you and Sodac that have something to gain by making sure she doesna escape. There's plenty of men who dinna have land to lose who'd help her out of pity."

Liam scowled. "I dinna think of that."

"Ye should have. I told ye last night that ye must keep yer sister tucked away or lose that land." McQuade glared at his sons. "Make sure ye dinna forget again. We must take her back to Red Stone on the morrow and shut her away."

"Maybe she should slip off her horse." Sodac raised an eyebrow with his question.

"Nay. She's a pair of hands that earns gold for our coffers. There's another thing ye have to learn, boy . . . no to waste. Bronwyn can be as useful as any other servant. I would have smothered her when she was a babe if murder was on my mind. It would not have been hard to dispose of her while covering up my deed."

"But the land . . ." Liam persisted.

"'Tis ours so long as she does not breed. Besides, my marriage to her mother might have been dissolved if we had no living children. I needed Bronwyn to keep her mother because she never gave me any sons." McQuade eyed his sons. "Shaming Bronwyn in front of the court will see to keeping good offers from coming to my door. I can refuse them all by saying she's soiled and I'll no see any man saddled with a slut that bears my name. No man of mine will dally with her. Once she's back at Red Stone, Scotland will forget that I even have a daughter." McQuade suddenly chuckled. "And the best part is, I got to blame it on Cullen McJames. If what she says is true, he'll wear the stain without ever having sampled the delights of knowing her. A fine revenge for all the trouble he's caused me."

Liam and Sodac joined their father in his amusement. But Erik sobered quickly.

"Get on with ye. Before she sets out for the Weavers Guild."

Liam and Sodac rushed toward the door, eager to follow in their father's footsteps by keeping their hands tight around every measure of land belonging to the McQuades. Erik watched them, satisfaction brushing aside the chill that had assaulted him. Most likely it had been the ghost of Bronwyn's mother, trying to smite him for his actions, but the spirit had better get back to her grave because it was her own fault for giving him a daughter. He'd married the woman for the land and he intended to keep it any way he had to.

McQuade walked back toward the entrance to the great hall, but the guards refused him admittance. The king's order to bring Bronwyn had seen him waiting every day that he did not bring her with him. It was the only reason that he'd brought her today, so that he could enter the main hall. Important men attended court and he needed to be viewed as a powerful laird who had the right to enter the royal hall. Appearances were everything.

"Ye saw my daughter this morning."

The guards looked at each other. One of them gave a barely noticeable nod and the pikes uncrossed to clear the doorway.

Erik enjoyed the fact that the guards raised their pikes to allow him in. There was a ripple of annoyance from the men waiting that placed a smile on his face.

But what he didn't see was the figure that emerged from the darker shadows of the alcove. Raelin McKorey shook her head slowly. There was no place private at court. She'd learned that lesson her first month attending the queen. A wise person guarded each thought, holding it carefully inside lest it be used against you. She waited for many long moments before approaching the entrance to the hall. The guards instantly allowed her into the hall, recognizing one of the queen's maids. She thanked them with a shy smile; there was something else she'd learned the value of—always flirt lightly with the royal guard. It endeared a girl to them and made life so much easier. But there was a fine line to observe when dealing with men. Go too far and your reputation suffered. The gossips were vicious. They condemned without mercy any girl who even looked at a man too boldly.

Like Bronwyn McQuade.

It would seem that she should have listened to her brother after all. She was more than glad to hear it because Cullen McJames was a good man. It was just a shame that he was so interested in Bronwyn McQuade. She'd seen the truth of that with her own eyes. Envy bit into her as she threaded her way through the courtiers in search of Cullen. No man had ever looked at her with such a longing. Bronwyn was a lucky girl, to be sure. At least the gossips would be satisfied if the pair married. That was the only solution now.

* * *

"She's her father's daughter, all right. Nothing but a curse to every living McJames." Cullen rounded on James Stuart. "I dinna touch her with anything more than me hand."

"So she said."

The king's words deflated his anger. Cullen shook his head trying to make sense of the whole situation. "She did?"

"She did. It is her father who claims otherwise."

Cullen snorted. "Well I suppose I might remind ye that the man lied to ye the last time ye summoned me to court because of a charge he made against my clan."

"I've nae forgotten that." The king sat down, indicating with a wave of his fingers for Cullen to take a chair. 'Twas a privilege to be invited to sit in the presence of his monarch, but he didn't feel like taking his ease.

"But McQuade accused the girl in the middle of the hall. The gossips are taking it as gospel. He said she was yer whore."

Cullen snarled. The sound erupted from his throat without any thought. The ashen pallor of Bronwyn's face suddenly made sense to him. The court had been dining on her.

"That makes no sense. Why would the man want to ruin his own daughter's name?"

"He's a greedy pig. Daughters must be dowered if they are to wed well."

Cullen stared at his king for a long moment. His temper flared and he left the chair behind to pace. He suddenly recalled just how sweet Bronwyn had looked that day on the hillside, her face full of delight. Her eyes had sparkled and at first he'd thought he was imagining her. The woman he'd seen this morning was nothing like the one he'd dreamed of. That idea sent his temper up a few more degrees. He wasn't a man who hated, but McQuade was earning it. "McQuade is a menace."

James chuckled. "Now that is something that I shoulder more than ye do, my friend. The McJames are no the only clan that

McQuade raids. McKorey is shooting me daggers since I allowed McQuade and his sons back into the royal hall. McAlister is no doubt penning me a letter expressing his displeasure over McQuade being allowed the benefits of laird when the man raids his neighbors like a common thief."

Cullen offered his king a shake of his head. "Did I mention that I've no desire to be king?"

"There's many a day I feel the same." Jamie offered him a tankard. Cullen refused it with a quick shake of his head. Jamie chuckled.

"Ye had better watch out, Cullen. It looks like that lass has ye hooked."

Cullen scowled. "Can I no be angry because my name was dragged through the mud in this scheme?"

"Aye, but that's no the only reason ye want to run the man through. Ye were undressing the lass with yer eyes."

Cullen didn't answer. Since he didn't understand his thoughts on the matter there was no point in trying to explain anything to the king. "'Tis the truth that I thought her interesting when I met her. She denied me her name. Now I know why."

Cullen forgot the king for a moment as he considered just how satisfying it would be to have Bronwyn in his hands without her father and brothers around. She'd blushed for him. All their family issues aside, he'd sparked enough interest in her to turn her cheeks scarlet. Beneath his kilt, his cock stiffened.

James waved his hand. "I dinna want to know what yer thinking. Just remember that murder is a high crime, man. Even I canna change that. Ye'll have to find a way to deal with McQuade without running the man through. Yer free to leave court."

Cullen inclined his head toward his king before turning around.

"I could order her father to place her at court."

Cullen turned in a swirl of kilt pleats. "Do not." His voice cracked like a whip, full of emotions he didn't understand beyond knowing that he wanted to deal with Bronwyn personally. The royal guards standing silently behind the king moved their eyes to stare at him now. Jamie only grinned.

"Yer mighty defensive, lad. I've a mind to see what sort of daughter the man has raised."

With a shrug, Cullen returned the grin. "Since everyone seems to think I've already had the lass, maybe I should keep those wagging tongues from spreading lies for once. Providing ye have no objection to such a match."

The king's face turned pensive. It was hard to tell what the man was thinking; he hid his emotions with the years of wearing a crown.

"Have a safe journey, Cullen."

"Aye, yer Majesty."

The king lifted one finger. Cullen stood still, his breath freezing in his chest while he waited to hear his monarch's decision.

"Ye have my permission to wed the lass, providing she kneels at the altar of her own free will. She's nae like her kin and I'll nae see her forced to wed."

"But I have yer permission?"

"Aye, and my blessing. But promise me ye will nae name yer first son after me. We've too many James in Scotland nowadays."

Nae like her kin . . .

Well, that remained to be seen. Cullen ground his teeth as he covered the distance toward the doors. Fans opened and whispers rippled away from him like waves in a pond. His temper strained against his control, doubling his pace. One word made it clearly to his ears.

Blackguard . . .

He snarled softly, his pride stung deeply.

His honor demanded action now. McQuade had miscalculated if the man thought he might strike out without gaining McJames retaliation. The man had misjudged him greatly.

A McJames never took disgrace without a fight. Cullen was going to make a struggle McQuade would never forget. He strode from the royal hall, determination fueling his stride. There was no more to think about.

'Twas time for action.

"Yer daft." Druce swirled the ale in his mug around for a long moment. "But I suppose 'tis my own fault for teasing ye about the lass."

"I met her."

Druce straightened up, surprise on his face. "Yer pulling me leg, lad. I dinna want to believe ye had her as her father said."

"I dinna have her." His voice was rough, but he'd heard his honor questioned one too many times in a single day to keep his sense of humor. "But we spoke and her brothers caught us." Cullen didn't care for the look his cousin gave him. Thinking about having Bronwyn in his bed was not the same sin as doing it. "I havena touched her."

"Yet." Druce was done teasing. There was no amusement lurking in his eyes now. The man was pure concentration, his mind considering the details of what needed doing.

"Aye, yet." He was no liar. Cullen stared straight back at his kin. He wanted her, wanted her enough to steal her. Maybe men talked about such things often, but he'd never truly thought he'd find himself wanting any woman enough to kidnap her. Applying his charm to the art of seduction, now that was more his style.

"Is it just yer pride that is pushing ye to do what ye've been accused of, Cullen?"

Druce asked a good question. One Cullen wasn't sure about himself. There was only one thing he was sure of and that was that he was going to take Bronwyn or die in the trying.

"There will be blood spilt for sure if ye take the lass."

Cullen snorted. "There's been blood spilled near every season I can recall in me life by her father and his insistence that my father stole his bride."

"He's going to be in a full rage when ye take his daughter as well."

Cullen shot Druce a deadly look. "McQuade should have thought about that afore he accused me of deflowering her in open court. It is my right to take her to the altar now that her father has said I took her maidenhead. That is the only thing that will save me from being labeled a blackguard."

"That's a truth, sure enough, but ye'll be the one that has to endure her as yer wife. Yer friends will understand if ye dinna shoulder that burden."

"I do not hold all of Scotland's nobles as my friends." Cullen slid a dirk into the top of his boot. He was arming himself for battle and Druce knew it well. "There must be fifty letters being written by those at court talking about me and my lack of honor. I wager few will take the time to debate the reasons."

He eyed the edge of his sword in silence, his full attention on the task of checking the blade for nicks. Druce held silent until Cullen sheathed the blade.

"If that's yer decision, I'm going with ye." Druce reached for his own sword. "McKorey mentioned that he and a few of his men would be waiting outside the McQuade town house tonight."

Druce shrugged when Cullen gave him a confused look.

"McKorey has as much reason to want that family laid low as the McJames do. The McQuades raid his land as often as yers.

I hear Alarik was thinking of pressing the king for Bronwyn's hand himself."

"She's mine."

And the rest of Scotland could just forget that Bronwyn Mc-Quade was born to a father who was a lying bastard that could not recall that he'd lost his bride thirty-five years ago through nothing but his own actions. His mother never lamented it. She'd loved his father until the day a battle wound took his life. His mother had followed her husband before a year passed. They had loved each other so strongly that death was not going to separate them.

He refused to believe that he and Bronwyn couldn't work out a decent marriage. His brother had married an English woman and managed to find love. Besides, Druce was right—his pride was stung. The sort of annoying pain that would never dull unless he did something about it. McQuade had called him a defiler of innocent maids so it would serve the man right if he did take Bronwyn to his bed.

It was no more than the greedy, scheming laird deserved for his words. As for Bronwyn . . . she would adjust. His pride demanded action and Cullen intended to see the matter settled in his favor. The vicious gossip would transform overnight into words of praise when he stole Bronwyn and married her. If he didn't, finding a good match would become much harder with his own reputation painted black by McQuade's lies. No decent family would take him for a son-in-law because they'd think he was a marauder and defiler of any lass he came upon.

As he'd come across Bronwyn . . .

Chapter Four

Locked away.

Bronwyn felt her mouth go dry as she considered the men watching her. It was so strange the way she noticed them. It had never been a burning need of hers to roam or escape her kin, but seeing the burly retainers set to keep her inside her father's town home, she missed the choice keenly.

With a sigh she walked around the lower dining room. She was restless, so much so it was almost anxiety. There was no cause for her feelings but she could not cast them aside. Sleep felt like a torment best avoided as long as possible but she retreated to her tiny room to escape her brothers.

Their stares reminded her of hungry rodents.

But the room was too small to move around in. She could not even make eight paces before running into the wall and having to turn around. The shutter was open to allow fresh air into the house during the day. The fires used at night to warm the larger sleeping chambers left a thick haze of smoke in the hallways that the staff had to clear out each morning. Every shutter was opened to help the breeze sweep the house.

A large splash from somewhere below her window drew her attention. Standing up onto her toes she peered down at the back of the house. Water glittered in the torch light. Two iron basket torches were set on either side of the kitchen door. Instead of a step, there was a ramp that led to the back door. It was more practical allowing for wheelbarrows to deliver heavy casks. The ramp also made it simple to cast used bath water out of the kitchen to flow down the gutter. There was a thick wall surrounding the back door to add security to the house. A wooden gate set into it had a sturdy wooden bar braced across it. The flicker from the torches shimmered off the bell hanging on the gate. There would be a cord that ran through the gate to the alley behind the house. Merchants could ring when they wanted to bring their wares into the kitchen. Only the master and his guests used the front door. There were no retainers at the kitchen door because of the barred gate.

A bath sounded good. Bronwyn sighed. At least it would be better than trying to sleep.

Cullen would be waiting in her dreams . . .

A shiver shook her. She felt heat travel across the delicate skin of her face in another blush. It was absurd, the way her flesh responded to him when he was not even near. With a snort of distaste she picked up her hairbrush and began pulling the tie off the end of her braid. She needed to set her mind to forgetting the man. The men standing guard gave her all the information she needed. Her father was going to see her living under his roof until she died. Red Stone was set in the heart of McQuade territory. The walls had never been besieged much less breached.

Sadness washed over her as she brushed her hair free. It fell around her in a soft cloud of honey silk. As she slipped her fingers down a portion of it, two tears escaped her eyes. No bridegroom would ever see her with her hair unbound. Somehow, knowing that was a hard fact, made it hurt. Perhaps she had been guarding a secret bit of hope that she might in fact marry, but now that was gone. Swept away by her own father's powerful hand. And there were girls who lamented the fact they were not born the daughter of a laird.

What was . . . was.

Reaching for her small bundle of belongings, she found her clean chemise and stockings. Clean skin would be nice. Maybe she would even sleep after her bath. Opening her door, she peered into the hallway. She listened for the creaking of the wood floor but all was silent. Using soft steps, she headed toward the back stairs that the servants used to bring food up from the kitchens. They were narrow and dark with only two tin lanterns set to light them. There wasn't even a door at the bottom; the steps simply ended in the kitchen.

Two maids were sitting at a small table. Their voices were soft while they chatted. One worked a lump of pastry dough while the other chopped leeks. They both stood as she entered.

"Evening, ma'am."

Only the older one spoke, the younger maid watching, her fingers gone still on the pastry.

"I thought to bathe."

The younger girl dusted her hands off using her apron. She turned and pushed the iron bar that held large caldrons inside the fire pit over the flames. There was a faint sizzle as water that had been dripping down the side of the copper caldron connected with the heat of the fire.

"Shall I build up the fire?"

Bronwyn shook her head. The glowing embers suited her mood. Besides, she did not want to call attention to where she was. Perhaps it was a small thing, but knowing she was not being watched felt better.

"There is no need to waste wood."

The maid took her words kindly, thinking her a frugal woman.

With winter due to encase the city in snow and ice any day, being wasteful for one's comfort was unwise. She'd heard that many a noble daughter lingered in their baths while huge fires blazed to keep them toasty warm.

That had never been her lifestyle.

But that was not something to lament. She was strong and sturdy. Her hands added to the good of everyone at Red Stone. The respect she had was respect well earned, not demanded like her brothers often did.

There was a rush of water. Bronwyn turned to watch water running down a wooden trough and into the tub sitting near the door. The maid waited until the tub was half full and then quickly pushed a thick slab of wood across the trough where it went through a window. Outside there would be a large rain barrel set up at the roof level. It would catch rain water and gravity would allow it to flow into the tub when the wooden shingle was removed.

It was quite a modern bathing convenience.

Only the hot water needed to be added. Bronwyn set about removing her clothing as the fire heated the water. She laid aside her skirt, doublet, and stays. Next came her stockings and boots. Placing her brush on the table top she pulled a bar of soap from the store box.

When the copper kettle was steaming, the maids dipped large ladles into it. They added enough hot water to raise the level of water by half a foot. Reaching for the hem of her chemise, she pulled her last garment off. The maids had returned to their work. Having them in the kitchen did not bother her; bathing was rarely private.

Sitting down in the tub, she worked the soap across her skin. She was oddly aware of the smooth texture of the water. Her nipples were far more sensitive than she could recall them ever being. Her body felt alive with some sort of anticipation.

It made no sense at all, but when she rinsed her hair, the water stroked her cheeks, sending little ripples of pleasure through her.

When she stood up, the night air brushed across her nude body, but she wasn't cold. She felt bold and free. A blush stung her cheeks and she reached for the toweling quickly. There was wickedness twisting through her blood tonight. A taunting desire to immerse herself in thoughts of Cullen McJames and what a man did with a woman.

Since she carried the charge of guilt, her mind wanted to know what the sin felt like. It would seem that she was as foolish as she was unlucky. Nothing good would come of her mental wonderings.

She worked the fabric through her wet hair for many long minutes to remove as much water as possible. Lifting her clean chemise from the chair, she let it cover her body and reached for the hair brush. Standing close to the fire, she drew the bristles gently along the strands of her hair, lifting the strands so that the heat from the fire would dry them. Soon the linen of her chemise began floating gently around her knees and her hair became a soft cloud.

She did love being clean. The church might call it wicked but she could not deny that she enjoyed the way her skin felt after a bath. With a sigh she reached for her stockings and covered her lower legs with them. She stepped into her ankle boots and laced them for the return trip to her room. At night the rats could make it into even well-kept town homes. In the crowded conditions of the city, the vermin were desperate to find food. Walking barefoot was an invitation to spread disease. Red Stone was much cleaner.

A rush of cold air made her shiver when the back door was opened. But there was no splash of water against the cobblestones. A startled gasp from one maid made Bronwyn turn in a flutter of unbound hair. A hard body collided with hers, turning her around once more so that her back was pressed to his front. Fear spiked through her as she bucked wildly, a snarl rising from her throat.

The sound never passed her lips. One hard hand sealed it inside her mouth. There was iron strength in that hand, such as she'd never felt. The dying firelight glittered off the spinning blade of a dirk as it sailed across the kitchen to embed its deadly blade several inches into the table a mere foot from the younger maid.

"Nae one sound, lasses. Not a one or the next dirk goes through yer hand."

Recognition was instant. Her memory recalled Cullen McJames's dark voice. Her fear died in a sizzle as her temper erupted. The maid's eyes grew huge while they stared at the slowly vibrating handle of the dirk.

Bronwyn jerked against the arm holding her, rage making her stronger. His grip slackened for a moment and she twisted violently, even biting at the hand lying across her mouth.

There was a soft hiss from Cullen but his body twisted and moved at the same time. His hand slipped away from her mouth but gathered up most of her hair. He twisted it around his hand, jerking her head backward. She opened her mouth to yell but a wad of fabric was pushed between her open teeth, smothering the sound. His larger body pushed hers forward until she was pressed against the table, her hands becoming useless when he leaned his body weight against her back to imprison her against the hard surface of the table.

"Now imagine my surprise to find ye here in the kitchen, lass."

Bronwyn spat the cloth out of her mouth only to feel a thick strip of leather sliding through her open teeth. Cullen tightened it down around her head, pulling some of her hair as he made sure her tongue was trapped and useless.

"And here I thought I'd have to search through the house for ye."

A garbled sound made it past her gag. Cullen leaned down across her body, letting her feel his strength. His breath brushed against her ear, enraging her with how easily he subdued her.

"Easy, lass. I've no desire to bruise ye."

Dark shadows moved past the kitchen. Blinking her eyes, she watched as men quickly bound the two maids without a squeak out of either of them. The ease and smoothness of their action enraged her further. She screamed behind her gag, pushing against the tabletop. There was a soft word in Gaelic from her captor before her arms were folded behind her in an iron grip.

"I warned ye, Bronwyn."

There was no lament in his voice, only solid determination. More leather was wound around her wrists and a good way up her forearms before it was knotted firmly. He kept his body against her legs, pinning her to the table. Her head knocked against the hard surface because she refused to stop struggling. The pain from each collision only spurred her on. She bucked and jerked, snarling through the gag.

"Such a temper."

She cursed when she heard the soft desire in his voice. How dare he? She suddenly stiffened to the point that every muscle felt as if it might snap. Cullen slid his hands down to her waist and over the curves of her hips before continuing right along the sides of her thighs. The touch shocked her. Her heart pounded inside her chest so hard it felt as though it might burst. With only her chemise, she felt the heat of his hands. He pressed her thighs together with that iron strength of his and bound her legs tight at the knees with another length of leather.

He stood up when it was knotted, releasing her from the tabletop. Bucking upward, she was rewarded with a hard connection with his chin. He grunted and satisfaction surged through her in spite of the sharp pain that jabbed into her head from the blow.

He leaned over her once more, his body forcing hers back to the tabletop.

"Enough, lass. Ye hurt yourself more than me." He remained there for a moment letting her feel his strength, his power. Her temper burned but she was helpless against his larger body.

"Play with her later, Cullen. After we've quit this house."

One of the shapes in the dark finished tying the older maid to the table leg. He leaned across the table to keep his words a mere whisper.

"Aye. Fortune has smiled on us. No reason to tempt her to turn sour. I have what I want."

Cullen stood up, releasing her. He turned her around and bent one knee so that his shoulder lowered to her belly level. He moved forward and straightened up in one fluid motion so that her body tumbled over his wide shoulder with an ease that horrified her.

It was far too simple . . .

She refused to yield, keeping her head up. Her neck strained, the muscles aching. The only thing she gained was the sight of both maids' legs stretching out on the floor. They were bound to the thick legs of the table so that they might not even push over things to gain attention. The table was too heavy for them to move, even together. With night having fallen, they might not be discovered until dawn.

That would be far too late for her . . .

Despair raked its unrelenting claws across her when she felt the night air on her thinly covered body. More shapes moved in the dark as Cullen lifted her up alongside the wall that had seemed so hard to escape but an hour past. Hands gripped her and pulled her over its top with ease. She heard the horses before she saw them in the dark. A narrow alley ran between her father's house and another town house. There was the dank scent of water from the kitchens that used the alley to drain their waste water toward the main gutter.

She was handed up and pulled atop a horse.

"A pity I had to bind ye so tight. Now ye have to travel like a sack of goods."

Cullen's voice held a note of amusement that sent her struggling once more. Her effort earned her little. He pulled her over his saddle, her head hanging down on one side. A sharp whistle and the horse moved, its hooves splashing through the water. She kicked frantically, trying to gain attention, but the horse kept moving and there was no shout of alarm from her father's men.

Instead she felt that hard hand of her captor pressing her down onto the back of his horse. Her head began to spin in a dizzy circle as it filled with too much blood. Bronwyn resisted the pull of darkness but there was no fending it off for long. She went lax as unconsciousness claimed her.

Cullen felt the change in his captive. He stroked her back, testing her compliance. He ran one hand lightly over the soft curve of her bottom and yet she remained still. He hadn't expected to find her in her bath. The light color of her chemise drew a frown from him. A bound woman lying across his saddle might draw attention that he didn't need. Pulling Argyll to a stop in a shadow, he looked around.

"Cullen, cover her with this."

Druce tossed a length of McJames plaid toward him. Pulling Bronwyn upward, he leaned her against his chest and wrapped her quickly in the wool. At least it looked as though she were simply sleeping. A common enough sight on the road at night.

Alarik McKorey watched him with a brooding expression.

"Treat her kindly, McJames, or I'll regret aiding ye." He turned his horse about, his men following suit. "Ride strong, man."

"I owe ye, McKorey. I'll nae forget that."

Alarik nodded his head before riding into the street once more. Cullen waited until the man was a good measure away before he and Druce took to the road. He urged his horse forward, needing to cover much ground before first light. Gaining McJames land was critical and every man behind him knew it. Only the faint sound of hooves meeting dirt, and leather shifting, filled the air. The crescent moon offered them the perfect darkness to carry their prize home. The wind stirred up the dry leaves on the ground like whispers of the past and other brides that had been carried away by moonlight.

Bronwyn lay against his shoulder, her body lax throughout the night. Cullen pressed a hand against her heart to feel for its steady motion. Deep satisfaction filled him as the hours passed along with the miles.

She was his. For honor's sake. For peace. For the rest of their lives.

Chapter Five

Her bed was moving.

Bronwyn frowned but opened her eyes when she felt the bite of the leather at the corners of her mouth. A hard, male arm was draped across her body, the hand cupping her hips far too familiarly. Her teeth ground against the leather, grinding it with her fury. The chest behind her rumbled, increasing her anger. Dawn was chasing the night away, the pink sky telling her that she'd slept the entire night.

The hand holding her hip slid up to cup her chin. She was sitting sideways across the horse, one thigh completely numb from the constant bouncing. Cullen raised her face to meet his stare.

"Good morning to ye, Bronwyn." Satisfaction coated his words. Bronwyn ground her teeth against her gag in reply. He chuckled, his fingers gently smoothing over her jaw.

"I think I'll leave that leather between yer teeth for a bit longer." He slipped a finger beneath it, testing how tight it was. The concern baffled her. The man was abducting her. She jerked her head, pulling her chin out of his hand. All traces of tenderness evaporated from his face, leaving only determination staring at her.

"We'll be discussing that a wee bit later, Bronwyn. But be assured that I will touch ye."

She snorted at his attention and refused to look at him.

He was too attractive.

She hated her body right then. Finding anything to like about her captor was intolerable. She needed to find her pride and refuse to notice that he was such a handsome man.

Well, Satan had been a cherub before falling from grace, too.

The last of night was rapidly giving way to daylight. They had left the city and the side of the road was rocky. The grass had turned brown now with the colder temperatures of the nights. Her toes were like ice in her boots. It was little wonder considering she was wearing only her chemise and stockings. A length of wool was wound around her and even up over her head. In spite of that she was freezing, a hard shiver shaking her. The hand on her hip moved, stroking her waist as though it were the most natural thing. As though he had the right to touch her.

She swallowed roughly. He had *taken* the right.

A rough breath rattled past her gag and there was no stopping the flood of despair that swept into her thoughts. Each pound of a hoof sounded louder than the last as the road kept falling away behind them. She had gone from being the property of a father who detested her to being the possession of a man who held good cause to hate her blood. It was disheartening, to say the least. Keir's face floated in her mind as she considered never seeing her brother again.

Or worse yet, hearing that he had taken up his sword to defend her. Her father would revel in another reason to rain violence on the McJames clan. Blood would be spilt and it sickened her.

The sun rose completely while she was lost in her dilemma. She felt the steady beat of her captor's heart against her shoulder and tried to wiggle away from it. The powerful stride of the horse threw her back until she gave up and remained still. She noticed the scent of his skin and tossed her head but there was no escaping. She'd never noticed that men smelled different. It touched off a current of awareness that made her quiver. The skin on her face recalled vividly how his fingers had felt against it.

He suddenly pulled his horse to a stop.

"There, lass." Ahead of them was a large stone tower. It was constructed of lighter castle stone and the morning sunlight made it look as though it were golden.

"Welcome to White Tower." The man beside them spoke to her. His face lit up as he looked at the tower with its large curtain wall that surrounded it. Set up on a rise, White Tower held the high ground, making it a formidable fortress.

The man beside them spurred his horse forward. Cullen stroked her hip once more. She turned her head and glared at his boldness. The look in his eyes sent a shiver down her spine because it lacked all remorse. Worse than that, there was a firm determination burning in his eyes that said the man considered it his right to touch her.

"My cousin Druce is lord of White Tower. It's the first castle on McJames land."

Bronwyn turned her head away to hide the fear that spiked through her. Cullen captured her chin, returning her face to where he could see it.

"Best that ye understand that there is no man who will help ye leave McJames land, Bronwyn."

She hissed at him, unable to fling the scathing retort that formed in her mind. She didn't need help. He was not the only one who knew how to make their way in this world.

"I suppose that sound means ye disagree with me." A hint of amusement edged his words now and it sparkled in his blue eyes. "'Tis nice to know that ye are nae a disappointment as far as yer spirit goes."

He chuckled but didn't waste any more time on talking. She felt his body move as he dug his heels into the sides of his horse. The huge beast took to the trail with amazing speed, covering the ground far faster than any mare she'd ever ridden. Before long they passed under the open gate of the outer wall. It was an iron one, held high by thick ropes on either side of the road. The inner yard was full of men and women working. Curious eyes moved over her but there wasn't a hint of disapproval. Quite the opposite. Many of the men grinned when Cullen allowed his cousin Druce to lift her off the saddle. The blue, yellow, and orange colors of the McJames's kilts surrounding her burned her eyes. The length of wool wrapped around her slithered down the moment she was stood on her feet.

A soft sound of distress made it past the gag when the bindings on her hands held them behind her. Her chemise was thin and the sunlight bright enough to illuminate her body.

"Here now, lass."

Druce grabbed the fabric and tossed it awkwardly around her body. The fabric didn't have anything to hold onto and it continued to slip toward her ankles in spite of his efforts.

Cullen ended his cousin's struggle by scooping her off her feet. A cheer went up from his men as the brute carried her up the steps that led into the tower. An arrogant grin covered his face as hers flamed scarlet.

To be sure, she hated him.

"Bastard." Bronwyn spat the word the moment her lips were free. She glared at her tormentor.

"Now there's the thing yer father hates me most for. I am legitimate. He won my mother away from yer father fair as could be and married her."

"Arrogant son of a thief."

Cullen clicked his tongue in reprimand. He held a dirk up in front of her eyes. "Careful, lass. Wound my feelings and I'll leave ye trussed up."

Bronwyn bit into her lip before she ended up earning a lesson from the cad. Her arms ached and her body was nearing its limit of endurance before she wet herself like a babe.

"If ye enjoy a foul-smelling captive, by all means leave me helpless."

The playful expression disappeared from his face instantly. He reached for her arms and she felt the steel of the blade kiss her skin. With one sharp jerk the binding loosened, allowing her to work it free. He cut the one holding her knees before she got her hands completely loose.

"I'll leave ye for a moment."

Bronwyn shot a stern look at his departing back. She wanted to spit a retort at him, but the needs of her body took precedence. It was indeed humbling to know that she was dependent on his goodwill to use the garderobe in private.

However, 'twas better than wetting herself.

Emerging from the closet that housed the necessities, she looked around the chamber. It was furnished with a large bed, hung with wool curtains that would keep the occupant warmer at night. The garderobe was set out a few feet from the rest of the room to allow the waste to drop into a barrel set below it. That barrel would be emptied often to keep disease and the stench from becoming a menace. It was a step up from chamber pots, to be sure, and one not found in many castles. Looking at the doorway of the closet, she noticed the newer stonework that edged it.

Besides the bed, there were two wide chairs sitting in front of the fireplace. They were built in the "X" fashion with padded seats and wide arms for resting your hands on. Both were huge, though, reminding her of how much larger Cullen was than herself.

Her chemise floated around her knees when she moved, making her keenly aware of how little clothing she had on her body. The soft linen was almost transparent; tonight when the fire was lit it would be. But she didn't have many options to cover herself. The length of McJames plaid was lying on the floor. She reached for it out of pure instinct to keep things tidy, folding it before her eyes really saw the McJames colors. She froze with it stretched out between her hands.

Never once had she thought to touch a McJames plaid.

It felt oddly intimate. Coupled with her new captivity, she felt possessed already and the man hadn't even stolen that kiss yet.

Be silent, Bronwyn . . . Longing for kisses is sure to land you in trouble . . .

The thoughts inside her head were wicked.

The hinges groaned as the door pressed inward. Part of her wanted to drop the plaid to show her defiance but the practical side of her brain reminded her that she'd be left standing in her shift if she did. Pride or modesty, she could not have both.

She dropped the McJames plaid.

Cullen's face was unreadable. He held the door wide for a young maid who stared at the dropped plaid as if it were a Bible flung carelessly to the floor. Her hands were full with a tray; she walked to the table and placed it down. She turned quickly, displaying the length of McJames plaid that was draped down her back, held by a belt at her waist and secured to her shoulder with a brass broach. It was the mark of a woman of the clan and she wore it proudly. She dipped down to pick up the wool lying on the floor. But Cullen pulled it from her hands when she went to pass him. She offered him a quick curtsy before disappearing into the hallway.

Cullen released the door and it fell closed with a heavy thud. He wound the plaid around his fist before slowly running his eyes down her length. It was a bold reprimand for her insolence. But Bronwyn raised her head, refusing to duck her chin. He was not her father, nor her brother or kin. Cullen McJames was her captor and she owed him nothing save contempt.

"Ye have lost yer mind, McJames. Stealing brides is a barbaric custom best left in years gone by."

Cullen raised one eyebrow. "Yer the one that is losing yer grip on what is what if ye think I am going to stand by while yer father calls me a blackguard who soils his neighbors' daughters."

"Do ye mean to say that ye dragged me here because of yer pride?"

He lifted his hand with the plaid. "Isn't that why ye dropped this when ye have nothing on but a chemise?" He tossed the plaid onto one of the chairs. "Or maybe ye're in the habit of displaying yer body to men."

"I am not." She said it too quickly. The heat edging her words betrayed just how much her father's words had hurt her. Cullen didn't need to know that she was as wounded by her father's words as he was. Discovering they had something in common felt wrong considering the man had abducted her. She could not look to him as a compatriot.

"But ye would rather let me see yer nipples instead of wearing a McJames plaid."

She crossed her arms over her chest but realized that the hair on her mons must also be showing through the thin fabric. Moving toward the bed, she tore the top coverlet back and yanked a sheet free.

"I would not even tell ye my name when we met."

He grunted. "I wondered about that."

"Good." She wrapped her body in the sheet while glaring at her captor. He granted her no mercy but stared at her the entire time, his eyes keenly observing her struggle to gather up the shreds of her modesty.

That eyebrow rose again but this time so did the corners of his lips. Amusement flickered in his eyes. "Ye enjoy knowing that I wonder about what sort of a woman ye are?"

Bronwyn hesitated. He was cleverly setting her words against her. She had never considered that he thought of her, too, but had believed that her dreams were something she alone experienced.

"This is nonsense." She crossed her arms on her chest. "Ye need to come to yer senses and end this game ye're playing with me." She didn't like how needy her words sounded.

"I assure ye, Bronwyn, 'tis no a game." He lost his teasing air, his face taking on a determined expression that sent a chill down her back. "I plan to wed ye."

She gasped, startled by his announcement. The man was boldness incarnate. "It is a game. Always with men there is the struggle to win. I am nae the first woman that has been taken to be held up as a prize between two arguing men. Or clans." Bronwyn shook her head, offering him a kind look in the hope that it might appeal to his sense of fairness. "Have done, Cullen, and send me home. My father will never change his ways, nae even for me."

Especially not for her . . . but it was her home and she had nowhere else to go. Better the devil she knew than the unknown one facing her. A husband had the right to beat his wife. At Red Stone, she had Keir and work she enjoyed doing. Cullen might lock her in a tower room with only enough necessities to keep her alive.

He moved toward her, closing the space with slow strides, his nearness making the breath freeze in her chest. The differences in their heights became obvious when she was forced to tip her head back to look up at him. She was too aware of him, too conscious of how little she wore and how much her skin longed to be stroked by his hands. Her feet scooted backward in retreat.

He stopped when she moved, a frown marking his mouth. "I'm sorry for that, Bronwyn."

He was, too. It stunned her, such caring from a man her father called enemy. There was honest sincerity in his eyes and it made him far more attractive than she'd already decided he was. It was so tempting to sink into that feeling and allow it to wrap around her. But how did she trust this man who had hauled her away from her family? She was his prize, nothing more.

"I won't marry ye." It was the only threat she held. His eyes narrowed when her words hit him.

"Then ye'll watch our first child be baptized a bastard."

Bronwyn gasped. She reached out before her stunned mind started working again, her hand delivering a sharp slap to his arrogant face. The sound was startling in the quiet room, but Cullen grinned at her, sending her temper into a full blaze again.

"That is a mean-hearted thing to say to a woman. It's the mother that is called slut when a babe is born out of marriage."

"Is that so?" His expression was guarded.

"It is."

"And yet I am the one saying that we should marry now,

afore our child is conceived." He paused, running his eyes down her length to pause on her flat belly. "If ye refuse me, ye'll have no one save yerself to blame when the gossips call ye a scarlet woman."

Her eyes narrowed. The man was far too cunning, but she refused to be trapped by his scheme. "I am no planning on having yer child. Why do ye think I refused to tell ye my name? I am no interested in ye. Not a bit." She propped her hands on her hips, making a stand that she couldn't truly back up. If the man was of the mind to force himself on her, there was little she might do to stop him. A twinge of something that felt like disappointment pierced her heart. She didn't want to think of Cullen as a man who would rape her.

Which was ridiculous. The man had kidnapped her. She had no reason to think highly of him. Better to expect the worst; it would hurt less that way.

"No a bit?" His lips twitched, rising into another grin that annoyed her. "Well now, it seems to me that ye were blushing back on that hillside. Just like ye are now."

She covered her cheeks with her hands and they were hot. "It is nae more than my temper."

" 'Tis much more."

He reached out in a motion so fast she stumbled trying to avoid his hand. She straightened up against the wall, any further retreat impossible, and his arms plenty long enough to span the distance between their bodies. His hand pushed her loose, flowing chemise flush against her body. But he did it with absolute control. There was no bite of his superior strength, only perfectly applied pressure. He cupped one breast, his thumb gliding across the hard point of her nipple.

"If ye are nae interested, why is yer nipple hard?"

His opposite hand pressed flat against the wall behind her, caging her between his arms. The knowledge that he could handle her more roughly held her in place to preserve the small distance he granted her. She stiffened as his thumb rubbed her nipple. Never once had she believed that so small a touch, so tiny a contact between two people, might spark such a torrent of sensation. It flooded her, shaking her with its intensity.

"I am cold, ye daft man. Ye stole me in my chemise."

And she was a liar, God forgive her.

"I've noticed that, fair Bronwyn. 'Tis the truth that I've enjoyed the sight of ye." His lips formed a sensuous expression that was sinfully carnal. "It kept me alert all night long knowing how bare ye were beneath that McJames wool."

"Exactly the sort of thing a blackguard would say. Have ye no decency?" She sounded too desperate for her taste but she was running short on reasons to deny him. Her life at Red Stone was nothing so wonderful. A ragged breath shook her, warm delight flowing through her. It was for sure that no man wearing her father's colors had ever made her blush.

"I'm not the one refusing to wed. I believe most would say that I'm behaving correctly by insisting that we go to church and marry. Before temptation gets the better of us both."

He chuckled, leaning closer. She felt the brush of his breath against her lips now and her mouth went dry. His lower lip quivered in anticipation, her gaze lowering to his mouth as she wondered what his kiss would be like.

"It will be my pleasure to help ye warm up." His voice was husky and dark with promise. His thumb moved once more across the top of her nipple. The hand on the wall moved, capturing the back of her head, his fingers threading through the strands of her unbound hair. Her hands sprang up between them, pushing against the hard wall of his chest.

He took her mouth, sealing her gasp inside. He tasted her lower lip with the tip of his tongue before invading her mouth.

The hand on the back of her head held her in place while he tilted his to the side so that their lips met. She jerked in his embrace, out of sheer surprise. There were too many signals rushing through her, too many sensations to understand. When her back left the wall, his hand slid smoothly around her body. Her skin hummed with enjoyment, everywhere he held her. Beneath her hands, she felt the steady beat of his heart. Her fingertips joined her lips in discovering a bounty of pleasurable sensations that she'd never experienced before. His lips pressed hers open, demanding a deeper intimacy while he pulled her up against his body. Heat flared through her. She twisted, attempting to understand why she liked his kiss so much. Her body urged her to return it, move her mouth in unison, to taste him.

A soft moan got past their joined lips.

She was leaning back against the wall again a moment later. Cullen's hands pressed flat on either side of her head, imprisoning her without touching her. A dangerous look flickered in his eyes, one that reminded her of a predator that needed only one move from her to trigger the instinct to pounce.

But he was breathing as hard as she was. She placed a hand on his chest before thinking about it, acting on the impulse. Her fingertips pressing against his warm skin and feeling the hard beat of his heart.

His blue eyes captured her gaze, locking and searching her eyes for a long time. Her heart slowed down from its frantic pace, but not all the way to normal. Excitement still pulsed through her, triggered by the scent of his skin.

She liked it . . . the way he smelled. Shocking, mysterious, and slightly overwhelming, but there was no denying that she found it attractive. The flare of hunger in his gaze mesmerized her. Her pride enjoyed knowing that she aroused him.

"Will ye marry me, Bronwyn McQuade?"

His voice was husky and rough. It tempted her with that edginess because the part of her that had lamented never having a husband wanted to say yes.

But she refused to be another blow in a feud. It would be nothing but a way to strike at her sire, and her father would use it as an excuse to shed blood.

Possibly Cullen's blood.

Pain nipped at her heart. The frustration of her entire life ripping and tearing at her conscience. There were no good choices, only ones that would hurt others.

"Ye have stolen me, and that is no way to begin a marriage."

He snarled softly at her, his fingers curling. But she refused to take back her words.

"What do you suggest, Bronwyn? Should I have ridden up to your father's gate and asked to court ye?"

His eyes narrowed, heat flickering in them. "Or would ye have met me on the border land?"

"I swore I'd never return there. 'Twas a foolish thing to do, riding so far from Red Stone. I've no excuse to offer. 'Tis a fact that I'm too old to be acting like such a child. Riding off without any thought for the world around me."

She pushed her way past him, ducking under his arm and not caring if he did allow her to do it. She didn't want him to see the lament in her eyes. "There was enough trouble from our meeting to last me a lifetime."

"Aye, that's true enough." His voice rose betraying his anger. "What do ye call this tale spinning around the court that I used ye?"

Her face flamed scarlet. "I never said that."

"But ye dinna voice an objection when yer father was saying that I used ye to all in earshot either."

Bronwyn stared at him in shock. "I dinna get a chance. The king took him away as soon as he said it."

"He is a liar." Cullen pointed one thick finger at her. "Listen to me well, madam. I'll nae wear the stain of this. We'll marry and that's the end of the matter. That will leave the gossips with nothing to say except that we did things out of order. That is forgivable. Neither of us will wear the mark of sin as long as we wed."

He was far more noble than any man she knew. She stared at him in awe for a long moment, absorbing the look of integrity on his face. It looked very fine indeed.

Bronwyn shook her head. Cullen wanted her to agree to wed him. Once that was finished and the bedding completed he might begin to extract vengeance on her. She did not know his true nature, knew no one who might tell her what sort of man he was. To trust him was a huge leap of faith and she stood to lose a great deal if it proved he was playing her falsely. Once she was his wife, the law and the church would be on his side.

"My father intended to return me to Red Stone. Set me free. That will end the matter."

"No to my satisfaction, it willnae." Cullen transformed into the warrior she'd known he must be. He hooked his hands into his wide belt, the corded muscles showing from the rolled-up cuffs of his shirt. He still wore his great sword, the hilt rising above his left shoulder. There was no sign of the tender concern she'd witnessed earlier; all that showed from his eyes was pure determination.

"Returning ye home will nae cleanse my name and that of my clan." He stood firm in his belief, his face hard and unrelenting. "As laird, yer father should know what weight his words carry. If he expected me to ignore the stain, he was very much mistaken."

"Yer quarrel is with my father, not me."

Cullen offered her a slight break in his stony expression.

"And yer father's quarrel with me is something my father did before I was even born."

"Which is why there is nothing to be done about it. My father will nae change his ways, no matter what ye and I do. Better to not risk offending God by taking marriage vows that are insincere."

He pressed his lips tighter together. "I'll tell ye only once, Bronwyn, never say that I don't keep my vows. If I make a promise, 'tis for sure that I will stand behind my words."

His voice was solid and edged with determination so sharp it was tempting to surrender to his wishes, just listening to him. Many a wife wished for so devoted a spouse. In truth, there were far too many mothers who wished for a wedding to cleanse the illegitimacy from their children. But Cullen wasn't simply smitten with her, the man wanted more than her affection.

"I will not be the weapon ye wield against my father. Have done with this. Enough blood has been spilt already between our clans. I dinna want to give anyone an excuse to fight in the spring."

Cullen snorted. "Obviously ye need time to adjust to yer situation. What I'm offering is the opportunity to put an end to the fighting and the gossip." His expression tightened. "And that is what I will have of ye, Bronwyn. One way or the other. I'll wed ye whenever ye decide. If that is in front of a midwife, so be it."

He turned and strode toward the door. The hinges groaned once again when he yanked it open.

"There's a meal for ye on the tray. Any of the maids will tell ye where the bathing tubs are. Try to leave the tower and ye'll be returned to the chamber I'm sleeping in."

Her eyes widened. "For what?"

His lips twitched up, hunger flickering through his eyes

once more. "For me to keep ye warm as a husband should. I suggest ye think about that before testing the alertness of my cousin's men." Cullen inspected her with his eyes once more, his gaze lingering on the small points of her nipples where they poked against the supple fabric of her chemise. "Or don't. I've been thinking about ye far too much since meeting ye. I'd just as soon overwhelm ye and have done with all yer arguments."

"Well, I would not."

He chuckled but it wasn't a nice sound. There was a dark promise lurking in his eyes now, one that set her heart to racing again. "We'll rest the horses for a day and then I intend to take ye to Sterling."

"I won't wed with ye, Cullen McJames."

He smirked at her before moving into the hallway. "Yes ye will, Bronwyn, because I will nae allow any man to blacken my name. No even yer father. The McQuades will learn that a McJames will nae take dishonor from their hand. Yer father thought a union between us something to talk about . . . well, I intend to have the last word on the matter. And that is a promise."

The door shut with a hard thump. The sound pierced her heart with a finality that nearly stopped it. Sterling was the earl of Alcaon's main residence. Brodick McJames was Cullen's older brother, his only brother. The man had wed himself to an English woman who brought more land to his holding, English land. Her father had launched new raids on the McJames in his rage. She doubted Brodick would make Cullen send her home, but she had to clutch at the tiny seed of hope that the earl might decide he didn't need more trouble from the McQuades.

It was far more likely that the earl would order her starved until she took her wedding vows.

She snarled as she turned and smothered a scream behind a

hand. Her father and his endless greed! She stood a captive in naught but her chemise because of a dice game thirty-five years ago.

Men . . .

They used women. Pain slashed through her, her eyes burning as she struggled not to shed the tears that welled. It was a futile effort. The wet drops sliding down over her hot cheeks as she looked around the room, desperately trying to think of a solution.

There was none.

Both her father and Cullen wanted nothing but to make her dance to their tune. Perform like a string puppet to amuse them and place gold in their hands.

Now it seemed even her body was betraying her. She wrapped her arms around herself because she ached. Her skin was alive, every nerve ending tingling with awareness, craving another stroke or touch from Cullen. Each nipple remained hard, the fabric of her chemise stimulating the sensitive buds. Both mounds felt swollen and far more tender than she had ever noticed before.

The needy ache bled lower until it settled between her thighs. Never once had she burned for a man. For certain, she had heard talk of it. That thing that otherwise obedient daughters slipped off into the night to sample because they could not resist the hunger for it any longer.

Lust . . .

She'd listened to many a sermon on the evils of it. In sooth, she'd shaken her head when overhearing the maids talking about their sweethearts. Wondering how they might be so foolish as to follow love anywhere. Love was the path to ruin, the church preached it, even Shakespeare wrote it in his plays. This was her retribution for judging others, this chastisement from her own flesh.

More tears spilled down her cheeks. She abhorred crying but seemed unable to stem the emotional tide washing over her. The fact that she was in a strange home, however finer it was than her own chamber at Red Stone, only increased her feelings of dismay.

It only served to increase her awareness of her fate. Bronwyn suddenly hissed. She wiped the tears off her face, grinding her teeth at her own weakness. She refused to endure without attempting to guide her own destiny.

She was a McQuade after all. Her brother Keir was a man worthy of respect, so she would endure and discover some way to return to the life she had earned. Staying meant trusting that Cullen was not the same as her own brothers, Liam and Sodac. She would be a fool to think the McJames was any less a warrior for his clan. Once she was at Sterling, it was very likely that she'd be shut away like the prisoner she was. Any wedding performed would be nothing but more chains to keep her in the stronghold of her father's enemy. Her father raided the McJames. She had no reason to suspect that any of them would like her. Cullen had stolen her to clear his name, nothing more. Better she dwell on how to escape, for it appeared that the only person she knew was telling her the truth was herself. There was still God, but she doubted that the angels would appear to set her free. There were plenty of stolen brides in Scotland to prove that.

No, if she wanted freedom, she would have to escape. She would worry about what to do with that freedom once she held it.

She moved to the door, inspecting it. There was a heavy bar slide on the inside that she might use to lock it. But that would lock her inside the chamber. She reached for the handle only to stop halfway there. There would be no easy escape from the tower yard, especially in her chemise. If she wanted to succeed, she would have to plan carefully.

Instead she walked back to the tray of food. She was too angry to be hungry but she picked up the bread and cheese, stashing them behind the pillows on the bed. Then she went to the door and pulled it open. Finding herself a dress would prove more challenging, but she was up to it.

She would not yield. Not now, not ever.

Cullen McJames could choke on his pride.

So could her father.

He needed some rest but his body wasn't interested in sleeping. Beneath his kilt his cock was hard. In the kitchen he found Druce bathing.

"Och now, ye look like a demon."

"Shut up, Druce. I'm nae in the mood for teasing."

There was a splash as his cousin poured a bowl of water over his head. He shook it out of his eyes and shot Cullen a glare. "Now there's the thanks I get for riding all night. Even gave up me plaid."

"I appreciate it." He just felt like strangling Bronwyn at the moment. "That woman is stubborn."

Druce laughed. "And ye and Brodick wonder why I'm nae married. Show me a female who's biddable and I'll take her to church quick."

Cullen unlacing his boots then shook his head. He didn't want biddable. It was a sure thing that Bronwyn's stubbornness wasn't what he'd planned on when taking a wife, but he couldn't deny the way it stirred his blood. He wanted her and his cock was still hard from tasting her sweet kiss.

He moved the water trough Druce had used to fill the tub he was in to another tub and pulled the shingle free to fill it. He didn't bother to add hot water but stripped off his clothing and sat down in the cold water. Druce made a poor attempt at smothering a chuckle.

His cousin laughed outright when Cullen turned a deadly glare at him. But he tossed a chunk of soap across the distance. Catching it, Cullen worked it over his skin, concentrating on the task in an attempt to ignore that demanding bit of flesh between his legs. He'd never been so hard, at least not when he wasn't with the woman who had sparked that interest.

"She says she'll nae wed me." And that stung. The feeling took him by surprise. He wasn't sure what he felt for Bronwyn. Having his pride within her striking range was sobering and a bit unsettling, too.

"She's nae the first abducted bride to say that when the question is first put to her." Druce was serious now. "The taking is not the hard part. 'Tis the convincing that takes a clever man."

And so it would. Cullen dumped water over his head to wash his hair. He liked being clean. Half of the nobles in court didn't value a good bath as much as he did. They stank like manure piles.

Bronwyn smelled sweet. She tasted sweet, too. He finished his bathing and stood up with his cock still firm. Kissing her might have been a mistake because sleep was going to prove elusive with her taste clinging to his lips. It was more involved than that, though. The way she returned his kiss, shyly, proving her inexperience, was what burned in his thoughts. For a single moment she'd tried to return his kiss, mimic his motions with her own mouth.

It had been sweeter than anything he'd ever experienced.

He smoothed out his plaid on the table that had been placed in the bathing room just for that purpose. The front legs were slightly shorter than the back ones. Wooden pegs had been set into the center of it to hold a belt steady while a man pleated the fabric in even folds. Most men used the foot of their bed to lay out their kilts, but Druce had seen the benefit of having a table constructed for more ease when donning the garment. This way he didn't have to bend his back all the way over to pull the belt around his waist. The pegs held the belt steady and all ye had to do was back up to the wooden surface once the pleating was done.

Druce watched him buckle his belt with a firm hand.

"Yer nae going to get some rest?"

Cullen scowled, his cock demanding he go to bed but not for sleeping.

"No now."

Druce chuckled while pleating his own kilt. Cullen didn't remain in the bathing room to hear the man's amusement.

He scoffed as he walked through the hallways toward the front entrance. Bronwyn McQuade had managed to kill his sense of humor. He stood on the front step, watching the activity in the yard as the sun began to arch back down on the horizon.

Now that was something he was going to have to fix. Right after he warmed the lass up. A grin lifted his lips as he considered the way she moved in his embrace.

Aye, warming her up was going to be a pleasure.

His pleasure.

"Och now, look at ye."

Bronwyn grimaced as one of the older maids spied her. The woman shook her head and shot a stern look at the two women who tried to tell her to ignore Bronwyn.

"Yer a sad lot, letting a girl walk around in her chemise and it being November." She clicked her tongue. "Come on with ye, child, there is no point in sneaking about like a specter. Everyone knows who ye be."

Of course they did.

Her sarcastic thoughts didn't change the way the woman stared at her.

"I'm called Lydia. Come on with ye and let's see if we can't find something for ye to wear."

"I'd be appreciative."

Lydia smiled at her. The woman considered her with a critical eye when Bronwyn stepped all the way into the kitchen. She suddenly smiled.

"Yer about the same size as Murain be. She's due to birth her first child next month so she has nae need of her long stays." Lydia nodded, obviously pleased with herself. "Go on back to yer chamber and I'll send someone to fetch some of Murain's clothing up to ye. Let's nae be letting the men see ye walking around like that."

Bronwyn nodded, keeping her mouth shut. She needed the clothing, and offending Lydia by insulting her clan was not going to endear the woman to her. Turning around, she paused in front of one of the large windows that allowed light into the kitchens. There was costly glass covering the window in six inch squares held together by lead. Such windows in a work area were the mark of a rich household with a laird that didn't begrudge his servants comforts. Red Stone had wooden shutters that were slid open in fair weather. When it rained, the kitchen was shut up tight and the servants had to endure the dark.

The kitchens faced the stables. Cullen stood next to his horse. He was rubbing the animal with steady motions. There was tender concern in his touch. That same thing she had glimpsed in his eyes for a few moments.

Her father and older brothers never took care of their own mounts. They considered it their right to have others do the labor.

There was a grin on Cullen's lips, reminding her of how he'd looked the first time she'd met him. Part of him was still a mischievous boy who enjoyed playing. But there was also a side of him that was a hardened man.

"Och now, stop undressing the man with yer eyes," Lydia scolded her in an amused tone. That set a few of the maids to giggling. The woman moved up behind her, cupping her shoulders with her hands. "Although, I'll admit to understanding yer fascination with that one. He's a fair bonnie sight."

"Not to me, he isna."

Lydia chuckled at her. Bronwyn frowned, moving her attention away from Cullen. She needed to learn about the grounds if she intended to escape. The stables were large with many men and horses in front of it. Even through the window she could hear a blacksmith working somewhere nearby. What drew her notice was the doublets that were tossed over the rails of the stalls inside the stables. Obviously the retainers stored the outer garments there in case of nighttime raids that called them from their beds quickly. Many of the retainers most likely slept in bedrolls laid out on the floor of the main hall after it had been cleared for the night.

And she had a length of McJames plaid in her chamber, enough for a kilt on her smaller frame. The idea took root in her mind—maybe the inhabitants would notice a woman, but would they stop a young lad from leaving?

"Yer eyes tell a different story, lass." Lydia gave her a gentle push. "Go on now, that chemise is too thin by far. Yer shivering."

She was, but hadn't noticed. Bronwyn worried her lower lip as she cast a last look at Cullen. No, she had not noticed the chill while looking at him. She was tempted to ask Lydia what sort of man Cullen was. But the woman was a McJames, so she'd likely defend a fellow member of her clan.

She quickly climbed the narrow stairs back to the floor with

her chamber in it. Relief swept through her when she was
once again behind the door. Her belly rumbled but she didn't
want to eat the bread or cheese she'd hidden. But there was a
small bowl of porridge on the tray. It had gone cold while
Cullen was in the room with her.

While he was kissing her . . .

Bronwyn snorted at her thoughts but she still recalled in
vivid detail the way his mouth had felt against her own. The
way he'd slipped his tongue across her lower lip, tasting her
like aged whiskey. She shivered, caught in the memory. Her
skin flushed and her heart accelerated. That tremor of anticipation returned, only this time it was stronger and more exciting.

Picking up the McJames plaid, she pushed it beneath the
pillow on the bed where her food was hidden. She refused to
listen to the warning voice inside her head. The church preached
against women dressing as men but the scriptures would not
be helping her out of this mess. There were many who believed any female who dressed as a male was possessed of the
devil. Bronwyn shook such ideas out of her mind. She would
try it.

Before Cullen got around to warming her up again.

Reaching for the cold porridge, she ate it in spite of its lack
of taste. There were small bits of fruit stewed into it that at
least were sweet. She'd have forced herself to consume it if it
tasted like dirt. Strength was the key to her liberation. An
empty belly would see her failing.

She mustn't allow her body to weaken. Cullen would seize
the opportunity to bend her. She might be fascinated by the
boy in him, but it was the man who posed the threat. Her own
body turned traitor under his touch. Her father might detest
her, but he could not wipe her thoughts from her mind such
as Cullen did with his kiss.

She would not be prey to him. The only thing she truly had was her own sense of being. As humble a possession as that might be, she refused to relinquish it to the lust Cullen unleashed in her.

Maybe she would not go back to Red Stone at all. The idea lingered in her thoughts while her logic told her what a bad concept it was. The world was a harsh place without a clan. If she returned to Edinburgh alone, she might end up in a whorehouse, or worse, on a ship bound for the Muslim countries because their law forbade enslavement of fellow followers of Islam. Christians were sold for gold in those places.

She could not go to court. Her father would find her there and the king might give Cullen permission to wed her. Such was the way of men, using women to settle their accounts.

Lying down, she tugged the bed curtains closed to block out the light. Her mind wanted to turn her circumstances over and over but she forced herself to sleep. She would need the strength when she made a run for it.

Chapter Six

"There now. That's much better." Lydia propped her hands on her hips to survey her work. "There's no need for ye to be near naked all the day long after all. I'm sure the laird will see about getting ye clothing."

"Laird?" Bronwyn looked at Lydia in confusion. "I thought his older brother was laird."

"Oh, to be sure his brother is the earl and Laird McJames, but his father never absorbed the title their sweet mother brought to the McJames because he had two sons. Cullen Mc-James is Laird Lampart. It's a baronial that he holds in his own right." Lydia clicked her tongue and reached out to adjust the sleeve of Bronwyn's dress. It was a pretty green wool that had brown edging and over sleeves for more warmth. It was too lightweight for the heart of winter that was coming, but finding a good dress to wear was lucky. Clothing was made for each person's body, trading it about was asking for boned stays to jab into your hip or the doublet to dig into you beneath your arms. Most girls didn't have but two dresses, and only replaced them when they were worn through. Sewing took time and it often had to be done once a full day's work was behind you.

"Please thank Murain for allowing me to wear her dress."

Lydia grinned. "Young McJames sent her a piece of gold already. She needs that more than a dress she'll no be able to wear anytime in the next year."

The dress would allow her to walk around the tower, to get closer to the stable, but knowing that Cullen had paid for it made her wish she could refuse to wear it. A jolt of guilt crossed her mind. It would seem that men were not the only ones who followed their pride.

She would wear the dress, and without a hint of concern for the gold it had cost her captor. It was his fault that she needed anything from him. And she would not feel grateful toward him either. She was a hostage; it was her duty to scorn the man responsible for her plight.

Indeed, it was.

Frustration set her teeth to grinding. Her feelings were all jumbled and unrecognizable. She actually liked the things Cullen did, approving of his conduct.

She was acting like a fool.

The sun was setting and she had only one day to escape the confines of this McJames stronghold. Sterling would be near impossible to escape. It was not just the castle she would have to work her way free of, but she needed to get off McJames land before she was run down by Cullen and that stallion he rode.

"I'm nae surprised that ye did not know of his title. Those brothers stick together. It makes the McJames stronger because they are not fighting among themselves like so many sons do when their father leaves this world."

Bronwyn nodded agreement without really thinking. She could see Liam and Sodac fighting once her father was gone. Keir suspected as much; that was why he was always keeping a personal hand on the investments and books of Red Stone. Liam and Sodac would be foolish to push him out when he kept the silver flowing into the McQuades' hands. All lairds had tenants, and from there they received rents due, but it took a clever mind to double and triple that money by investment. Without Keir, her brothers would see their share dwindle quickly.

Her belly rumbled again because of her meager meal.

"Come on, lass, let's feed ye. It's near time for supper."

"I'd like that."

More important, she'd enjoy the chance to escape the chamber. Lydia led the way down the stairs and through a few larger rooms. The scent of roasting meat sent her belly into another long rumble that Bronwyn tried to ignore. If supper was being laid on the table, most of the White Tower inhabitants would be making their way to the tables lest they miss the last warm meal of the day. Supper was always served while there was good daylight remaining to clean up after the meal was eaten. Candles and firewood were resources best used sparingly, so the inhabitants rose with the sun and settled in for the night when it surrendered to nightfall. Overhead a bell began to ring, echoing through the stone walls.

"See there? Supper is being served."

Lydia didn't give her the chance to slip away, instead reaching down and clasping her wrist. Bronwyn stared at the hold, fighting the impulse to jerk her arm away. But that would not do her cause any good. Better to allow Lydia to think her frightened enough to comply.

"Here now. Supper smells good today."

The main hall of White Tower was a large rectangular room. It had a raised ceiling that was circled by hallways on the upper floor. Bronwyn marveled at the soft sounds of music drifting down over the rapidly filling tables. Music was a treat, something normally reserved for feast days and celebrations.

Celebrations . . .

Her eyes widened as the hall quieted when Lydia pulled her

into it. Men turned to look at her, curiosity on their faces. Smiles abounded and many raised their tankards to her. Lydia kept her moving at a steady pace, but Bronwyn recoiled when she got a look at the head table.

Cullen sat there with his cousin, Druce. Next to them was a bishop in his white short robe and black square-topped wool hat. A gold cross hung around his neck as a symbol of his office within the reformed church. One of the new changes James Stuart was making to the Kirk of Scotland, bishops were beginning to show up as the governing body of the church. They held high position by royal command. Refusing the instructions of a bishop was something no wise person did.

To write and seal a marriage contract, you needed a bishop. She saw the glint of candlelight flickering off the heavy signet ring affixed to his right hand.

She stopped moving, forcing Lydia to drag her or release her. The maid turned to look at her, but Bronwyn was staring at Cullen.

Of all the sneaky things . . .

The man smiled at her and reached up to tug the corner of his knitted bonnet. He wore a doublet that was buttoned up to mid-chest. The creamy linen of his shirt showed through the open front of the sleeves. But he had the cuffs of that shirt secured around his wrists. It was far more formal than he'd been that morning, warning her that the man intended to press her to take vows tonight.

Well, not if she didn't get close enough for that bishop to speak with her. She suddenly hated the dress, because no man of the church would invade her chamber if she was wearing nothing but a chemise.

"May I present my bride, Bishop Shaman." Cullen's voice bounced down the length of the hall. Druce's men let out a cheer as they lifted their tankards high. Bronwyn shuddered, her cheeks turning red with rage, but the bishop crooked his finger at her. There was no way to refuse his command without painting herself a disobedient Christian soul. She'd end in the stocks if she offended the man.

Bronwyn forced her feet forward and her teeth into her lower lip. Finding herself locked into wooden stocks for public humiliation wasn't a pleasant idea. The offender would do their time no matter the weather. Often they were whipped while helpless to ensure they felt the disapproval of the entire community. Children would be brought by their schoolmasters and mothers to gaze upon her and learn what the penalties were for denying the authority of the church. Of course, it would all be done in the interest of purging her soul and teaching her her place so that God would not be offended by her lack of humility.

The church was the one constant in a land where clans ruled absolutely on their ancestral lands. No one refused a bishop, not even the king did so publicly.

Cullen McJames was not fighting fairly. First stolen kisses, and now a bishop! She was right to suspect him. A wedding performed by a bishop would be impossible to dissolve. Cullen and his brother could petition the king for her dowry armed with the seal from that signet ring. All the time, she might be locked away, only kept alive so that the McJames might gain money for her. And it was also a fact that she would not have to live very long, only a few years for the McJames to have claim to a share of her father's holdings.

Cullen might lay with her but once to consummate the union before taking his hot kisses to a McJames lass who didn't have the blood of his enemy flowing through her veins.

She ground her teeth, a hot flash of jealousy surprising her.

"Come along now, the bishop is no a man to be kept waiting, dear." Lydia tugged on her wrist. Bronwyn sealed her emotions behind a blank expression and walked toward the high table. She stopped and lowered herself in front of the bishop.

Bishop Shaman nodded approval at her. A small ripple of conversation went through those watching. The man stood up and the hall instantly fell silent. Bronwyn felt every set of eyes in the hall on her back.

"Marriage is a holy estate, free of sin. All true Christian souls should strive to marry and refuse lustful wonderings."

There was a mutter of agreement while heads nodded.

"Join us, my dear." The bishop extended his hand toward the empty chair at the high table. That simple gesture was as solid as chains being locked around her.

"Ye are too kind, yer Grace."

And Cullen was too sure of himself by far . . .

The only available seat at the high table was next to Cullen. A groom pulled a heavy X chair back for her. The man pushed it toward the table the moment she sat in it, trapping her between Druce and Cullen. Maids instantly began serving the table in fine fashion. If she hadn't known that she had been abducted and therefore not expected, she might never have guessed, because the meal was so lavish.

As far as celebrations went, it lacked nothing. There was mulled wine and roasted meats. Candied fruits graced the table along with dried ones being mixed in with breads. The bishop dined well, clearly enjoying the rich fare.

Unfortunately, she enjoyed none of it because Cullen was enjoying himself far too much at her expense. She waited until Bishop Shaman was engaged in a loud conversation with Druce before turning her wrath on the man sitting so smugly beside her.

"I told ye nae."

His expression might be playful, but when she looked into his eyes she noticed the burning determination. He offered her no quarter. His face might not be painted blue for fighting, but it was certainly the image of a hardened warrior.

"And I warned ye to consider yer options." He shot a hard look at her. "But I'll be most interested in listening to how ye plan to tell the bishop about yer desire to nae wed with me."

"I will tell him."

Cullen lost his amused expression. His lips pressed into a firm line as hunger drew his face tight. "And I will inform him of what yer father told one and all. That I have had ye."

"That is a lie." She kept her voice low because her heart jumped at the very idea. The lust he'd stirred in her flared up at the mere suggestion of his touch now. It was truly a poison. Once infected, she was doomed.

"Yer father did say it, that part is no a lie."

"But ye haven't . . ." She failed to voice the last few words because they felt like some sort of surrender.

He smiled, an unpleasant expression that was full of hunger and promise.

"I will."

He grasped her hand, imprisoning it in his larger one. She was instantly aware of how his skin felt against hers, how much she enjoyed the touch.

His touch . . .

Cullen leaned closer, angling his head toward her. Two of his fingers stroked the underside of her wrist. Her breath caught in her throat, her heart accelerating while he stroked her delicate skin once, twice more.

"Dinna doubt it, Bronwyn. There's too much passion between us."

His fingers slid over her inner wrist and up to the hollow of her palm. A deep shiver shook her, forcing a soft gasp out of her lips. His face shone with satisfaction, deep, hard male satisfaction.

"'Tis only lust."

He shrugged. "That has its place between a man and wife, too. But this is more. Ye felt it the day we met. It was more than lust that colored yer cheeks."

She shook her head, but Cullen suddenly straightened, looking beyond her. There was a chuckle from Druce and another from the bishop. Horror flooded her as she turned to look at the man of the clergy.

Bishop Shaman looked pleased, enormously so. He clapped his hands together, making a loud pop. With a satisfied smile he rubbed his palms against each other with glee.

"Come, my children, let us settle this matter between ye."

The bishop stood without looking behind him. The grooms pulled his chair back before the powerful representative of the church knocked his shins against its legs. There was hustle all around the head table as the staff made sure the bishop's desires were granted quickly. All the chairs were pulled back. Bronwyn frowned but stood up.

Cullen didn't release her hand. Possibly because he knew she'd rather duck into the kitchen than follow the bishop to any place where the matter of her marriage might be settled.

That's no quite so . . .

Temptation was a demon because it whispered to her, reminding her how much she did like his touch. Escaping Cullen meant sealing her fate when it came to marriage. She would never know a man's kiss again unless she wanted to make the gossips correct by becoming soiled.

She looked at Cullen's hand where it was clasped around her wrist. He held her limb lightly but securely. The skin of her inner wrist was keenly aware of each of his fingers and there was no trying to tell herself that she disliked the way his skin felt against hers.

Or the way he kissed.

Her eyes moved up his arm, staring at the linen of his shirt still buttoned around his wrist. No man had ever dressed formally for her. She'd always considered it a useless waste of time, the rules that supposedly went with courting. But she suddenly felt plain with her hair hanging down her back in nothing more than a single braid.

Druce led the bishop to his private receiving room. It didn't take very long for them to cover the distance. It was a comfortable room with a large fireplace. Windows ran along one wall, and hanging over them were draperies made of velvet. The fabric was worthy of a king. She reached out to gently touch it because it was too much of a temptation. Her hand glided along the surface of the fabric, as soft as a baby's new hair.

"Well now, my children."

Bishop Shaman clearly enjoyed his position and the duties that went along with his church robes. The man settled himself in a large X chair that had ornately carved hand rests in the shape of lion claws. There was a carpet beneath the legs of the chair, spread out over the stone floor, adding another touch of luxury to the room.

Two grooms had followed them and they silently set up a traveling desk on a side table. An inkwell and quill were pulled from within the desk along with a sheet of paper. Her throat constricted as she watched one last item come out of that desk. It was a finger of sealing wax and a candle. Held in a short holder, the groom lit it and placed the wax near it. Her gaze flew to the bishop and the signet ring sitting on his right hand.

Aye, Cullen McJames was a warrior, all right. The man didn't plan to allow her any chance to escape him. But she understood. His honor was at stake.

Yet so was hers. It was a poor child who shamed her parents. Even though her sire hated her, there was a lifetime of church teaching that forbade her to judge her father. Indecision gripped her so tightly, she forgot to breathe. She stared at Cullen, trying to understand why she had to reject him. She was truly torn, but one truth stuck in her thoughts. She knew her life at Red Stone. There was respect there. Even friends . . . well, maybe not friends but people who were kind toward her. She went where she wanted, had the things that she needed. Her attention settled on the blue, yellow, and orange of the McJames plaid. At Sterling there would be no kindness for a McQuade. Cullen would use her to strike back at his enemy, but she would be the one who would have to live her life among a clan who detested her blood.

It was a bleak prospect that even the hot attraction brewing inside her belly could not warm.

"Bronwyn McQuade."

Her mind snapped back to the man sitting in front of her. The bishop eyed her with a stern look.

"Cullen has made a petition to me for license to wed with ye." The bishop's voice dropped a few notes as he applied his considerable authority over her.

"That is a matter best taken to my father."

Cullen snorted. "That is nae possible and ye know it." Exasperation laced his voice.

"As an obedient daughter I must refer ye to my father. It is tradition." She lifted her chin, refusing to negotiate.

"So is marrying to end a feud."

"Exactly." Bishop Shaman slapped his hand down on top of one armrest. The sound startled her with how loud and final it was. The bishop raised one hand. "Sometimes it is necessary to dispense with some traditions in favor of the greater good."

Bronwyn felt the trap closing around her. "I cannae wed without my father's permission."

"Ye mean ye willna." Cullen stepped closer, his eyes dancing with impending victory. "Which is why I stole ye."

She gasped, her eyes widening. The determination in Cullen's eyes scraped across her composure, making her angry at his manipulation of her life. It might not be much, but it was hers. She would not be his prize, used to soothe his pride.

"I do not want to marry any man who seeks me for retaliation against my kin."

Cullen's face changed; it wasn't a softening but a shifting in his expression from solid determination to hunger.

"I want ye for more." His voice was softer now, deeper. Heat flowed into her cheeks and her lower lip went dry. Before she thought better of it, she licked her lip. His eyes instantly dropped to her mouth, sending a quiver through her belly.

Bishop Shaman cleared his throat. Cullen flushed for a change and turned to look toward the man. His humility was short-lived though. He tilted his head and shrugged.

"Now ye see why I'm set to get married."

"I see quite clearly." The bishop didn't sound as somber as she would have expected. Instead there was a twinkle in his eye and a grin curving his lips. He gestured toward his men with the desk. One picked up the quill and dipped it into the ink. There was a dull scratch as he set it to the parchment.

"We'll see to this agreement and set down the legal document." Cullen and Druce both nodded agreement. "And then I shall hear yer vows."

Bronwyn felt that grip on her throat once more. She shook her head and Cullen growled. The sound was low and full of impatience. But it was Bishop Shaman who demanded her compliance.

"Are ye refusing to wed?" He leaned forward to peer at her. "I've never been to McQuade land. Is yer father a Christian?"

Now true fear sent its icy touch across her. This was dangerous ground for anyone who didn't want to end in prison for suspicion of witchcraft. The church would expect her to take the honorable union that Cullen was offering because it would cleanse her of the sin her father had said she'd committed with Cullen. To refuse marriage with him was to say she preferred immorality. The bishop could have her lashed until she repented of her sinful ways. But if she married Cullen the man might beat her simply because she displeased him by being the daughter of his enemy.

Druce and Cullen knew exactly what they were doing. It was a harsh and unrelenting war on her personal refusal to take marriage vows.

At least Cullen hadn't raped her.

She stared at him because having a bishop ride roughshod over her wasn't the worst thing he might do. He could use the superior strength of his body to force her thighs apart without so much as a soft kiss to make it pleasant for her. It would not be the first time a bride was claimed in such a brutal fashion.

That kindness tempered her anger. Bishop Shaman cleared his throat.

"Explain yerself, Bronwyn McQuade. Are ye a Christian?"

Lowering herself into a curtsy, she stared at the floor attempting to collect her thoughts. She didn't have time to waste on ideas of how well Cullen was treating her at the moment. She dare not trust in that.

"Yes, yer Grace, I am a Christian."

He laced his fingers together, staring over them at her. "Then why are ye hesitating to kneel before me and take vows that will grant ye the mercy and forgiveness of the Lord?"

"Because I have not sinned with any man. I am pure and there is no need for me to marry."

"Yer father said it in front of a hundred witnesses."

Bronwyn glared at Cullen. The man was saying enough to damn her without admitting that he hadn't had her.

But Cullen was tightening his grip around her. He looked at the bishop. "And 'tis nae just a matter of her reputation, 'tis a blight on the name of McJames. I canna seek another bride without her father's words haunting me. No family will want their daughter associated with me now that I'm called a blackguard. Marriage between us is the only thing that will set it straight."

She shook her head. "It is a sin for a daughter to disobey her father. A breaking of a commandment."

Cullen stared at her and the look on his face made her shiver. "I have the king's permission to wed ye."

"That canna be!" For that would change everything, her father was bound to obey his king.

"Enough." Hard authority rang through the bishop's voice. He stroked his gray beard for a long moment, considering her first and then Cullen.

"Having the king's permission negates the need for yer father's blessing on the match. We must consider what the gossips will continue to say if you do not marry. Better to set a good Christian example even if you have not yielded to lust. There is also the matter of the fighting between yer clans that will be stopped." He paused and drew a slow breath. "I agree with this match and shall marry you."

"I will not wed him." The words slipped past her horrified lips.

The bishop's eyes narrowed. "Yer Christian soul will be the better for it, madam."

She stammered while trying to think of a way to placate the man without getting married tonight.

"Of course, yer Grace. I simply meant that I am nae in a proper state of mind to take such holy vows tonight."

The two grooms frowned, the quill pausing in midair.

The bishop's forehead creased. "Go on."

Bronwyn took a shaky breath, needing the time to think. "It is just that this morning I awoke bound and gagged. My soul is still heavy with anger." She lowered her chin meekly. "Not a proper frame of mind to be taking sacred vows. I need time to prepare . . . and . . . forgive."

The last word stuck in her mouth. She had to force it out without hissing. Cullen glared at her, that flush coloring his face once more. Bronwyn looked back at the bishop, lest she lose the argument because she failed to hide the lust Cullen inspired in her. The bishop held the power to see her wed on his whim, and no one in the room would admit that she had not agreed. The wax seal would be pressed down onto the parchment and she would be bound by both church and law. Cullen could use the document to partition the king for dowry from her father. It could become a battle that would take years to resolve, or the king just might decide to side with his bishop. James Stuart wanted Scotland organized by the time he took the crown of England. Installing bishops was his way of making sure there was a church that answered to him.

Although it would serve her father justly for being greedy enough to raid his neighbors, she would not surrender her body and honor for a sire who detested her.

"Well spoken." The bishop nodded approval. "And a testament to yer Christian soul. One must be humble and penitent when kneeling before God."

Cullen lifted his hands toward the man. "Only a wedding will prevent her kin from attempting to claim her back, through bloodshed, yer grace. They'll come with their swords unsheathed."

"That is no change. My father has been raiding ye for years."

Cullen smiled. His eyes glittering with victory. "Which is why we should marry to put an end to this fighting."

"That is very true." Bishop Shaman drew in a long, deep breath and blew it out again before deciding the matter.

"I will wed ye tomorrow. After morning service."

The quill began scratching across the paper once more. It sounded like a cannon blast announcing her execution. She felt the blood drain from her face.

"So be it. Tomorrow morning."

Cullen was furious. She heard it in his voice and turned to stare at him. A gasp left her lips when she looked at him. Here was the warrior her father must have faced in battle. There was nothing kind in his expression, no hint of the teasing boy she'd witnessed before. There was only determination. Hard, solid, and inescapable.

It stole the breath from her and every shred of composure. There was no more will to stand up to him, only to run before the heat from his eyes melted her.

With a hasty curtsy, she quit the room. Her heart was pounding so hard, it felt like it might shatter the bones holding it inside her chest. Her breath was raspy and her stride fast. She turned the corner and made it to the end of the next hallway before a hand clasped her wrist, dragging her to a sudden halt.

A scream formed on her lips, but never made it past the hard kiss Cullen pressed against her mouth. He hauled her up against his body without any softness, his arms pressing her tightly to his body while his mouth ravaged hers. He cupped the back of her head in a sure hand, tilting it so that their mouths fused. Heat poured through her, running down her spine like molten steel. Her hands were pressed to his chest and she was unable to resist the urge to stroke him. She wanted to touch what she could never have. Needed to discover what it felt like to have nothing between her skin and his.

He broke the kiss when she stroked him. His breath was ragged and she felt his heart hammering beneath her fingertips. His eyes shone with hunger as he placed his own hand on top of hers, keeping her skin against his.

"I'm going to have ye, Bronwyn, and that is a promise."

He truly believed it, but her pride rebelled. She shoved against him but he didn't move a bit, his strength imprisoning her easily.

Too damn easily for her pride to bear.

"Ye are only going to provoke my father further with this idea of yers."

The chest beneath her fingers rumbled when he chuckled. "It is more than an idea. The bishop is affixing his seal to the document as we speak. Tonight is yer last night as a maiden."

"Yer assuming I'm pure."

His expression changed to one that was dark and disapproving. He lifted his hand, freeing hers. He stroked her cheek in a soft motion that sent a torrent of sensation down her spine. She shivered, unable to control her response.

"Dinna say things like that, lass. A maiden deserves to be treated gently the first time a man touches her. Dinna say things that will tempt me to forget yer deserving of that tenderness. My patience has its limits."

"Is that why ye've been such a brute to me? Ye think me a virgin?" She sounded like a shrew but couldn't seem to stop herself from firing cutting words at him. She was desperate to shield herself from him. The man seemed to see too much of who she truly was deep inside, far more than anyone ever had. Besides, his words offered her hope that he didn't plan to use her roughly. She wanted to believe in that, wanted to think that he'd be the man she'd dreamed about.

Reality was rarely so kind.

"I only apply the force necessary to overcome yer struggles. The choice is yers on when it will stop. I willna let ye escape me."

"Ye mean choose to yield to ye. Bringing yer bishop here to force me onto my knees at the altar. That is no choice. Dinna delude yerself by thinking I wed ye of my own free will."

She shoved at him and her hand smarted, but he snorted before letting her go. She hadn't realized how much she was fighting his hold because when his arms opened she stumbled backward until the wall stopped her. Her head smacked the stone with a thwack. Bright stars danced across her vision for a moment. There was a sound of disgust from Cullen.

"Ye need to have done with this struggle. 'Tis done now." He shot her a hard look full of determination. "Ye will be my wife tomorrow." His expression softened for just a moment but that kindness vanished almost in the same moment that it appeared. "'Tis a good match between us. Good for more people than most unions."

Guilt hit her hard. Slamming into her conscience with the possibility that he was right. It would be a grand day indeed if one wedding stopped the hostility. But there was more than one laird's daughter who had kneeled in submission to her father's enemy in the same hope only to have the feuding continue. Scotsmen didn't give up their arguments easily.

"My head aches." And that was the truth. There was too much to consider, too much to worry about befalling her. She felt so alone that she ached with it. Every shred of confidence she normally had missing now.

"I know the feeling."

There was a small hint of the playful boy in his words now.

A glimmer of hope flaring up in that empty place inside her. Forcing her weak need for comfort down, she pushed away from the wall before she did something foolish, such as surrendering to his will. That would be all well and good for the hour it took him to seduce her, but the sun would have no mercy on her in the morning. Nor would her clansmen.

"I think it best if I retire now."

He nodded. "Since ye told the bishop ye needed tonight to set yer thinking right, aye, 'tis time to find yer bedchamber."

She began walking and he followed her. The hair on the back of her neck rose. Each step felt as if it took a long time. The blood was rushing past her ears so loudly she had trouble hearing anything. She felt as if he could read her like the ink on a page of parchment.

But he was watching her and that stiffened her resolve to escape.

She climbed the stairs and heard the soft step behind her. Sweat actually began to bead on her forehead and she quickly wiped it away. The door of her chamber looked like a sanctuary, but Cullen's arm crossed it before she could open it.

"Stay in yer chamber, lass, or I'll do what needs doing to keep ye."

She couldn't keep her temper in check. She shot him a look full of loathing but bit back the scathing comment that formed on her tongue. His eyes narrowed but he pulled his hand back when she remained silent.

"All right, then. I see ye understand me."

"Ye're clear, there is no doubt of that."

Once inside, she shoved the door shut. It made a loud thunk when it closed, satisfying her need to escape from the scrutiny that surrounded her.

But there was no escape from her desire to flee White Tower. Her cheeks burned as she admitted that she was now running from herself. Cullen unleashed something inside her that was uncontrollable. It was thick and needy, urging her to provoke the man just so that he'd touch her.

But that was a coward's game. Oh, she knew it well. Had seen many a girl in Red Stone toy with and tease the men until they reached for what the lasses dangled in front of their noses. It rarely ended well. Even those who gained marriage from their lovers when their bellies swelled often lived with discontented husbands in unhappy homes.

She craved his touch.

It was a harsh truth, one that lent her the strength to remain awake until the castle settled in for the night. She watched the moon rise and climb higher into the sky.

Unlacing her bodice, she quickly shed the green dress. She hoped that her chemise might look enough like a shirt at night to serve her needs. Reaching beneath the pillow, she took the bundle of food and set it near the door. The bed gained a longing glance from her, but she lifted the McJames plaid and began pleating it along the mattress.

Tearing a wide strip from the bottom of her chemise, she folded it in half and worked it beneath the evenly pleated wool. She yanked another strip off her chemise and tied it firmly around her breasts to flatten them. It was uncomfortable and would likely begin to hurt before too long, but two plump mounds swaying on her chest would end her ruse quickly.

Bending over backward, she grasped the ends of the first strip and used it to tie the kilt to her waist. Men used sturdy belts, but the strip of fabric would serve for tonight.

Her hair was a glaring reminder that she was not a young lad. There was no hat in the room. She settled for stuffing the tail of her braid into the high collar of her chemise.

She peeked into the hallway and all was silent. Being careful to close the door without a sound, she started down the hallway toward the stairs. Every step sounded too loud. Cool night air blew up the stone steps from the yard, making her shiver.

How did men ride with bare legs?

A tin lantern was left on the ground floor of the keep. A fat candle flickered inside the round tin shell that had cuts scattered over it to allow light to spill out. An iron peg was driven into the stone of the wall for the lantern to hang from. The tin protected against fire in case the wind blew the lantern to the floor. There was always light in the keeps in case of emergency.

Outside it was dark. Clouds kept the moon from illuminating the yard. A perfect setting for escape. Men were stationed up on the top of the towers, and fires burned in iron-cage torch holders, but it was still dark on the ground.

Winter was truly here because the yard was blanketed in a white layer of fresh snow. Bronwyn stared at it in horror. Each step would be visible. More frightening was the fact that she had little protection from the chill. Many died on the roads when they were foolish enough to venture out.

Swallowing hard, she gathered her courage and took the first step into the snow. It was still soft and she sank to her ankle. The ice was bitterly cold, chilling her foot, but she took the next step. Her breath was a wispy cloud in front of her face, the thin fabric of her chemise poor comfort against winter's touch. Shivers began running up and down her legs as she moved toward the stable. The leather of her boots was wet now, the heat from her body melting the snow. Her fingers were stiff when she reached for the latch holding the door shut.

A hard male hand captured her fingers, closing around it completely.

"I warned ye, Bronwyn."

Chapter Seven

Cullen pulled her back against his body. A hard shudder shook her as her skin eagerly soaked up the warmth from him. His breath teased her ear while he folded his arm around her body, keeping her hand prisoner within his grasp.

"But I'll confess that I'm happy to see ye dinna mind me."

"Release me." She sounded too breathless, too relieved. Shame choked her.

"Never."

His arms opened for a fraction of a moment. A hard push on her shoulder turned her around to face him. In the dark he was a huge shadow that loomed over her. Beneath the linen strip, her nipples drew into hard points. Her belly quivered, the muscles tightening with anticipation. His face was only angles in the darkness but she had never seen so handsome a man before. He was the embodiment of strength and she found it mesmerizing.

"I will never let ye go, Bronwyn, and I will be happy to prove it to ye."

He grasped her waist and tossed her upward. Her weight didn't seem to tax him. Those solid arms clasped her against his body, her waist above his shoulder. She tried to remain stiff, refusing to bend over his back, but he turned and the momentum sent her head downward. One arm clamped across the back of her thighs. She pushed on his wide back to rise up but he bounced her and her breath left her lungs in a whoosh when she landed on his broad shoulder.

"Enough, Bronwyn. Ye are caught. I dinna want to fight with ye."

"I know what ye want from me!"

She snarled at him but the sound lost much of its venom against the expanse of his back. He reached the steps and bore her up them quickly. The lantern in the keep twinkled as she was carried back up to the second floor. Cullen pushed a door wide and shoved it shut behind him.

A squeal left her lips when Cullen flipped her off his shoulder. He caught her in his arms like a child, cradling her with an arm beneath her knees and one behind her back. He held her for a brief moment before tossing her onto the bed.

His bed.

He looked like a warrior from the tales repeated in the kitchens of raiders that ravished along with stealing.

But it excited her.

The dark expression on his face should have frightened her. Instead she remembered every time he'd used only enough of his strength to subdue her. Somehow, in spite of all of the reasons not to, she'd grown to trust him.

"Aye, ye do know what I want, but if I was intent on hurting ye, I'd have already taken it without a care for yer feelings."

She scoffed at him. "Pulling me in front of a bishop is being concerned for my feelings? I think not. That is so that ye can petition the king for my dowry."

The bed shook when he landed on top of her, his weight smothering her and pinning her flat on her back. He grasped her wrists, holding them harder than he ever had.

"I could have taken ye roughly this morning to ensure ye wed me tonight, too, Bronwyn, but I dinna."

He pressed a hard knee between hers, spreading her thighs in one swift motion. "Even now, I could fuck ye without a thought for yer own pleasure, but I won't."

He pushed up off her, standing in front of the bed once again. Reaching out, he grabbed one ankle and attacked the lace holding her boot closed. A scowl marked his face, his grip tight on the back of her foot. With a tug he pulled the boot loose and sent it sailing across the chamber.

"I should have taken yer shoes."

He had the matching one off her foot in a few more quick motions. A look of triumph lit his eyes. Even in the meager light the room offered from the glowing coals in the fireplace, she noticed that look of victory in his eyes. But she was too shocked to resist. Too stunned to see him undressing her instead of taking what he wanted.

She rose up onto her knees to face him. "It wouldn't have stopped me."

He drew a sharp breath. His eyes locking onto hers.

"Which is why I'll nae relax my guard on ye."

He reached for the end of his belt. He tugged the three-inch-wide tail of leather back so that the brass spikes holding it tight released. The evenly pleated wool of his kilt slid down his legs but he caught it up and tossed it over a chair before it hit the floor. His legs were bare, except for where his shirttail covered him to a few inches above his knees. She realized that he'd come after her without his boots or sword.

"Ye have more courage than plenty of men I've met. I may have stolen ye to right the wrong done to my family name, but I'm keeping ye because I have nae ever met a woman that is yer equal."

The compliment stunned her. "But ye don't know me. Not really. Any woman would resist being hauled away by strangers. That is no something extraordinary, Cullen."

"It is more. I felt it on the afternoon when neither of us knew each other's name. Just a man and a woman meeting, and the attraction that was there between us."

He reached up and grabbed his shirt at the shoulders. With a swift tug he drew it over his head. Her breath froze as the crimson light coated his upper body. Every muscle was sculpted into hard ridges. But her eyes dropped to the hard length of his cock. It stood out from his body, swollen and demanding.

"Call it lust or attraction, Bronwyn, but I intend to call ye mine."

He reached for her and she recoiled with a soft cry. He captured the sides of her makeshift kilt and lifted it into the air. Her entire lower body was held aloft, stealing her ability to escape. But the strip of fabric she'd used to tie the wool to her waist was not strong enough to keep the kilt around her hips. Cullen pulled it over her hips and down her legs.

"It is almost a shame to strip this from ye. I enjoy seeing my colors on ye."

"Ye would." Flipping over, she came back up onto her knees but farther back in the bed. There was a solid wall behind the headboard, but at least her chemise fell down to cover her thighs. "Raping me will not break my resolve to not wed ye."

His expression tightened. "And what is the matter with that? I plan to make ye my wife. Wanting to see my colors on ye is a mark of respect." He drew a stiff breath. "I may have stolen ye, but I've no touched ye once without controlling my strength."

There was a reprimand in his voice that hit her hard.

"I know." The admission tumbled past her lips because it was so very true. Her body suddenly quivered as she teetered on the edge of uncertainty. Part of her trusted that he wouldn't take her roughly, but a lifetime raised as his enemy warned her not to expect kindness from him. The future stretched out so uncertainly, she shivered.

"Tell me ye'll marry me in the morning, Bronwyn."

She was tempted. Excitement pulsed through her to surrender her body while the night shrouded them. There was no clan color in the ruby glow of the coals, only two people. Standing there in front of her was the only man who had ever tempted her.

And she was sorely tempted. "I . . . I dinna . . ." She clasped a hand over her mouth, sealing her emotion fueled words inside.

The bed rocked as his knees landed on it. He captured her body, drawing her up against him in a swift, secure motion. One hand captured the back of her head, tilting her chin up so that her lips were ready for his kiss. His embrace felt so good, she trembled.

"Maybe ye would prefer I prove my worth as a husband to ye first." There was a hint of mocking in his voice but it was also tender. "I do enjoy a challenge, lass."

The hand across her back stroked her bare skin and she shuddered as sensation raced along her spine. He cupped one side of her bottom, pushing her toward his body until they were flush. The hard length of his cock pressed against her belly, sending a wave of heat through her that settled deep inside her.

"I promise to do my best to satisfy ye." His hold was unbreakable. "I would never rape ye, sweet Bronwyn, but I will seduce ye."

A whimper left her lips as he kissed her. But it wasn't a hard, demanding one like the one he'd taken in the hallway. He kissed her gently, tasting her mouth, the tip of his tongue slipping along her lower lip before seeking entrance into her mouth. The hand cradling her head kept her still as he pressed her jaw open to deepen his kiss. It felt too good to resist. Every point of contact between them was pleasurable. It was as if her skin had never really felt before, never truly shown her how much delight she could feel.

She kissed him back, mimicking his motions while trying to learn how to return his kiss.

"Aye, lass, that's the way. Kiss me back."

There was a husky tone in his voice that made her bold. Lifting her hands, she slid them along his arms. His skin was so warm as to almost be hot. Soft as satin, it covered muscle that was iron solid. A soft groan filtered through their fused lips. Her eyes opened in surprise.

"Aye, I like it when ye touch me, Bronwyn." His hand moved and slid down the column of her neck. Sensation shook her instantly, her head tilting to one side without any thought. It was pure instinct to offer herself to his touch.

"As ye enjoy me touching ye."

There was a hint of determination in his voice now. One that unsettled her. He was so much stronger and her trust for him so fragile. He stroked down along her arms until he caught the hem of her chemise. He drew it over her head in a soft whisper that was mercifully quick.

"Now that is a sin, lass."

His eyes were focused on the fabric binding her breasts.

"Truly a sin to disguise such a beautiful body."

He reached for the binding, tearing the cloth with his greater strength. It rent in two, the sound echoing in the silence. Her breasts rejoiced as they were freed, the soft globes falling into their normal teardrop shapes.

He cupped each breast, his fingers gently massaging them. A soft moan passed her lips as her eyes fluttered closed. There was too much sensation to add sight to what her brain had to understand. She was being swept out to sea, where there was enough water to cover her completely.

"I've dreamed of tasting ye since I saw ye on that hillside."

His voice was rough with emotion. Opening her eyes, Bronwyn shivered as he moved toward her. He laid her back among the bedding, his hands still cupping her breasts. His thumbs brushed over each nipple and she arched toward his touch.

A strangled cry passed her lips when he kissed one nipple. His lips were scorching hot against her skin. But he did not stop there. Gripping the soft mound, he returned to suck the hard tip into his mouth. She twisted as heat pooled in her belly. It bled into her passage, making her keenly aware of it. She was hungry for more touches, ones that ventured lower.

Cullen didn't disappoint her.

His hand smoothed down her body, moving across her ribs and onto her belly. The tip of his tongue flicked across her nipple before he trailed soft kisses down the side of her breast and up the side of the other one. His hand roamed lower, teasing the skin above her mons. Anticipation knotted her muscles so tight, she twisted and turned, unable to control her motions.

She wanted that touch. Actually needed it, for some reason. Her thighs were already slightly open, but Cullen moved one knee up along her leg to spread her for his conquest.

It was a conquest, a final action that would complete what he'd begun when he'd demanded her name in the meadow. He pulled his mouth from her nipple and loomed over her when his hand stroked the curls decorating her mons. Their eyes met in the dim light, and even with nothing but embers, she saw the hunger in his gaze.

He pressed a kiss against her mouth that was demanding. Parting her lips while his fingers delved between her thighs, she kissed him back, uncaring about anything but the urges burning through her. Half of his body lay across hers, pinning her gently but completely to the bed.

She cried out when his fingers found the little button at the top of her sex. So much feeling flooded her from the first graze across it, she tried to escape but he held her down, a soft chuckle shaking his broad chest.

"Do ye like that, Bronwyn? I promise ye, it gets better."

The man kept his word.

Sweat covered her skin when he began rubbing her clitoris. Soft, teasing circles that sent intense pleasure up into her passage. Each minute that he continued built her hunger. For the first time in her life she realized that she was empty. Her body was made to cradle the hard cock pressing against her thigh.

And she craved it.

"No more teasing, Cullen." She didn't recognize her own voice. It was too sultry, too hungry.

"Aye, sweet Bronwyn, it is time to be done with playing."

He rose above her, spreading her thighs with his wide hips. The hard tip of his cock nudged the opening of her body. He held still for a long moment, looking at her beneath him. A glitter of satisfaction crossed his eyes as he pushed forward into her spread body.

She was too tight. As much as she craved being filled, his flesh was hard and the walls of her passage ached. She shuddered, pain twisting up her spine to cut through the haze of desire clouding her thoughts.

"Trust me, lass. I dinna take pleasure in hurting ye. I swear I never will."

He lowered his body over hers, catching enough of his weight on his forearms to keep from smothering her. But she was pinned completely beneath him, unable to escape the next thrust.

Her fingers turned to claws on his shoulders. Her fingernails cut into his skin, making him grind his teeth. Every bit of control he had was straining against the need to bury himself deep. Her passage was soft and wet with welcome but he pulled free before thrusting smoothly into her once more. He would control the urge to ravish her. For the first time in his life he understood the value of a pure woman. Her body had never welcomed another. It was so stunning, his head spun when he pressed his entire length into her. She quivered beneath him, drawing a deep breath to steady herself. Tears glistened on her cheeks but she didn't sob, didn't make a single sound to complain.

"Now we'll get back to the feeling good part."

She blinked, her eyelashes wet from her tears. Her hands released their grip as she realized what she was doing. He moved slowly, riding her with long strokes to rekindle the fire in her. A shaky breath rattled past her lips when she realized there was no more pain. Leaning down, he kissed her. Her mouth opened to admit his tongue. Her hands gently stroked his shoulders and it was by far the most arousing touch he'd ever received. Soft and hesitant but sincere.

He found the few tears that had made it past her resolve. He kissed each one, sending a new trickle from her eyes at the tenderness of such concern. The burning pain had dissipated into a dull ache now, her body stretching to accommodate his hard flesh. Yet it was more than that. Each thrust sent a little ripple of enjoyment up into her belly. Her body began to arch toward his thrust out of instinct. There was no thinking about doing it, her hips lifted and a sigh passed her lips when more delight filled her.

"That's it, lass."

His voice was husky and edged with a raggedness that hinted that she was giving him the same amount of pleasure. That idea made her bold. She lifted faster and watched his face. A tic jerked along his jaw. Her body was warm again, the heat swirling and pooling deep inside her. All the sensation was tightening around the flesh impaling her. She wanted to move faster, needed to feel him deeper inside her.

He seemed to feel the same. Cullen captured her head, holding it prisoner while his body pressed her down into the mattress. His breath was ragged and hers came in soft pants. Their bodies strained toward one another and she held onto him, wanting him closer.

Her eyes fell closed as her spine arched completely. Even the slight pain from where he held her hair so tightly didn't bother her. She was too absorbed by the bubble of delight growing in her belly. It swelled and tightened until it broke. Pleasure suddenly ripped through her, stealing every last thought. Her mind swung around in an insane kaleidoscope of colors and sensations that held her frozen in the moment. There was so much pleasure, the intensity of it so great, she cried out, unable to keep it contained.

Her eyes popped open when she heard an answering groan from Cullen. The bed rocked almost violently as he thrust hard and fast into her. His hands tightened around her head as he groaned long and deep. With a hard thrust he buried his cock deep and she felt the warm spurt of his seed fill her. She quivered, her breath rattling while a soft sob left her lips.

'Twas a deed that could no be undone now.

Her mind wanted to wage war against the implications of feeling him inside her, but there was still too much delight rippling through her body to move. Her flesh was satisfied in a way it had never been before. Even knowing that her innocence was gone didn't alarm her enough to keep her from slipping into slumber. Her body was more than happy to drift away while enjoying the last glow of pleasure. The stress of the last day had drained her, and Cullen was keeping her warm. It seemed to be all she needed. He rolled off her and gathered her against his body. Her head ended up on his shoulder, the sound of his heart filling her ear.

"I'll keep ye warm, lass."

And he would. Cullen felt her go lax against him. His own body was sated and fatigue was nipping at his mind. But he wanted to savor the moment. Wanted to indulge in this moment where she lay so complacent against him. The dawn would bring renewed struggles from her, he had no doubt.

Yet for the moment Bronwyn was sleeping against him.

Aye that was worth remaining awake for.

Dawn woke her.

Bronwyn lifted a hand to rub her eyes. It wasn't very bright light, but the gray of winter. She stared at the windows, trying to recall where she was. Her nose was cold because the bed curtains were not drawn and the fire long gone cold. But her body was basking in the warmth of the man beside her.

"Good morning, lass."

Cullen held her still when she would have jumped away from him. With a solid arm around her waist, he kept her tightly against him. The night rushed back at her, her memory recalling every detail. Between her thighs there was a dull ache when she moved, confirming that her mind was quite correct in what it remembered.

"I trust that there will be no more debate over the subject of taking marriage vows."

Horror flooded her as she heard the voice of Bishop Shaman. Turning her head, she looked across the room to see the man eyeing her and Cullen critically. Druce McJames stood there as well and grinned when she looked at him. Her face turned hotter than a summer day. Lined up next to Druce were Lydia and three other women. Not young maids, but mature women who were there to see the sheets she was lying on.

The jubilant air in the room made her stomach tighten with nausea. She felt more helpless than when Cullen had tied her up and carried her out of her father's kitchen.

Lydia moved forward. "Well now, up with ye. There's a wedding to dress for. I hear your mother is gone from this life, so I shall see ye to the chapel in her place."

She pulled Bronwyn's chemise from the floor and shook it out. The maids grasped the bedding and rolled it down, baring her and Cullen to everyone.

The brute held her still as they finished the job.

Turning her head, she glared at him, but found solid determination on his face. There was no hint of relenting in his eyes. None.

"There is going to be no question on just when I took yer innocence, Bronwyn."

He stood up, taking her along with him from the bed. Her gaze dropped to the sheets. Her gasp was lost as Lydia laughed. A dark stain marred the surface of the sheet. Cullen set her free but the women surrounded her. They inspected her from head to toe, even lifting her arms to see all of her body.

The bishop observed it all. Druce at least didn't look at her nude body. But Cullen's clansman walked closer to the bed to inspect the sheet. He nodded approval before tugging the fabric off the bed.

"I'll take charge of this." He walked to the window and the maids hurried to push the shutters open for their laird. With a sharp snap of fabric, Druce set the sheet hanging out the window. A cheer rose from the yard below. Bronwyn felt her throat tighten. The noose was tight against her throat now.

"I will see you both in the chapel before you break yer fast."

The bishop spoke too happily for her pride to suffer. She glared at them, at all of them who were helping to form a cage around her. With brute strength and church law she was being broken to their will.

"I will not wed."

Cullen was already in his shirt. He scowled at her. "Bronwyn . . ."

"I told ye I wouldn't and I won't. Nae even now that ye have taken what my father accused ye of." She lifted her chin high. "Ye've earned what the gossips are saying now."

"Do you accuse this man of rape, Bronwyn McQuade?" The bishop's voice cracked like a whip. "By yer own admission and the evidence before me he has had yer innocence. Do ye cry rape?"

The chamber was silent, the tension thick. Cullen watched her, waiting to see how she would answer. She shouldn't care about his feelings, but saying rape would provide her with more time to avoid him. The bishop would have to hold a hearing. But she would have to lie to do so.

She couldn't, not after the way he'd handled her so tenderly.

"No. There was no rape."

Bishop Shaman grunted. He touched all of his fingertips against each other and peered at the three women that had inspected her.

"Is there any sign of force?"

They all shook their heads, one of them lending her voice to the question. "Nae even a small bruise, yer grace."

Bishop Shaman nodded then glared at her. "Ye have passed the night with this man, Bronwyn McQuade. I believe ye have given him yer innocence and therefore ye have sinned against church law. You will marry for the good of both yer souls as well as for the example such will set for this Christian community."

She backed up, shaking her head while reaching for her chemise to cover her body. The bishop snorted with displeasure.

"Persist in this rebellion and I will have ye placed in the stocks until ye repent. Perhaps on your father's land loose morals are allowed, but among the McJames, the law of the church is enforced."

He turned his disapproval on Cullen. "I will be waiting in the chapel. Are ye set to obey my will, son?"

"I will be there as soon as I dress."

Bishop Shaman nodded approval at Cullen's quick answer. He sent one more stern look at her before leaving the room, his black robe floating in the morning air. Druce rubbed his palms against one another.

"Well now, I suggest ye get dressed, lass. It will be a mighty cold day to stand in the stocks in nothing but that bit of linen. As delightfully charming as it is on ye."

Her temper snapped when one of the women chuckled in response to the jest. Grabbing one of her shoes, she threw it across the room at Druce. He ducked and laughed harder.

"Enough of yer taunting me! I swear I've a mind to satisfy God's will just so that he'll hear me when I pray for ye to be stricken with love for a woman who will no have ye."

Cullen surprised her by laughing. His eyes twinkled as he shooed the women toward the door. "There is nae such thing as a woman my cousin canna have, Bronwyn. If she says nae, we'll just have to steal her, like we did ye."

She threw her other shoe at his mocking face.

He raised an arm to deflect it and scooped her up a second later. He spun around in a circle and she grabbed at his neck to steady her head. He stopped a moment later, one hand wrapping about her braid to hold her head in place.

"Enough now, lass. There is two feet of snow in the yard. I'd hate to see ye shivering in the stocks on our wedding day."

"But ye would allow it." She hissed at him, pushing against his chest, but the man held steady. "Ye and yer bishop that ye brought here to torment me."

"Aye, be very sure that I enjoy winning. Yer father will nae bend to this union easy, I know that well. But Jamie will take the word of one of his bishops."

He released her and bent down to retrieve her boot. "But if ye have it in yer mind to challenge the church, I suggest ye put yer boots on before being led to the stocks."

"Brute."

All traces of teasing melted from his expression. Hunger flickered in his eyes now. "I promise to warm ye up when ye have taken yer vows. Before or after the stocks, that's yer choice, Bronwyn McQuade. But ye will be my wife."

He picked up his plaid and belt where it lay on the chair from the night before. Slinging it over his shoulder, he walked toward the door.

"I'll make a poor wife, that's my promise to ye."

He turned back around to look at her. His gaze was filled with heat as he looked her over from the top of her head to her feet, lingering on her breasts and the nipples that showed slightly through her chemise.

"I disagree. Ye've passion inside ye that will see ye becoming a fine wife to my way of thinking. 'Tis understandable that ye dinna trust me, Bronwyn. But only time will see us learning about one another. 'Tis for sure that our bed will nae be cold."

"Ohhh . . . trust a man to think lust is all a couple needs."

He shrugged and taunted her with that boyish grin. "It is nae so bad a place to start." His expression sobered. "At least it is better than dwelling on the fact that yer family is full of vipers who plot to blacken my name or run me through."

He left and the sound of the closing door was as piercing as a gunshot. Horror held her in its grasp as she stared around the room. The cold wind whipped up through the open shutters of the window, chilling her legs. But she heard the snap of the sheet as it flew outside the window. It was the noose tied around her neck.

It had not been rape.

Her father would scream that it had been, but she knew better. In sooth, she wondered if she were truly the child of Erik McQuade because she could not lie as he did. It was a harsh burden to carry, knowing that your sire was not an example to follow.

Cullen was.

She stiffened as the idea blossomed inside her thoughts without warning. There were so many reasons for her to distrust him but she could not deny that here was a man worth admiring. If she were not a McQuade, wedding him might be a happy moment. Instead she was besieged by the ideas of what next spring would bring. There would be blood spilt on both sides. Her father would accuse Cullen of rape and no one would get close enough to her to hear her deny it. The entire sordid mess would be paraded before the court.

That was not the part she feared. It was the hot tempers of her brothers and the night raiding that they favored for venting their spleen. The farmers would pay the price along with the retainers who followed their lairds into battle.

Even Cullen might fall victim to burnished steel.

And what lay before her this winter at Sterling? A McQuade inside the fortress of their enemy, what would be her plight there? Many a man acted well in front of a bishop only to throw off his sheepskin once he was no longer in sight of such a powerful man of the church. Cullen wanted a child. Would he beat her if she failed to conceive quickly? Would he raise his hand if she birthed him a daughter? Would he . . .

Bronwyn shoved the disturbing thoughts away. She would be weeping in another few moments.

She walked closer to the window. A blanket of white glittered in the dim sunlight. The stocks stood empty on one side of the yard. Every castle had them. It was more civilized than whipping. Faster than starving her until she yielded. As much as she might wish it otherwise, no one could endure endlessly. She would bend to the cold at some point.

As ye yielded last night to the pleasure.

A knock on the door interrupted her thoughts. Lydia appeared with the green dress in her arms.

"I wish there was something finer for yer wedding." She bustled into the room, another maid following her with a pitcher of water. She poured it into the large wooden bowl on the dressing stand and steam rose from it. No one catered to her so well at Red Stone.

But that didn't mean that her life at Sterling would be any better.

Lydia began pulling the braid from her hair and brushing it. Numb with her doubts, Bronwyn stood still while the maids tended to her. It should have made her happy, thinking of home. But it darkened her mood, settling in her heart for some strange reason.

But she refused to wear the green dress. Lydia looked at her as if she was insane.

"What are ye going to wear then? Surely not only yer chemise?"

"Aye, that is exactly what I will wear and nothing else."

The maid looked at Lydia and the woman rubbed her hands together for a few moments. Bronwyn turned on them.

"The man wants a wedding made with a stolen bride? Well,

he shall have me as he took me. In my shift. Best that he begins to understand that I bring nothing else to this union."

Her pride might be a greater sin but she put her boots on and tied the strip back around her breasts to help hide her nipples. With a deep breath she walked toward her wedding.

May God have mercy on them all.

Chapter Eight

Her husband was displeased with her.

The muscle on the side of his jaw was twitching and the ones in his neck were corded. Bronwyn smiled sweetly at him as a meal was served to them. Druce was still gleeful, making her appetite flee. Cullen frowned again when she only toyed with her food.

"Enough, Bronwyn. It's a full day's ride to Sterling. Have done with our quarrel until we reach home."

The word home made her throat constrict but she refused to allow him to see it. Picking up her spoon, she used it to begin eating the porridge in front of her. It was still half warm and her stomach approved.

She was amazed that something so life changing could be accomplished in so short a time. Their wedding hadn't taken half an hour. Her cheeks warmed as she considered that deflowering her had actually taken longer.

That was only because her husband had a care for her pleasure as well as his own. Peeking at him, she studied the man she was bound to. He was ruthless in his way. But not a brute even if she'd labeled him one. There was many a reluctant bride that earned the back side of her groom's hand when she dared to tell him nay.

Cullen had seduced her instead. More heat colored her

cheeks. Well, in truth he'd used a combination of overwhelming her along with soft seduction when she was too blinded by desire to resist any longer.

"I enjoy seeing ye blush."

Lost in her thoughts, Bronwyn dropped her spoon when Cullen spoke. He wasn't frowning at her any longer. A playful light had entered his blue eyes and his lips curved up, the effect transforming him into a handsome devil.

"I've never seen a lass so fetching as ye when yer cheeks turn color for me."

He held up a hand when she started to reply. "Have pity on me, Bronwyn, and let us nae bicker at my cousin's table again."

"Ye assume I was going to say something cross." Heat crept down her neck because he was correct. She had been ready to argue with him about the cause of her blush.

Cullen grinned at her. "What I assume is that ye are nae complacent to my will."

A soft sound of amusement left her lips. She could not help it, the way he teased her made her smile. Her new husband winked at her.

"Does that sound mean that there is something we agree upon?"

"I suppose it does."

He stood up and reached down for her hand. With a firm grasp he pulled her to her feet.

"The weather will nae be our friend today. Best we begin our journey."

With a sharp whistle Cullen walked out of the hall. His men pushed their benches out at the lower tables, many of them grabbing up rounds of bread that they tucked into their leather doublets for the journey.

Cullen didn't stop until they were standing on the stone steps that led to the yard. Horses were standing in the now muddy snow. The wind blew up beneath her chemise, making her shiver. The surge of pride that had seen her wed in her shift was about to cost her on the long hours spent in the cold.

The huge stallion Cullen rode was waiting for his master. The beast tossed its head, snorting out white clouds from its nostrils.

"I've nae introduced ye to Argyll." Cullen pulled her along with him toward the animal. He reached up and ran a sure hand along the horse's muzzle, slipping his finger into the leather straps to check its grip. Such an action showed that he paid close attention to the animal's care, not trusting it completely to those who served him due to his position.

"He's a fine animal." And there was no denying it. Stallions like this were expensive and rare.

"And a good friend."

Cullen watched her hand as it petted Argyll. He stood close to her, maintaining his grip on her hand. He pulled it down to straighten her arm and keep her close.

"I've a mare for ye to ride today."

Bronwyn heard the warning in his voice. Looking behind Argyll, she spotted the smaller animal. The length of McJames plaid she'd been given was draped over the neck of the horse. Standing next to the stallion, it was clear how much smaller the mare was. But it was a welcome sight, a horse for her to ride by herself.

Her hand was suddenly free as Cullen reached for a bundle strapped to his saddle. He looked curious as he pulled a dirk from the top of his boot and began poking at the fabric.

"Who would sew something closed that ye need while traveling?" The frustration on his face amused her because it was clear that the man was not used to picking out seams.

"My sister-in-law's younger sister gave this to me. I don't know what it is. Truthfully, I forgot it was tied to my saddle."

"Well, I suppose 'tis nice to know that I was distracting enough."

He paused, a twinkle in his eyes. "Is it now?"

Bronwyn shrugged. "Dinna let it swell yer head."

He chuckled and returned to slicing open stitches. "Wed but an hour and yer rising to the chore of telling me what to do."

The fabric gave way. Cullen replaced his dirk and pulled a folded garment from within the bundle. He shook it out and held it up. It was a woolen surcoat, with linen lining and deep over sleeves. It would button up to the neck and was also constructed with deep slits up the sides to accommodate riding. Her chilled limbs quivered just looking at it.

"Bonnie told me that I would need it." He looked at her, his gaze lingering on the hard points her nipples made in spite of the binding she had over them. "And so I do need it."

"Who is Bonnie to be giving ye her clothing?" Suspicion flared up inside her. Was there a mistress waiting on his return? A McJames woman who would be snuggling up to him now that she had taken her wedding vows?

"My sister-in-law's sister, and too young a lass for the tone of yer voice, Bronwyn."

With a swish he flipped it around her shoulders. Her chilled skin begged her to lift her arms and slip her hands through the arm openings. Cullen watched her, waiting for her to accept the garment. Her pride argued against it because it meant another form of submission to their marriage, but her flesh demanded to be shielded from the winter chill.

"Come, lass, save yer arguments for things that do not place yer health at risk. Bonnie sent it for ye."

"Yer brother knows what ye set out to do?"

"Aye."

Her hands slipped through the arm openings and a tiny

sigh escaped her lips when she felt the weight of the fabric settle onto her shoulders. A flicker of satisfaction filled his eyes as
he fastened a few of the buttons. Satisfaction shone in his expression as he ran a hand along the surface of the wool. It was
fine, thick wool, the highest quality.

"Be angry at me if ye like, lass, but I do enjoy knowing I provide for ye." His expression went hard for a moment. "Because ye are mine."

"As ye keep telling me."

"I am hoping ye learn to remember it. Dinna make me
chase ye down on the road, Bronwyn." His voice was stern but
tempered with something that sounded like tenderness. She
held her chin steady, refusing to answer him by word or gesture. It was bad enough that she was his captive. She refused
to become obedient to his will.

He grunted and waved her mare forward. "As ye like, madam.
Be assured that I will keep my word to keep ye."

A page brought the mare close and Cullen grasped her waist.
He set her in the saddle with an arrogant look that made her
temper flare.

"Dinna be so proud, Cullen McJames."

But it also hit her heart because the man wanted her and
was proud of having her. She should detest it. But she had
never been one to lie to herself. There was a part of her that
was looking forward to being Cullen McJames's wife. He
flashed her that boyish grin once more.

"Dinna be proud of having ye for my wife? Why would I no
be happy about that, Bronwyn? 'Tis the truth that I am quite
proud this morning."

He swung up into the saddle, then raising his fist into the
air, cried, "Sterling!"

He rode through the gates, her mare following along with
his retainers. Several banners flew with his crest on it and that

of his brother. She was given a place of honor among the ranks of men and truly it warmed her heart.

She only wished that she had more confidence in it lasting past her arrival at Sterling.

The day's journey was long and hard. Bronwyn gritted her teeth before noon. She wasn't used to hours in the saddle.

And she was not used to being sore between her thighs.

She swung her leg over and sat side saddle until her hip went numb. She shifted the other direction and endured a few more hours, but she was as close to begging as she had ever been before the towers of Sterling came into view.

It was bitterly cold. The surcoat was not enough to keep her teeth from chattering. The length of McJames wool lay across the horse and she gave in. Wrapping it around her body, she even tugged it up over her head. Snow drifted down on them in soft flakes. How often had she watched them falling from the shelter of a window and considered the white flurries magical? With no fire to warm her, the snow took on another side. A cruel one as it pulled all of the heat from her body, beginning at her fingertips and then up to her knuckles.

She might not have survived on the road if she had made good her escape.

Knowing that did not cheer her any. The towers of Sterling came into view and the men who rode with Cullen sent up a cheer. They were returning home, and as they climbed the rise toward the sprawling castle that was the seat of the earl of Alcaon, she heard the bells on the walls begin ringing.

A true welcome.

She pulled her mare to a stop and stared at the castle. It was built in a series of towers connected by a large curtain wall. The flags on the walls were blue and gold, telling her that the earl was in residence. All of it was constructed of gray castle

stone, no doubt where its name had once come from. It was a
place she had heard so much about but never expected to see
with her own eyes.

It was possible she might never leave its heavy walls.

"It's too cold to linger out here, lass."

Cullen spoke gently but he hooked her around the waist
and pulled her off her mare. She landed in front of him with a
bump that sent a bolt of pain up through her abused body.
But he was warm. She shivered as she felt the heat bleeding
out of his body like an oven. The hand holding her against
him stroked her side in a soft motion.

"I dinna realize ye were so cold." Disapproval coated his
words. With a kick, he sent Argyll toward his home.

"'Tis nothing more than any other is enduring."

He lifted one hand, displaying his leather gauntlet. "But my
men are prepared for riding out in the weather."

"I suppose ye should not make a habit of stealing women
then. Since captives do not have the privilege of preparing for
the journey."

A twinkle of mischief sparkled in his eyes. "Ye think not?"

"Indeed."

She sounded waspish but did not care. Cullen rode through
the raised gate. People were crowded onto the front steps and
faces peered out of the windows. All the shutters were open in
spite of the winter chill as the household staff looked down to
see their laird returning. She saw their white linen caps lining
the window openings.

"I dinna know about that. It's been a grand adventure, trying my hand at stealing ye. I'd be lying if I said I dinna enjoy
carrying ye off to my bed."

He pulled the horse to a stop as she hissed at him.

"Stop yer bragging."

She slid off the back of the horse herself and sunk into the snow up to her ankles. She was suddenly thankful for the numbness in her feet because at least she couldn't feel the ice. Her ankle boots were mere leather ones, meant for spring. They served well enough inside during the winter. Cullen and his men wore knee-high boots that were lined with thick wool and sealed with wax to keep their feet dry.

Bronwyn shivered as she looked at the steps crowded with curious McJameses. Standing in the snow wasn't the best option either, but she remained in place as her body began to shiver.

"Come, lass, I'll introduce ye to yer new home."

Cullen swept her toward the door with a firm arm behind her back but her legs refused to walk. Her knees knocked against one another in a clumsy attempt. It was frustrating beyond endurance. Concentrating on her feet, she tried again, this time making it a few paces before her knees collapsed.

"And ye wanted to escape in this chill."

Cullen swept her up against his chest. There was murmuring from those watching and more than a few grins. Clearly she was providing welcome entertainment for a winter afternoon.

"I would have kept walking, even in the snow."

He frowned, but they had reached the top of the stairs. The earl stood there with his wife just inside the doorway and out of the weather.

Brodick McJames swept her with a critical eye. Cullen didn't put her down even when she squirmed.

"May I present Bronwyn McQuade, my wife."

The earl raised a dark eyebrow. "Yer wife?"

"Witnessed by Bishop Shaman and Druce. Our good cousin flew the sheet with his own hands."

Bronwyn hit him. "Put me down."

Brodick's wife Anne peered at Bronwyn. "Why isn't she dressed?"

Cullen shrugged before setting Bronwyn on her feet. Her knees wanted to buckle but she forced them straight.

"Och, well, it turns out I stole her away right after her bath."

Bronwyn glared at the humor in his tone, but Anne's eyes opened with alarm.

"That is barbaric." Her delicate English accent lent gravity to her words. "And quite unkind in this winter chill, I might add. She's half frozen."

"I plan to warm her up."

Bronwyn growled but Anne stomped her foot beneath her skirts. The earl's lips were twitching as he tried to resist the urge to grin.

"The pair of you are a disgrace." She shot a particularly pointed look at her husband before turning around to look at Bronwyn.

"I see it falls to me to offer you hospitality." She dropped a small and practiced curtsy. "Please follow me and we shall find a warm bath for you."

Anne turned back around to look at Cullen who was still grinning like a triumphant boy fresh from a victorious fist fight. "We shall see how many toes she still has after your handling."

Both men frowned, their brows creasing.

Cullen looked troubled, his keen gaze sweeping her. The concern bothered her, nipping at her conscience. She was made of sterner stuff than the countess hinted at and for some reason she liked Cullen knowing it.

"I refused to wear the dress they gave me at White Tower."

Shock registered on Cullen's face. Anne looked incredulous. "But why?"

"Because he stole me. So I wed him in the only thing I had.

Better to understand that such a wedding will not bring anything more than what he stole."

Her teeth chattered because she couldn't keep them clenched when she was speaking. Cullen closed the space between them, scooping her off her feet before her teeth stopped hitting themselves.

"Put me down."

"Nae." He was striding down the hallway, uncaring of the attention pointed at them from every door frame. "Anne is right. Ye're freezing and that's my doing."

"And walking would warm me up."

He sent her another one of those determined looks. "So will placing ye in a hot bath."

Bronwyn held her tongue, mindful of those watching them.

"Aren't ye going to call me a brute?"

"I should." But she wouldn't. Not with so many watching. The man was as proud as she, but he wasn't a laird drunk on his own power like her older brothers. Cullen earned the respect being given him. She admired that even if it rubbed her own pride.

They entered a huge hall filled with benches and long tables. One end had a raised dais with another table, but there were chairs there instead of benches. The kitchens would be behind it, so that food might be served up hot and with the least amount of walking.

Cullen carried her through a doorway and the air became wonderfully warm. Her cheeks stung as feeling returned, the tip of her nose actually feeling colder by contrast.

"But ye didn't."

He set her feet down but held her securely against his body. Cupping her chin, he raised her face so that their eyes met. "Why is me question."

She squirmed because his gaze saw too much. "I just didn't.

That is all. As difficult as ye might find it to believe, I am not a shrew by nature. This is yer home. I'll save my temper for places where it will not be overheard."

He didn't believe her, or maybe he was simply frozen with shock at her explanation.

"I thought ye promised me a warm bath."

"So I did, lass."

He released her and Anne strode into the bathhouse with another younger woman who looked very much like her.

"Away with ye, Cullen."

"Nae."

Anne propped her hands on her hips. "Do not say nay to me, sir. Bonnie and I shall see to the bathing on the women's side. If I need another set of hands, I'll send for your sister."

Bronwyn's gaze flew to Bonnie and the girl was young. A ripple of relief swept through her before she could bury her feelings. Cullen grinned.

"My wife was grateful for the use of yer surcoat, Bonnie."

Anne scoffed at his humor. "There is two feet of snow on the ground. She'd have been content in a smelly saddle blanket."

"No content, but I agree that she'd have no argued."

"Enough from you. Be gone before she takes to beating some manners into you. I confess that I'm of the mind to help." Anne gave Cullen a shove, and he feigned a stumbling step backward.

He turned to look at Bronwyn, offering her a good-natured grin. "Careful, Bronwyn, Anne rules Sterling with an iron fist."

Bronwyn offered him a flutter of her eyelashes. "If that is so, why aren't you more respectful to her?"

"Well spoken." Anne shook her head. "I believe your brother would have a few words with you, Cullen."

"Aye, I imagine that's true enough."

He gave her a long glance. "But I'm still wanting to know the answer to me question, Bronwyn. We'll see about that later."

He turned in a swirl of McJames kilt and left. Bronwyn wished she didn't find his form so enticing, but her eyes were glued to his wide back until it disappeared.

"What does he want to know?" Bonnie was young enough to ask the question. Her sister, Anne, tried to warn her but the younger girl refused to be put off.

"Why I didn't insult him." Bronwyn sat down on a stool and began fighting with the laces on her boots. The leather was wet and stiff with ice, and her fingers still half frozen. "Who can understand why a man would need to ask such a question."

There was a splash as water began filling one of the high-backed slipper tubs in the room. There were three of them and a trough that could be moved between all of them. It was built up at an angle and most likely connected to a water reservoir in back of the ovens. The snow and ice would fall into it and melt with the aid of the heat from cooking. It most likely ran the entire length of the kitchens to supply the bathhouse. It was a wonderful convenience, allowing bathing all year.

"Who can understand the way men think." Anne spoke more to Bonnie but Bronwyn found herself agreeing.

Anne took over the chore of removing her boot for her. Bronwyn stared at the woman, unsure of how to act. She had feared that being a McQuade would cause her trouble at Sterling, but it was for sure that an English woman would find Scotland far less welcoming. For the moment, her worries paled compared to what Anne must have faced when she married Brodick McJames.

Anne pulled the boot loose at last. She looked up and offered a soft smile.

"I find myself often wondering what Brodick is thinking when he asks me some of the things he does."

It was an attempt at kindness. Bronwyn returned the smile but busied herself with disrobing.

"I'm happy that Cullen remembered to unwrap the surcoat." Bonnie spoke with the carefree tone of youth. She crossed the room and took the garment from Bronwyn's hands.

"Does that mean everyone here agreed with this idea of stealing me away from my family?"

It might have been wiser to keep such a barbed question to herself, but the words spilled out. Bonnie looked stunned and Anne sighed. The countess reached for Bronwyn's chemise and tugged it over her head.

"Your father's charges made Cullen determined to confront the situation. Truthfully, it was not the first time stealing ye was discussed." Anne gave her a hard look. "And by different men all intent on ending the raids."

Bronwyn stepped into the tub and winced. Her toes smarted as the warm water broke winter's grip on her flesh. Her entire body ached in one fashion or another, her mind hurting worst of all as she tried to fend off self-pity.

"Many marriages are made for less." Bonnie had lost her sweet tone. Bronwyn looked up because there was too much sorrow in that voice for one so young. She stared at Bronwyn with glistening eyes. "I was married to force my sister to return to England. My husband is a terrible man."

"Yer very young to have a husband . . ." Bronwyn's words trailed off because guilt slammed into her when she realized how much better off she was with Cullen. Bonnie had gone pale with just the thought of her husband.

"Too young, and he will never set hands on you." Anne spoke with confidence. "Waste no time on the matter. I'd sooner ship ye to the highlands than allow that to happen."

Bonnie did not obey her sister. Her teeth bit into her lower lip but she remained silent.

The sounds of bathing filled the room. Bronwyn didn't know what to say, so she busied herself with washing her hair. The soap was fresh smelling and she wrinkled her nose when she realized that the only thing she had to wear was her chemise. After three days, it was unsavory at best. Her bathing didn't take long and she stood up. A length of toweling was held up by Anne. The personal service from the mistress of the house was surprising. It was also the height of hospitality.

"Thank ye."

The countess smiled.

Another woman entered the room. This one was older and wore a good wool dress with a McJames plaid draped down her back. It was drawn up over her right shoulder and secured with a brass broach.

"I've brought a few things for her, and since it is winter, we'll put some of the girls to needle tomorrow to make the rest."

The woman inspected her with keen eyes. A hard look glittered in them that Bronwyn understood. That was the strife that had been caused by her father's greed. Anne and Bonnie were English and had not lived with the deaths that had happened in years gone by, but this woman had. Bronwyn shivered under the woman's wary regard.

"Well now. I'm Helen. We'd best get that hair dried before ye take ill."

Helen's words were surprisingly pleasant. Bronwyn discovered that she was too tired to worry about what might happen later. For the moment she was among women and there was a camaraderie that was worth savoring. In a world run by men, every female had doubts. She was not alone in that. Knowing that helped fill in a small amount of the empty place she'd noticed yesterday.

Bronwyn sat in front of the fire, brushing her hair until it dried into a fluffy cloud. The new chemise was fresh and welcome. Anne put the surcoat back over her so that she could leave the bathhouse. But she held onto the shoes, tiny wrinkles appearing on the bridge of her nose.

"These are soaked clean through and smell like a horse."

"I'm not surprised. I believe I've lived on one for the better part of three days." Bronwyn looked at the pitiful lumps her boots had become. "But 'tis all I have."

"Not so," Helen declared as she placed a pair of bedchamber slippers on the floor near her feet. "Ye have a McJames husband now. He will provide well for ye."

She slid her feet into the slippers. They were lined in soft wool to keep her toes warm. She began following Anne through the hall without question because her mind was too busy. Besides, she had no other idea of where to go.

A McJames husband . . .

Bronwyn wasn't sure if she was more stunned by the word "McJames" or "husband." A tiny quiver went through her belly as she realized that night had fallen. Most of the shutters were tightly closed now and tin lanterns had been set along the hallways to provide light. Yellow dots danced on the stone floor, the winter wind stirring the candle flames.

Her wedding night.

Even if they had celebrated it already, it was, in fact, her wedding night. Cullen would be waiting for her. Heat began to warm her skin as she thought about walking to a room where everyone knew that she would spend the night with a man and that they would not be sleeping immediately.

It was amazing to think that half an hour in front of a bishop could change something that was forbidden into a thing she was expected to do. Many labeled it a chore, but she had enjoyed it.

But what was it?

A wifely duty? A sin?

A need . . .

Her cheeks burned scarlet as she thought about the *action*. Oh, she knew plenty of words for it. Some of them more coarse than others. But she couldn't deny that she had enjoyed those moments in Cullen's arms. The sheer pleasure that had taken control of her had been mind numbing. To think that it was expected of her now was pure temptation. Since he'd bent her to his will, she might lay back and indulge her body in its craving for his touch.

The church would not frown on her.

Yet her clan would.

Did she care? She wasn't as sure as she had been two days past.

It was a dilemma that made her bite her lower lip.

Anne paused in front of a large door. She pushed it inward, holding it wide for Bronwyn. Candles burned in bright welcome on the table in the room. There was a fire in the hearth adding warmth.

"I remember how lonely it was my first night at Sterling. Believe me when I tell you that the McJames men are very good at helping to change that." Anne went back into the doorway. "I will see you at breakfast."

"Thank ye." Her voice lacked true sincerity, so she kept it low. She meant no disrespect, but she was not an accomplished liar, either.

Anne didn't linger. The door shut, leaving Bronwyn in the chamber. It was large and round because it was in one of the keeps that made up Sterling. On the second floor, there were windows that were covered in curtains. Curious, she moved toward them, fingering the expensive velvet fabric. Brushing one aside, she gasped at the glass behind it. Small panes of expensive glass were held together with lead to form windows that would allow light into the room even in foul weather. There were hinges that would allow the sections to be opened so that fresh air might enter the room. She touched the glass lightly, marveling at the smooth texture. Her fingertips could feel the chill of winter through it. They were large windows and that was a luxury because it allowed heat to escape even with the heavy curtains. But it would allow the air to be fresh in the chamber.

There was also a chimney for the hearth for the smoke to rise up and out of the chamber. The bed itself was clearly made for a man. It was large with thick curtains hanging on the sides of it. The fluffy coverlet that was turned down looked inviting. She was suddenly so tired of struggling. Lying down in a warm bed tempted her almost beyond her endurance.

"Yer hair is beautiful, lass."

She stiffened, each muscle straining. Turning around, she looked at the man she'd wed. His hair glistening in the candlelight told her that he'd bathed as well. He wore only his kilt now, his sword slung over his shoulder. He let the weapon down to rest against a wall near the side of the bed that was closest to the door.

"I should have stolen ye the first time I set eyes on ye."

"That's insane." She meant to sound firm but her voice was breathless.

Cullen shrugged, the thick muscles on his chest moving with the motion.

"Maybe, I'll no deny that ye have that effect on me."

He had closed the distance between them. With each step he took, her body responded. Sensation flowed down over her skin, awakening it. Her breasts became more aware of the fabric of her chemise, the nipples tingling as they recalled what his mouth felt like on them.

"Ye shouldn't say such things."

He reached out to finger her hair. Enjoyment flickered in his eyes as he reached up higher and slid his fingers through it. "There is no one here to judge what we say, Bronwyn. I often wonder why the church is so concerned about the matters between a man and a woman, anyway."

"That's close to blasphemy, Cullen. Ye'll be the one in the stocks if ye are overheard."

"Maybe, but I suppose ye might just consider that fair because you almost landed in their rough grasp this morning."

She suddenly laughed, the sound bubbling up past her lips before she realized it was coming. "Ye are such a boy sometimes."

His hand closed in her hair and gave it a gentle tug. He was grinning as he repeated the motion. "Since I've pulled yer hair, does that makes me a naughty boy?"

"It does indeed. But give me a moment and I shall find a tree to cut a switch from."

His expression changed. The teasing light vanished as desire replaced it.

"'Tis too cold for that, besides, it would nae stop me. I'm nae in the mood to behave properly."

Neither was she . . .

Bronwyn quivered as she recognized how much she agreed with him. Her body was pulsing with needs that it wanted satisfied. She wanted more than she'd had last night. Needed to touch him more. The surcoat was suddenly too warm and the chemise rough against her sensitive skin.

But the need to touch him was stronger than her desire to

rid herself of the discomforts. Reaching forward, she stroked his chest with her fingertips, tracing one sculpted ridge of hard muscle. His skin was hot and smooth and his nipple drew into a hard point as she moved her hand toward it. Would he like it as much as she had if she leaned toward him and sucked it? Her hands slid over it and his skin rippled with a shudder. That little reaction made her bold. Closing the last step between them, she tilted her head and gently placed a kiss on his nipple.

"Sweet mercy."

He growled through his teeth and grasped her head in his hands. But he didn't pull her away. Flattening both her hands on his chest she stroked him as she parted her lips to gently suckle his nipple. His chest rumbled with some sound that was half growl and half moan.

It filled her with confidence.

Parting her lips, she allowed the tip of her tongue to tease the little tip. The grip in her hair tightened and she trailed soft kisses across his chest to the opposite nipple. Closing her lips around it, she offered it the same teasing affection.

"Ye learn too fast, Bronwyn."

Cullen pulled her head away from his chest, raising her face so that his mouth hovered above her lips. "But I'm no complaining."

He pressed a kiss onto her mouth. It was demanding but slow. He tasted her lips, sliding his across hers in a soft motion that stole her breath. She shivered as delight filled her. Slipping her hands up his chest, she held onto his shoulders, urging him closer.

He sent his tongue into her mouth, invading and demanding, but she opened wide for it. His tongue found hers and stroked it. He teased it again and again until she followed his lead. They thrust and tangled for a long moment before he lifted his head. Desire made his face fierce but it didn't alarm her.

What it did was excite her. Her passage heated up, her clitoris throbbing gently between the folds of her sex.

"I need to see ye." His hands slid out of her hair. "All of ye."

He didn't reach for her surcoat, but watched her with need etched into his face.

"Show yerself to me, Bronwyn."

It was a command but one edged with desire. She had never thought a woman might have control over such a strong man, but she did in some odd fashion. He'd stripped her last night but wanted the gift of her surrender tonight.

She wanted to know what that power felt like.

She reached for the buttons on her surcoat, watching his face while he waited for her to comply with his demand. There was no logic to the idea, only the rush of confidence that filled her. For the first time in her life she felt beautiful.

The buttons slid quietly from the buttonholes. Only the first few were closed. She shrugged out of the heavy wool in a few moments. Cullen stood still, giving her his absolute attention.

"More." He croaked the single word when she stopped.

She drew her finger along the edge of her chemise instead. He frowned, his jaw twitching.

"Sweet tease. Be careful, lass. That's a game two can play."

She brushed past him, walking toward the hearth. The fire would make her garment transparent and she knew it. The heat caused the hem to billow softly around her calves.

He chuckled softly, following her in a lazy pace that reminded her of stalking. A mocking grin decorated his lips. With a hard tug he released his belt and his kilt slid down his hips. He caught it up and tossed it aside.

Bronwyn couldn't help herself, she looked at his cock once

again. It was standing straight up from his lower belly, the head crowned with a thick ridge of flesh. Knowing that she'd already taken it didn't keep her from wondering if he was too large. The flesh looked impossibly thick and long.

He suddenly captured her, closing the distance with one long step. She gasped, but he laughed at her and clicked his tongue in reprimand.

"Distractions often prove fatal."

He pressed another kiss onto her mouth. This one was hard and unrelenting. His tongue speared into her mouth, boldly demanding what his body wanted. He grasped the sides of her chemise and pulled it over her head.

"Much better."

He didn't take time to look at her nude body. Scooping her up, he turned and settled her in his bed without hesitation. The bed rocked and he kicked the bedding down to the foot.

"Now to return the favor."

He grasped both her breasts in a light grip, and leaning down, licked one nipple, sending a shaft of pleasure straight down her spine. She twisted with the intensity, reaching for something to hold on to. Her hands closed on his shoulders as he sucked her nipple into his mouth.

A soft cry hit the canopy above her but she didn't recognize it as her own. It was too wanton, too passionate. Cullen was unleashing something she had never known lived inside her. She twisted as need clawed through her passage. It seemed to build much faster now that she understood what satisfaction felt like. Her clitoris was begging for attention, her thighs already open in invitation.

Cullen appeared to agree. He slid a hand down her body quickly tonight, stroking her skin but not hesitating at the top of her mons. He parted the flesh protecting her clitoris in a smooth motion.

The first touch made her moan. Pleasure spiked up into her belly. He lifted his head from her nipple to watch her face. That single fingertip pressed slow circles onto her clitoris. The pleasure overwhelmed her and her eyes fluttered shut as the intensity hit her all at once.

All she wanted to do was feel.

"Do ye like that, lass?"

Her eyes popped open because she couldn't believe he was asking about . . . about something so intimate.

That teasing grin was back on his face. He slid his finger down the lips of her sex to the opening of her passage. A new sensation hit her as he circled that opening, teasing it. Her hips lifted toward his touch, craving to be filled.

"Ye dinna answer my question."

"I can't."

He chuckled and slid his finger tip back up to her clitoris. "Yer voice sounds like it is working fair well."

He paused, not moving but only resting on the sensitive bit of flesh. The teasing look in his eyes hardened into a demanding one that she knew well now. The man wanted his way.

"Aye." She growled the word at him.

He chuckled in response, but his finger moved, sending sweet delight through her. It was tightening again, her belly becoming a pool of hot need. She craved the satisfaction that had ripped through her last night.

"Do ye want me?"

"Why do ye torment me?"

His expression softened. "Can ye nae believe that I want to hear ye tell me that ye crave my possession? And nae just because I know where to rub ye?"

There was something in his tone that touched her deeply. His hand had gone still again, but this time it was because he craved something from her that only she might grant him.

Sliding her hands up to his face, she cupped his cheeks and spread her thighs wide in invitation.

"I want ye."

He needed no more urging. His body covered hers, pressing her down into the mattress again. He didn't smother her but held his weight above her, giving her enough but not too much. She felt the hard tip of his cock slipping between the folds of her sex.

"I don't just want ye, Bronwyn. I crave ye."

He thrust slowly into her. The pace frustrated her until pain nipped at her.

"Easy, lass. It gets easier with repetition, I promise ye."

His words proved true when he slid deep without much more discomfort. She didn't ache as she had last night, only a few twinges as her passage accepted his entry once more.

"As ye told me, ye keep yer promises."

He withdrew and plunged back into her. "I do indeed."

She didn't want to talk. There was far too much sensation for her to think about words. Every inch of her body was one huge receptor. Every place their skin touched added to the wealth of delight filling her. She lifted her hips for each thrust from his, learning the rhythm. Each stroke of his cock slid along her clitoris, pushing her closer to the edge. His breathing became rough as hers turned shallow. She strained toward him, seeking release.

It hit her hard. Jerking and ripping at every thought, every idea. The wave of satisfaction was so strong it washed everything away leaving her gasping in limp surrender.

But Cullen joined her in that state, his body driving a few final times into hers before his seed erupted deep inside her. He pressed her hard to the bed as his seed filled her, a growl leaving his lips. But his arms quivered beneath her fingertips exactly as hers did. It was an unspoken thing, but she felt it, that moment when they were simply both slaves to the passion their bodies had for each other. For the moment it was enough to satisfy her pride. The need to struggle against him and their marriage died.

It would sprout anew in the morning, but she allowed it to lie dormant. The bed felt like a perfect sanctuary from the world where she was McQuade and he McJames.

He rolled over, shaking the bed when he landed on his back.

"I swear ye are a siren sent to lure me to my death." He sat up to grasp the bedding, pulling it up over them both. "But I'm going to die a happy man."

"If I'm a siren then ye are the sailor set to die on the rocks at my feet. We make the most tragic couple." She stared up at the canopy above her, suddenly fighting off tears. They burned her eyes as she resisted the weakness.

Cullen sighed. "Ye seem to forget that along with all the other things in this world there is still hope. I prefer to think about that more than the tragic fates that have befallen others. I plan to be the sailor who enchants ye so completely, ye cannot bear to watch me die."

"That's not the way the story goes."

"Ah, but it's a myth and I'm a modern man, composing my own tale of adventure."

"Well, I agree that ye are certainly no following anyone else's rules." And in all truth, there was a part of her that was enjoying it. To be wanted, even for reasons that she was suspicious of, was still being wanted.

Clearly her mind had gone soft.

He pulled her against him, scooping her up and pulling her into contact with his body. She wiggled, trying to regain some space, but he tucked her against his body, refusing her.

"Be still, lass. I promised to keep ye warm."

IN THE WARRIOR'S BED

IN THE WARRIOR'S BED

She hissed softly. "I cannae sleep like this."

His chest rumbled softly with amusement. "And why not? Ye have never tried."

She was too close to really hurt him, but she slapped a hand down on his chest and it popped loudly in the silent chamber. A second later her hand was captured in a warm hand.

"Enough for one day, Bronwyn."

She suddenly noticed what he smelled like. His body heat wrapped around her, combining with the satisfaction pulsing through her to drag her down into slumber. The fact that she was sleeping beneath the roof of her clan's enemy didn't seem to have any power against the warm arms wrapped around her. Her flesh was content and it ignored everything beyond the man holding her.

For the moment it was perfect.

The royal court of Scotland

"McQuade is demanding to see ye." Alarik McKorey didn't bother to hide his smirk from his king. Erik McQuade had stolen enough from him to make any sufferings on his part amusing. "Again."

James Stuart sighed. The queen sat beside her husband with her ladies near. They worked fine silk threads into embroidery in the private royal receiving room. Anne was making her husband's shirts, a task that showed affection when done by a wife for her husband. She looked at her husband. "I believe we have heard enough from that man to last a year."

The king looked at his queen. "I canna ignore him forever. The man is a laird and my treatment of him is watched carefully by the rest of the clans."

"The man should be so considerate when he talks about his daughter when others are watching him." The queen kept her voice perfectly smooth and soft, a credit to her tutoring to wear a crown, but there was no mistaking the subtle disgust.

"I believe Bronwyn McQuade will be marrying soon, if she hasn't already."

The queen looked stunned. She glanced quickly around the room, frowning at the lowered heads of her maids of honor. Not one of them looked her in the eye.

"I understand this is a particular custom among your clans, but I confess that I find it harsh. I hope you will understand why I don't remain to hear the man's displeasure over having his daughter stolen. I have a daughter of my own." The queen stood. She curtsied to her husband before gliding gracefully from the private receiving room. Her maids followed her, each one modeling themselves after her. Raelin McKorey remained, silently sorting the costly silks the queen had been using to do her embroidery. She carefully tucked ends and slipped them back into the queen's embroidery basket that was entrusted to her keeping.

"My queen has an interesting point."

Alarik offered his king a grin. "I do believe no man alive would dream of stealing the Princess Elizabeth."

James Stuart snorted. "Och now, they'll dream it sure enough. It's in the nature of a man to reach for something he sees above him."

"Except for a king."

James looked shocked but then laughed. "Och now, ye have that right. There's been a few times I've looked down and envied the lives of those not born to sit on a throne." He sobered though and pegged Alarik a hard stare. "I meant what I told young McJames. There had better have been care taken with that girl."

Alarik stared straight back at his king, his chin level. Raelin watched them from beneath her lowered lashes. A shiver raced down her spine. Men were hard creatures. They saw women as items that were fashioned for their use.

"Laird McQuade." The royal messenger announced Erik Mc-Quade with a tap of his staff against the stone floor.

"He may enter. Alone."

There was argument from beyond the large doors but the king did not relent. Laird McQuade entered and the guards closed their pikes across the doorway to bar the man's sons and retainers from the private receiving room.

"Alone or wait until I'm in the mood to receive ye in the outer hall."

McQuade glared at Alarik McKorey.

James Stuart held up a hand. "When you disturb me in my private chambers, you take my company along with me."

McQuade shook with his anger but he gave his king the quickest of bows before stepping farther into the room. The guards secured the doors behind him. There was an uproar from his sons that the heavy doors muffled but did not completely seal out.

"That stinking McJames has stolen me daughter!" His face was red and contorted with anger. He sucked in another breath. "I demand he be tossed into chains."

The king lifted his hand but Laird McQuade didn't heed the warning. He cussed.

"He's stolen my child! I demand his blood!"

The guards behind the king lowered their pikes. It was clear they didn't care for the way the man was bellowing at his monarch. McQuade scowled but held his tongue.

"Rather interesting that Cullen would see fit to steal her away when you told all that he'd already had her. What do you suppose is the man's motivation? Why steal a woman who lifted her skirts willingly?"

McQuade sputtered, outrage making his eyes bulge. "I'll deal with the thieving bastard myself!"

"Ye will not." James Stuart raised his voice and there was no missing the crack of authority in it. "Yer raiding is at the root of this problem, man. Did ye think ye could smear the names of yer neighbors and nae have them retaliate?"

"If they were any sort of real Scots they'd take the matter up with me, no me daughter."

The king gripped the arms of his chair. "Yer the one who brought her into the fight between you and the McJames."

"Because Cullen McJames soiled her and tossed her aside like a whore." McQuade opened his hands. "I came to ye for justice."

"It would seem that Cullen has not discarded her at all but intends to keep her. A wedding will satisfy the need for justice."

"I have no given her permission to wed! I am her father and laird!" McQuade returned to yelling. The guards at the back doors of the receiving room entered because he was bellowing so loudly.

The king, however, was calm. "And why not, man? It won't be the first couple that knelt on the altar after sampling each other."

"It will no wipe the stain off me honor."

James snorted in frustration. "What do you want? Cullen McJames rotting in chains?"

"Aye! And me daughter back on my land where she belongs."

"To what end, McQuade? Ye want to keep her unmarried and shamed for the rest of her days?"

McQuade quieted down. He considered his next words before replying. "I do not know as yet. Bronwyn has shamed me and her entire clan. I'll take her home as an example to the other daughters who think to disobey their fathers and clan."

The king raised an eyebrow. "Just how are ye planning to do that, man? I thought ye said she was stolen away?"

McQuade shook with his anger. "I want ye to order that thieving McJames to bring her back. He'll obey ye."

"How do ye know it was McJames who took her? There's more than one clan that would like to force ye into an alliance by marrying yer daughter." Alarik McKorey glared at Erik Mc-Quade, making it plain that he was one of them.

Erik McQuade spat on the floor. "I've witnesses. The way they tell it, there was more than one set of colors that helped with the stealing, but they only got a good look at the Mc-James that tied up me daughter and threw her over his shoulder."

Alarik shrugged. "The McJames are good friends. I've no doubt that if Cullen were the one who took yer daughter, there would be a few men that might help him. Considering the fact that ye labeled him a blackguard."

McQuade smiled. It was a slow, sickening twist of his lips. "Is that a fact? Well, since ye seem to think that stealing brides is acceptable, maybe it's time I married again meself." He glanced down at Raelin and the embroidery basket went tumbling right out of her lap when she stood up.

"Yer sister's ripe for breeding." He licked his lower lip. "I always liked plump tits best."

"I'll carve yer cock off, ye letch." Alarik had his hands around McQuade's throat before the guards made it across the room.

They trampled the contents of the queen's baskets beneath their boots as they tried to tear Alarik off McQuade. Raelin was pushed out of the way and ended up against a wall while the fight went on. She watched it intently, feeling that shiver cross her spine again. Her brother was in a full rage, but McQuade didn't seem to notice the younger man's advantage. He pulled a knife and plunged it toward Alarik.

The blade sliced through the air with a wicked flicker of light off its polished surface. Time slowed down and she heard her own heartbeats while the slashing blade was moving closer and closer to her brother's throat. The metal sliced into his skin, spilling crimson blood. Alarik let out a roar as he turned away, releasing his hold on McQuade.

McQuade stumbled forward now that Alarik wasn't there to absorb his attack, the knife dripping blood as it plunged toward the king still in his chair.

In one more heartbeat a guard thrust his lowered pike through the impending threat to his king. A sickening sound filled the chamber. The iron top of the pike embedded itself in Laird McQuade's chest, his own charge helping to push it deep.

The king's guards pulled him over the back of the chair and out of the range of McQuade's dagger. Bright red blood flowed over the pike and onto the rich carpets that lay beneath the king's chair. McQuade looked down at his lifeblood, a frozen expression of rage still on his face. He looked up, meeting Raelin's horrified stare.

"Ye stupid bitch. All . . . women are nothing . . . save . . . trouble . . . for . . . men." He wheezed, bloody bubbles appearing at the sides of his mouth. With a last effort he threw the bloodstained dagger toward her.

Alarik made a lunge for the dirk but was too far behind her to make any difference. Still frozen in slow motion, it seemed impossible to avoid the spinning blade. But she moved away from it, every second feeling like an hour. Her cheek burned as the tip of it slit her skin open. The soft gold silk of her dress turned crimson, ruined beyond saving.

"Holy Christ!"

Time resumed its normal tempo. More guards rushed into the room. Lairds who had been waiting in the outer hall pushed their way in. Liam and Sodac McQuade howled loud enough to shake the rafters when they found their father dead, his eyes still open and staring at her.

"Ye witch!" Liam screamed in an insane rage. He reached for her, his fingers stained with his father's blood. Alarik shoved him back, but it took more guards to subdue the enraged Scot.

"If ye want blood McQuade, try and take it!" Alarik snarled his eyes alight with the will to fight.

Liam spat on the floor, uncaring of the fine carpets beneath his feet. "What did yer bitch of a sister do to my father, McKorey?"

"Yer father was the one who insulted her by treating her like a common whore."

Liam's face turned purple with rage. He aimed that fury at Raelin. "Ye bewitched him! Ye devil's handmaiden!" He pointed at her. "Witch! I'll see ye burned for it!"

"Enough!" The king fought with his own guards, struggling to be heard over the rising voices of the men in the room. Accusations were flung out, one clan against another. McKorey retainers facing off with McQuade. Mixed into it was the royal guard trying to maintain order and protect their monarch.

Raelin watched in horror as McQuade men cursed her and strained to reach her so that they might murder her. Through it all, Liam McQuade watched silently, his face contorted with rage. It became his legacy as every man wearing his colors joined the fight to stamp out her life and that of her brother's clansmen.

Hours later the McQuade retainers rode away from court, their laird's body wrapped in his plaid. Hate blazed from their eyes in spite of the explanation given by their king. Raelin watched them from a balcony on the second floor of the palace.

Queen Anne laid kind hands on her shoulders. "It was not your fault, child."

It hadn't been, but there was no telling any McQuade that. She looked at the snow and shivered. Not because she was cold but because spring would bring more blood.

McKorey blood.

Chapter Nine

Sterling

"Well now, it seems yer husband's bed agreed with ye." Helen swept into the room with a cheery smile.

Bronwyn jumped, startled awake by the sound of the woman's voice. She had been sleeping so soundly it took several minutes to recall where she was.

"Ye slept past services and breakfast but no one thinks poorly of ye for that since yer so newly wed."

There was a soft laugh from the girl with Helen. She wore a neat wool dress and linen cap. But she did not have on a long apron like the other maids. Two of them were pulling the draperies open to allow more of the winter light into the room. One pushed on the slide lock to swing the pane of glass open.

"Here now, the mistress has not yet dressed."

Helen nodded approval at the girl.

"This is Sybil. She has served in this house for a decade and her mother before her. I brought her up to see if she suits ye."

Sybil had dark eyes that studied her with calm confidence. She lowered herself before snapping her fingers at the two under maids and pointing at the bed curtains.

"I don't need a maid."

Helen frowned and the two under maids cast quick looks at each other. "Ye are a baron's wife."

Sybil didn't appear put off by her words. The girl stepped up to the bed and offered her chemise to her. Helen watched with a critical eye.

"We've plenty to do, what with ye having not a stitch of clothing to yer name."

Sybil held the chemise perfectly so that all she had to do was raise her arms to get into the sleeves. The two under maids pulled the bedding down as the fabric of the undergarment slid over her nude body. It was flawless the way they worked together to help her rise.

Sybil even gathered up her hair and laid it down her back once the chemise was in place. "I understand that it will take time for ye to become accustomed to my service. But yer a Mc-James now and we take pride in serving our mistress."

"I've never had a maid, that's all I meant." The words crossed her lips before Bronwyn realized how they must sound. Four sets of eyes looked at her and then the two maids laughed. Oh, they tried to smother their amusement but it made it past their lips.

Sybil and Helen didn't find it funny at all. Both their expressions tightened as they took her words as an insult, an expected one but still a slight to their blood. As the laird's daughter, no one was going to believe that she was accustomed to fending for herself.

"Truly, I have always been treated as the other women at Red Stone. My father is not one for comforts. Everyone works." Sybil brought forward the surcoat. She looked pensive for a moment.

"Well, if ye are handy with a needle that shall be a blessing today. I sent one of the girls along to the sewing room to pull down some of the lengths of new fabric for ye to consider for a dress."

It was a test. A subtle challenge laid down to see if she was lying. It was one test she would have no trouble passing. Helen had laid out a comb and hair pins on the table. Reaching for the comb, Bronwyn pulled it through her hair herself but Sybil stopped her when she would have braided it in one long tail.

"Perhaps ye might allow me to braid it up, to keep it away from our work."

Helen pulled a small stool out from beneath the table. Sinking down onto it, Bronwyn surrendered the comb. Unless she wanted to be rude, she would have to allow Sybil to tend her.

But there was a part of her that was touched by it, too. It would not have surprised her to be left on her own at Sterling. With the years of raids from her father, there were plenty who had reason to detest her for her blood alone. But the four women moved around her without any outward sign of animosity. Sybil was gentle, her hands coiling her hair in a French braid that encircled her head. Breakfast was served to her on a polished silver tray while the two under maids righted the bed. They both paused at the door and curtsied to her before standing quietly near the door awaiting her needs.

Helen watched Sybil with a critical eye, making sure the girl performed to her satisfaction. As the personal maid to the countess, Helen made the choice of who would get important positions such as the maid to the wife of the laird's brother. Sybil most likely had been apprenticing for years, waiting for her opportunity to rise above the other maids.

But in spite of knowing that Sybil had most likely been looking forward to the day that she would have a mistress to maid for, Bronwyn could not sit still for very long. The food stuck in her throat because she had never once in her life eaten while others waited upon her. She did not know how to act or even how to continue eating. She felt like each bite was awkward or clumsy.

"I am eager to set to work."

Helen and Sybil both looked at the meager amount of food that she'd consumed, but Bronwyn was already on her feet.

"Let us go to the sewing room." She reached for the tray her breakfast was on, intending to carry it from the room lest the mice discover an easy meal and make a nest in her bed because they thought food plentiful in the chamber. Helen took it from her with a stern look that only age gave a woman. It did not matter that she was a servant and Bronwyn considered mistress. But there was a hint of curiosity in her eyes as she watched how naturally Bronwyn cleaned up after herself. She handed the tray to one of the maids before moving toward the door.

"If ye will follow me."

Helen was more accomplished in her position than Bronwyn had guessed. The woman had somehow managed to find the most tenderhearted women on McJames land to tend her that morning.

She encountered a far different attitude once she left the sanctuary of Cullen's chamber.

The women she met in the sewing room barely contained their snarls. A few of them watched her with critical stares, critiquing her every motion. Four rolls of newly woven cloth were awaiting her inspection. Tension knotted her neck as she realized how many sets of eyes were on her. Along the back of the long room were spinning wheels. Now that the harvest was in, the wool could be spun during the winter hours. There were three long tables for cutting of fabric. Three small looms were in a corner but what drew her eye was the two great looms at the far end of the room. The familiar sight felt like a sanctuary from the harsh glares she was enduring.

Reaching out, she fingered one bundle of wool but her voice failed her because her throat was tight under all the scrutiny.

A deep grunt echoed down the silent room. Helen narrowed her eyes at the offender but the woman didn't look contrite.

"As if I ever thought to see a McQuade compliment anything made by my hand. I should like to see ye do better."

"The mistress did not insult yer work, Gerty."

The woman's lower lip protruded as she propped a fist onto one hip.

"Please don't call me that." Attention shifted from Gerty back to her. Sweat trickled down her neck. Sybil looked at her confused.

"To address ye otherwise would be disrespectful, mistress."

"I am Bronwyn. It's the truth that I am not sure about even my last name this morning. The last few days have left me baffled." She glanced at Gerty. "Yer command of the great loom is to be admired."

The woman lost some of her condemning posture. "Have ye ever worked a loom?"

Her tone said she doubted it. Bronwyn lifted her chin, her pride rising to the bait. Perhaps her father was a greedy man who worked every pair of hands until they were exhausted, but she was no pampered chit useless for anything save bearing children and giving orders. She was a McQuade.

"I have indeed."

Gerty grinned in challenge. "I believe I should like to see that." She glanced at the second loom. "Mind ye, ye'll have to thread it first."

"The best place to begin when weaving."

It was also the most difficult part of producing cloth on one of the large looms. But she rose to the challenge, eager to prove her worth. After a week of being nothing but Cullen's pilfered goods, she wanted to be herself again. Someone who pulled her weight and earned respect while doing it.

At the very least, setting the loom for work gave her mind enough to focus on, all the eyes watching her faded into the background. It wasn't the first time someone had doubted her ability to be useful. But in a way it was just another link in the chain that had begun with her birth to a man who did not want her.

But Cullen wanted her because of who her father was . . .

It was a strange twist of fate. Bronwyn almost laughed at it but kept her mind on the loom she was stringing. Many of the women went back to working because she was still stringing it when the noon meal was set out in the hall. The kitchen bells bounced between the stone walls but she was too intent on her task to leave before finishing. Besides, there would be naught but a hall full of condemning stares waiting for her if she did go join the meal. She was not that hungry yet.

"Mistress, are ye not hungry?" Sybil stood up, stretching her back. She placed her sewing on the table, being careful to place the needle into a small cushion to keep it from getting lost.

"Go along without me. I want to finish."

Sybil appeared torn but lowered herself and left. Bronwyn sighed with relief. She looked around the room and found no one watching her. It seemed as if it had been a year since she'd had privacy. It wasn't as if she craved being alone but she did miss feeling confident in her surroundings. All the small things that went with life were so much more valuable than she'd ever given them credit for. Such as knowing details about the people surrounding her. Who was married, who was excited about a sweetheart that might soon ask them to wed. Whose sister had a new baby and whose mother was always interfering in her life. Who had a brother that was too wild for his own good and what dreams did they all share with each other during the work hours.

Being installed at Sterling was bleak because she knew nothing about anyone. It felt like a day without sunlight where she was trying to feel her way through the darkness. It was also cold. No friendly comments or jests. Nothing but hard stares while she was watched to see what she did and how well she performed.

Well, she knew her loom. With determination, she set the last few bobbins and drew the threads along their paths. She tested them gently to judge the tension. She had threaded the loom with a cheerful blue and loaded the shuttle with the same.

The same blue as Cullen's eyes . . .

The thought surprised her. Cullen snuck into her mind without warning, sending heat into her cheeks. A soft throb began hidden in the folds of her sex. Flashes of last night cut through her determination to see the loom threaded. But she didn't frown this time. At least there was something pleasing to think about.

And there was no mistaking that she found the man's touch pleasing.

More heat touched her face. It flowed down over her limbs beneath the surcoat. She was suddenly more aware of the lack of clothing she wore. Noticing the way her breasts hung free.

His hands felt amazing on her breasts . . .

With a shake of her head, she sat at the loom to begin weaving. Her nipples were hard pebbles beneath the wool of the surcoat. The chemise fabric felt scratchy against their taut peaks. Cullen did that to her. Somehow, the man made her body feel so much more than it ever had before. There was no sense to it and no way to control it either.

"Be careful, Bronwyn, Show a talent for that loom and ye may never be free of it."

She stepped on the floor pedal too hard, making a loud crunch against the stone floor. Cullen moved up beside her and ran a hand over the few inches of new cloth she'd just produced.

"I hear a good number of the women detest this loom." There was a soft hint of approval on his face that drew her interest. In fact she met his gaze, staring at that glimmer of praise like a child seeking affection. But all she saw staring back at her was dark suspicion.

"It takes a bit of practice, is all."

His blue eyes were as hard as stone.

"If that is the case, make sure ye do not miss meals. There is time enough for weaving. Ye don't need to go hungry in favor of a few feet of cloth."

Sybil was standing near the door along with three other maids. They cast their gazes toward the floor looking for all the world as if they were not listening but there was no way they might not hear what was being said. It was something she had often seen her father's servants doing. Attempting to disappear while remaining in plain sight.

"If ye miss a meal, yer personal attendants will as well." Cullen's tone was quiet but as hard as iron. There was no missing the reprimand. She bristled under the commanding tone, the noose returning to her throat once more.

"There's no need for me to be pampered by servants following me every step I take."

Cullen frowned at her. "But there is a need for me to know where ye are, wife."

He spoke the word "wife" with a hard tone that wasn't lost on anyone in the room. Suspicion edged his tone and it glittered in his eyes. Her temper rose until it choked every bit of patience she had.

Slapping the shuttle down, she stood up and for once Cullen's height didn't seem to impact her.

"By all means then, *husband*."

His expression tightened. "Aye, ye have that right. I am yer husband and ye will nae escape while yer maids are eating in the hall."

"Is that so? And ye are here to clamp yer servants about my ankles like fetters. Telling me that they shall go hungry if I dinna obey yer whim is the same as chaining me to a wall."

He remained silent for a long moment, his gaze cutting into hers, but she refused to lower her chin.

"It is not the same and I pray ye never have to experience what cold iron is like around yer flesh. Just as I'm setting Sybil to making sure ye dinna walk off into the winter snow."

Shame made it past her temper, drowning a good deal of her anger. Cullen stood watching her, his expression guarded. It was such a stark contrast from the man she had been daydreaming about a few moments past. The man who stroked her body until she floated away on a cloud of bliss seemed foreign to the one she faced. This was the warrior who fought against her kin. There was no leniency in him. Only determination to make her bend.

But she had tried to escape and could not blame the man for thinking that way. It was her own rash words that had him suspecting her of running off into the snow.

"I will not allow ye any opportunity to attempt an escape that will only endanger yerself. Ye willna last long out in the snow."

Both temper and shame choked her. Stepping closer, she hissed at him with every bit of uncertainty he unleashed in her.

"I dinna think of escaping but I should have."

He clasped her arm, keeping her close. "Why, Bronwyn? Tell me what displeases ye so?"

She turned and crossed the room.

"Bronwyn . . ."

"Have done, husband." She turned and glared at him. Fury drew his face tight but that suited her mood as well. "Ye want me on display in yer hall and that is what I am planning to do."

Like a prize.

With another swish of her surcoat, she faced the door and headed into the hall. Two burly retainers watched her, disapproval etched into their faces. Their presence made her grind her teeth. Her pace increased and the bulky coat became a nuisance. Grabbing a handful of it she lifted it so that it wouldn't get stepped on. Tripping herself would certainly put a crowning touch on the moment.

She was in a temper, no doubt about it and not even one with a just cause. It was frustration, pure and simple.

She heard the conversation drifting out of the hall before she came to the arched door frames that opened into Sterling's great hall. The scent of warm food filled the air, but the sound died away when she swept through the doorway. If she'd felt the weight of being stared at in the sewing room, it was nothing compared to the crushing sensation trying to buckle her knees now.

Sybil might call her mistress, but she was anything except respected by the inhabitants viewing her. Not a single man tugged on his bonnet. More than a few sneers were sent her way. She kept walking until she reached the far side of the hall. The shutters were open to air out the smoke that didn't rise up the chimneys. She stopped, looking out over the river that ran behind the castle. Its banks had a solid foot of ice on either side and chunks of it floated along with the current. She stood there with her back to the hall. Tears burned her eyes but she refused to allow such a weakness. It was foolish to expect anything else from her situation. Instead she drew in a deep breath of fresh air to clear her foolish emotions.

"Sit, Cullen." Brodick McJames sounded tired. Cullen glared at his brother. "Dragging her to this table will nae settle anything. One step at a time."

Cullen stared at the still form of his bride. Her back was straight and her chin level, her body rigid with defiance. His temper smoldered. She was in the hall but not eating by his side. Her literal obedience to his command rubbed his pride.

He cast a stern look at Sybil. "She's nae to eat except when by my side."

He was being ruthless, but he did not care. Her silent form cast a challenge that he was going to take and conquer.

Sybil dropped him a curtsy before escaping to a lower table to join the other maids. They cast nervous glances between his wife and him, all the while frantically eating.

"Excuse me." Anne shot him a disapproving stare as she left the table. Her husband reached for her hand but she avoided his grasp. "I will not watch that girl being broken like a hunting hound."

Brodick frowned as his wife swept from the hall, but there was a gleam of understanding in his dark eyes when he looked back at Cullen.

"I wish ye luck, Cullen, it looks like ye are going to need it."

"I have nae been unkind to her, brother." His voice was low but still carried the unmistakable edge of determination.

Brodick nodded. "I believe there is a difference of opinion between men and women on that subject. My wife finds it very unkind that ye stole Bronwyn away from her home."

"As if that is any different than ye arranging a proxy marriage with Anne's father without her knowing about it until it was signed and sealed." Cullen hit the tabletop with his frustration.

"Men are different from women." Brodick cast a pensive look at Bronwyn. "I bargained with Anne's father because of the good it would bring the McJames."

"Which is exactly what I'm doing."

Brodick lifted an eyebrow. "I've nae disputed that, brother. If I disapproved I'd have sent her back to Jamie with an apology for yer wild ways. And the promise that I'd bring ye to heel."

Cullen glared at his brother but his temper didn't alter the fact that Brodick held the authority to do exactly what he'd said. As the earl of Alcaon he was the only man on McJames land who could force him to relinquish Bronwyn.

"She's my wife now." He sighed, letting his temper go. Anger was no way to deal with Bronwyn. Her father had dealt her his fury for too many years. A grin slowly lifted his lip. Nay, the way to her was through her heart.

Brodick stared at him. "What are ye thinking, brother?"

"That my bride needs to be courted."

His brother chuckled at him. "Oh aye, I can see how warm and receptive she is toward ye."

Cullen looked at his bride. She was his and not just because he'd managed to drag her to Sterling. His claim on her was rooted somewhere deep in the center of his chest, born in those dark hours when she'd clung to him. Some part of him refused to accept the defiance her back presented. Oh, he could order her to sit beside him but what he really wanted was her to join him because she considered it her place.

"Now that is where you and I differ." Cullen smirked at his older brother. "Yer English bride doesna have the same temperament as my Scottish lass."

"Ye have the temper part correct." Brodick stood up, taking a moment to fill a large wooden platter with a healthy portion of the meal. He covered it with a linen cloth. "But I'll agree that a little tender attention toward one's wife has definite merit. Best of luck to ye, brother."

Brodick carried his offering off toward his chamber and Anne. Cullen turned his attention back to Bronwyn, only to find her moving back down the aisle with Sybil, and her maids still clutching rounds of bread in their hands.

His grin turned into a roguish smile.

His bride was still running, but this time he was going to sweep her off her feet with something she wasn't even aware that he might use on her.

His charm.

Her belly was rumbling long before the night meal was due to be put down. Bronwyn kept the loom working, determined to ignore her hunger. It was a pity she could not so easily dismiss the root of her problem from her mind.

Cullen was foremost in her thoughts in spite of her efforts to banish him. She seemed fixated on him. Tension knotted her shoulders and she took to worrying her lower lip. She felt trapped by the women he'd set to serve her and choked by the retainers that remained in the hallway. They were there to guard her, but what they really did was announce to every Mc-James that Cullen did not trust his wife.

Wife . . .

So now the word rose to her mind. It was a form of acceptance that she wanted to deny, but found herself lacking any true passion for such a task. It felt so useless. But that left her with naught but surrender and the word stuck in her throat.

A sweet smell drifted into the room and for a long moment she thought it was her imagination. But it grew strong, her nose telling her that it was some newly baked sweet. Her hands froze on the shuttle, her feet becoming motionless on the pedals. She felt her husband behind her before she caught sight of him by turning her head.

Her belly grumbled low and deep as the scent of fresh baked food grew stronger. Cullen lifted one leg and straddled the bench, one leg on either side of her hips. His back was pressed along the length of her own but she was fixated by the wooden bowl he lowered onto the new cloth she'd woven. Inside it was a ceramic baking dish with a tart still gently steaming. Two silver spoons were stuck into the golden brown crust and hot fruit was swelling up out of the broken pastry.

It smelled divine . . . and looked it as well.

"I learned something today." His teasing tone turned her lips up without her thinking about it.

"Is that so?"

The scent of the tart drew another rumble from her empty belly.

"It is. I now understand why spring is the best time for weddings. It makes it much easier to sneak off with yer new bride in the middle of the afternoon." He lifted one of the spoons and carried a mouthful of the confection toward her lips. "It is also a wee bit easier to talk the cook into baking a tart. That woman dinna want to part with her fruit stores. She claimed she was saving them for a feast day."

Bronwyn felt her cheeks color because she suddenly recalled that they were not alone. But the spoonful of warm berries was too tempting to resist. She opened her mouth, humming when the sweet connected with her tongue. Nothing had ever tasted so good. Not ever.

"I'm glad ye talked her out of them."

The chest behind her rumbled, a soft chuckle brushing past her ear. Another spoonful of warm fruit made it to her lips. He fed her like a small child, taking only a few bites himself. When the last bits were scraped off the bottom of the baking dish, he sighed.

"I can see that ye are going to be distracting, dear wife. My brother may take to chastising me for my lack of attention on my duties."

He rose, taking the bowl with him. Bronwyn turned to stare at him. A grin decorated his face and it was too handsome on him. No man should look so fine. He reached up and tugged on the corner of his bonnet.

"But it's worth it to see yer eyes shimmering, lass. I dinna care how much my brother blusters at me."

"He will not. 'Tis the dead of winter."

Cullen raised an eyebrow. "Ah, but I'd rather ye think he would. What is the point of stealing an afternoon hour with a lass if ye don't have to sneak away to do it?"

He winked at her, clearly enjoying the moment.

But she was, too.

He turned and his kilt flared out behind him. He was every inch a man but lurking inside him was a playful boy who touched her heart with his games.

The man touched her, too. Sending heat through her veins. Her hands shook when she resumed her work but she did not lament it.

Instead, she savored it.

*   *   *

Bronwyn stood up when the kitchen bells rang that evening. She paused to admire the length of cloth she'd produced. Gerty cast a critical eye at her but made no comment. The light was fading and the work would not resume until dawn. It was already growing cold in the long work room because firewood was not wasted here. Sybil waited for her near the door, her face a mask of concern.

Bronwyn felt her temper rise again. Forcing her to shoulder the guilt of Sybil and the other women was ruthless. She resented it but walked toward the great hall anyway. The scent of food made her belly cramp painfully. She gasped softly at the acute pain.

"Ye'll feel much better with a full belly, mistress." Sybil tried to sound cheerful but there was a guarded note in her voice that hadn't been there that morning.

"Perhaps." But it was even more possible she might choke on anything she tried to eat. Her afternoon treat was a pleasant memory when she considered the harsh looks she'd met in the hall at noon. She paused in the doorway but forced her feet forward in spite of her concern. Tonight there were smirks as well. Expressions rich with delight over her being bent to Cullen's will.

The maids were carrying platters of steaming food out of the kitchens. Her mouth watered just looking at it. Cullen sat with his brother at the table on the raised dais at the end of the room. Both watched her as she made her way up the aisle. Bronwyn stared at Cullen, seeing no other but the man who had talked a tart out of the cook for her between meals. He held a high position at Sterling but inside him was a playful boy she was growing to like more and more.

Cullen suddenly frowned, his gaze shifting to the men at the tables. He slapped his palms down on the table in front of him, making a loud sound that silenced a good amount of the conversations in the room. The attention focused on her shifted immediately to him. He stood up, moving his gaze over the room before speaking.

"It seems a few of ye have no heard that I have married." The last of the conversations died instantly along with the smirks that had been aimed at her. "Bronwyn McQuade and myself have entered into a union that is designed to bring better futures to both our clans. She is my wife."

Cullen held out a hand toward her. She was frozen on the first step leading to the laird's table, his words sending tears into her eyes. She blinked them away as a ripple of approval passed along the tables. Feeling so many eyes on her held her still for a long moment, staring at Cullen's hand.

It was a welcome sight, one she was hungry for in soul and heart. He remained standing. It was a mark of respect. The only person at Sterling he was bound to rise for was his older brother.

Actions often spoke louder than words.

Bronwyn paused in front of the dais. Lowering herself, she remained in the position for a long moment.

"Come and sit by me, Bronwyn."

She rose and climbed the stairs to join him at the high table. Confusion held her in its grip as she stared at Cullen. The man was her captor, deserving of her scorn, but he was also offering her respect. Even rival lairds gave each other respect in public. A large chair was pulled out for her. When she looked out over the hall once more, several hands tugged on the corners of bonnets. It was such a startling change that she blinked her eyes, wondering if it was her imagination. Conversation resumed and the maids began serving again.

"Ye are a puzzle, Bronwyn."

"No more than I find you."

He maintained his grip on her hand, their eyes meeting. He

studied her for a long moment. Mischief glittered in his eyes before his lips rose into a playful grin. Her stomach tightened with anticipation exactly the way it had the first time she'd laid eyes on the man.

Cullen's fingers lightly brushed over the tender skin of her inner wrist. Sensation raced along her arm. It was so intense she wiggled in her seat. He leaned close, his eyes locked with hers.

"So if I flirt with ye, sweet Bronwyn, will ye repay me by blushing prettily?"

She yanked on her hand, but all it earned her was a warm chuckle from him. His gaze lowered to her mouth. Her lower lip tingled, craving a kiss.

"Stop teasing me."

He leaned in closer, his gaze returning to hers. Hunger flickered in his blue eyes now, and her body recognized it instantly. Heat flowed through her, touching off a blaze of need.

"I assure ye, Bronwyn, I'm no teasing." His fingers rubbed over her inner wrist again and then up into the center of her palm. Never once had she realized that her hand might be so sensitive. A shiver shot down her spine and her breath froze in her lungs.

"Ye dinna answer my question." He pulled her closer. "If I pay ye court, will ye soften and yield to my seduction?"

"Ye have already had me." Heat blistered her cheeks when she realized what she'd said while sitting at a high table. A soft moan crossed her lips.

Cullen chuckled at her again. His eyes were lit with amusement, but not the sort you found in a boy. There was nothing innocent about the way he looked at her, his fingers playing across her skin with a finesse that shook her.

"We have not yet even begun to explore the arts of having each other." There was a promise lurking in his gaze now. She stared at it, fascinated by the intensity. Anticipation drew her muscles tight, her lower lip going dry. She licked it without thinking and froze when his gaze dropped to the tip of her tongue as it stroked her lip. His face flushed, betraying his own level of arousal. An unexpected wave of confidence washed through her as she recognized that she could affect him.

A maid sat a large platter on the table in front of them. Cullen jerked his fingers, tightening around her hand.

"Ye have managed to distract me." He carried her hand to his lips and pressed a slow kiss against her fingers before freeing her. "I believe this shall be the longest meal of my life."

Her heart accelerated. It was a ridiculous response but she felt it nonetheless. Her belly growled long and deep, breaking through her fascination with the man beside her. Cullen frowned. He reached for a knife lying on the platter. Stabbing it into a section of roasted pork, he transferred it to her plate.

"Eat, Bronwyn, and dinna let yer pride wage a battle that cannot be won."

"I wonder how ye would react if I told ye to ignore yer pride." She kept her voice so low he had to lean closer to hear her. Something flickered in his gaze that surprised her. It almost looked like admiration instead of the gloating victory she'd expected.

"I would no fare as well as ye have, lass." Another serving of meat landed on his plate. "'Tis a fact that ye weather this storm between our families far more gracefully than I could ever hope to."

It was an admission. Maybe she was foolish to grasp at it but he looked sincere. It was balm for her wounds, relieving the sting for a moment. Turning her attention to the meal, she took solace in those words at least long enough to satisfy her hunger.

But she felt him watching her. Heat returned to her cheeks

but she resisted the urge to look at him. Too many pairs of eyes watched them from the lower tables, but a good deal of the animosity seemed to be missing among the McJames retainers. She would not call their faces friendly, but at least they were not condemning.

It was something, a place from which she might look up and hope for a brighter future.

Maybe.

Chapter Ten

She was nervous.

Bronwyn hugged herself and marveled at the quiver making her insides jelly. Sybil stood near the door watching two maids turn the bedding down. The girl knew her job well. She took no task lightly when it came to ensuring that everything was correctly attended to for her mistress.

Watching the sheets being revealed sent gooseflesh down her arms. It was ridiculous to be so aware of the coming night. She wasn't a maiden any longer to wonder and fret about the unknown of the marriage bed.

That isn't what you are contemplating . . .

With a small sigh she admitted that the voice in her head was correct. She was thinking about what Cullen had said. Actually excited by the idea of doing more than being taken as she already had.

It must be wicked to feel as she did.

The maids finished and curtsied to her before leaving the room. Sybil remained until they had gone.

"Is there anything else, Mistress?"

"Call me Bronwyn." She said it hopefully but Sybil frowned and remained silent.

"Good night, Sybil. Yer mistress does not require ye any longer." Cullen appeared in the doorway, his hair still damp.

His shirt was sticking to his upper torso in dark patches where his skin had not been dry.

"Good night." Sybil lowered herself before leaving. Cullen closed the door behind her.

"Why do ye refuse the title of mistress? Do ye really prefer the staff no respect ye?"

"I've never been called mistress before . . ." Her words trailed off because Cullen's face tightened dangerously. He shut the door, still frowning.

"Are ye refusing Sybil because she's a McJames?" He asked the question quietly but she heard the anger in it.

"No. I would no be so hard hearted."

He drew a deep breath but didn't relax his guard. "I suppose I shall have to take yer word on that or I can no expect ye to trust me."

The suspicion in his voice agitated her. She lifted her chin. "I suppose ye shall."

It was half challenge and half admission. But the response she witnessed in his eyes made her aware of how her skin felt fresh from her bath. Her hair was lying down her back to dry in the heat from the fire coals, the thin fabric of her chemise wet from it. Her surcoat was already hung up, leaving her once more nearly bare for her captor.

Tonight it excited her.

Anticipation sent heat coursing through her. Need licked along her skin, awakening it. She felt the heat from the fire behind her but also the soft throb of passion in her passage. A yearning began building there, a need to be filled.

Cullen watched her, his gaze lingering on her body in a slow motion that traveled from her head to her toes. His expression changed, the suspicion melting away to be replaced by hunger.

"Sterling is a fine home, Bronwyn. Give its people a bit of

time to win ye over." He reached for the end of his wide leather belt and pulled it. His kilt dropped and he laid it aside with nothing but his shirt covering his skin.

"Ye mean give ye time." She felt vulnerable for some reason. As if she had no defense against him when it came to her feelings. The side of him that she encountered behind the closed door of their chamber seemed to be able to touch her heart. It was the single place that she called her own.

He offered her a grin. "Aye. What's wrong with hoping ye'll grow to like me?"

"We're already married."

"Och now, and ye think that should satisfy me?" He closed the distance between them with a playful grin on his lips. Reaching out he stroked her cheek with the back of one hand. She shuddered as sensation ripped through her.

"The first time I saw ye, I wanted to win ye over, lass. That has no changed." His lips came closer as his hand made a second pass over her cheek. "We're still the same two people who met on an autumn afternoon and drew sparks from each other. Admit that ye wanted me to kiss ye there in the meadow."

Her lips curved up in a guilty smile. "Maybe. But I'd never been kissed afore so maybe not."

His eyebrows lowered. "Never? I would have thought at least one man wearing yer father's colors would have braved his laird's displeasure to get a taste of ye." His gaze lowered to her mouth. "I was willing to challenge my king for ye."

She gasped, the sound barely making it past her lips before he claimed them. A strong arm slid down her back and around her waist to pull her tightly against his body. She was keenly aware of how hard he was compared to her softness. Her breasts pressed against his solid chest and her belly cushioned the hard shape of his erect cock. Heat flowed through her veins as he pushed her lips apart so that his tongue could invade her mouth. It was the sweetest breaching, one that she encouraged. She teased his tongue with hers, tracing it and stroking along its length. Her hands slid up to his shoulders, frustrated by the fabric of his shirt.

"I couldna agree more." He grasped the fabric covering her back and drew it up and over her head. Tossing it aside, he cupped her hips, holding her steady as he looked at her bare body.

"I think I'll order a fire built every night just so that I can keep ye nude." He slid his hand up her body to cup each breast. The soft globes fit neatly into his hands. He controlled his grip and brushed the nipples with his thumbs.

She wanted to touch him . . .

Be it surrender or something wicked born out of lust, she did not care. The rules and expectations that she had been raised with didn't seem to apply to this moment. She tugged on his shirt, seeking the warm skin beneath it. But he was too tall for her to remove the shirt like he had pulled her chemise from her.

She slid her hands down to where it ended over his thighs, a soft sound of triumph crossing her lips when she found his bare skin. She bent her knees slightly to press her hands against his legs. The muscles were corded and defined.

"Touch me, lass."

There was a note of enjoyment in his voice that surprised her. It lacked the mocking sound she might have expected. Instead she felt her confidence rise because she was affecting him once more. Her own weakness for him was suddenly acceptable as long as he was as susceptible to her touch.

"Touch me . . ." His voice grew rough.

Her hands were already sliding up in answer to that plea. Smoothing over his warm skin until she touched the soft sac that hung beneath his cock. He drew a sharp breath, his eyes narrowing.

"*More.*"

Her confidence made her bold. Reaching up farther, she closed her hand around his length. His staff was long and thick in her hand. The flesh stiff and hard. Both her hands gripped it at the same time. He shuddered, a soft growl echoing in the room.

With a quick motion he ripped his shirt up and over his head. The ruby coals cast him in crimson.

"Now stroke it."

His words were a command, but she didn't mind obeying. The rough breath he sucked in stole the authority from his stern command. Moving her hands, she worked them up and down his cock. A muscle began to twitch on the side of his jaw as his neck corded. Seeing him enjoy her touch sent a bolt of need through her hot enough to burn. Her passage was demanding the hard flesh she held.

Cullen leaned his head back, his chest rising in hard, fast breaths. She worked her hands faster and his hips began moving toward her softly. He looked back at her, his teeth clenched.

"Now for a bit of reciprocation, lass."

His hands grasped her hips in a firm grip. He lifted her right off her feet and up onto the table that was alongside the wall. The wood was warm from the fire but it was startling against her bare bottom. Her thighs spread around his hips as he moved closer to her. He released her hips and pushed her thighs farther apart.

"Put yer hands behind ye."

"Why?"

"Because it will thrust yer beautiful breasts upward."

She shivered as the idea filled her mind. "That must be wrong . . . wicked."

"We're married. I see nothing wrong with enjoying every part of the body God created for us."

"That is clear." Her voice was husky, surprising her with how wanton she sounded.

He chuckled, his hands sliding along her thighs. It was wicked but more exciting than she might ignore. Where their skin met, pleasure radiated. Her hands were already moving to the position he'd demanded. When she pressed them onto the smooth surface of the table behind her, it arched her back, thrusting her breasts up. He slid his hands all the way to her breasts to cup each one. He leaned down and sucked one hard nipple deeply into his mouth. She gasped because it was so hot. His mouth against her nipple felt like a brand. He flicked the tip of his tongue over it before lifting his head.

"Now I'll show ye the advantages of obeying yer husband."

He sank down between her spread thighs until his head was level with her open sex. She gasped, sitting up in shock, but he pressed her thighs wide with a hand on each one.

"Cullen . . ."

He looked up at her face. "I enjoy hearing ye use my name."

His voice was hard. His gaze returned to her folds and he leaned forward until she felt his warm breath against her spread flesh.

"Cullen, ye canna mean to . . ."

"I assure ye I do."

Her next words were lost as he pressed a soft kiss against her clitoris. She jerked because it was too intense. Pleasure shot into her passage so fast it was impossible to remain still. His hand moved around her thighs to grasp her hips in a flash. His grip was firm, keeping her in place, the tip of his tongue slipping between the folds of her sex and traveling up toward her clitoris. She wasn't sure if it was pleasure or agony that tore through her when he tongued her. All Bronwyn was certain of was that she didn't care if she died.

If this was wicked, then let her be damned because she could not refuse it. Pleasure gripped her tighter than it ever had. Cullen toyed with the sensitive little nub, flicking his tongue over it again and again until she sobbed. Her fingers curled on the tabletop, trying to grip it. Gooseflesh spread across her belly as every muscle tightened. Her breath came in hard pants and she began lifting her hips toward him, offering her clitoris to his mouth. She craved more pressure, more friction.

But he denied her. Cullen raised his head, keeping her hips prisoner in his grasp. Need clawed through her so fiercely it hurt. She cried out, every bit of pride drowned in her body's need for release.

"Look at me."

Lifting her eyelids felt impossible. She wanted to fall back into the swirling pool of desire and passion. A soft lapping across her folds forced her eyes to open.

"Call me husband."

His eyes glittered with determination. One hand slipped off her hip and down across her belly. Her clitoris began throbbing as his fingers neared it, demanding the friction that would send release ripping through her. But he rubbed her so softly, a single fingertip lightly brushing the sensitive bud, that all she felt was more need.

He would not relent. She saw it in his eyes.

"Husband."

"Ah, but do ye believe that, sweet Bronwyn?"

He stood up, magnificent in the glow of the coals, every inch of his body hard and sculpted. She craved that strength. Even his pride was attractive because it was something that made him the man he was.

Unrelenting and unbending.

"I wonder . . ." He sat in one of the X chairs, his gaze fashioned on her.

"Come here, wife. Yer husband demands ye."

Sitting up, she glared at him because her body was an inferno. One he'd ignited knowingly. But his cock stood straight up, telling her that he shared the same need.

"Is that so? Husband?"

"It is."

Slipping off the table, she stood still for a long moment. His gaze traveled over her nude body, the tic returning to the side of his jaw. The response made her bold, her attention dropping to his erection, her mind pondering whether or not he would be as susceptible to her tongue.

Wicked . . . but impossible to ignore.

Moving forward, she stopped in front of him. Her fingers trailing lightly over his length. A harsh breath and she leaned forward to tease him with her breasts.

"Shall ye put yer hands behind ye and let me have my way with ye, husband?"

A harsh grunt accompanied his reply.

"As ye wish . . . wife."

There was a challenge in his voice. One she cheerfully accepted. Kneeling in front of him, she closed her fingers around his cock. Hot and hard, the skin was silky smooth, the scent of his male skin slightly intoxicating. Leaning forward she glided her tongue over the ridge that crowned his cock.

"Sweet Christ."

He reached for her head and grasped her hair. Looking up, she found his eyes wide and focused on her. Surprise flickered in his eyes but it was the hunger drawing his face tight that spurred her on. Looking down, she began licking the length from the base to the crown. His breathing turned rough when she tasted the slit on top of the head.

"Take me inside yer mouth . . ." His voice was a husky whisper, as if he did not dare say it any louder for fear of divine retribution. But he wanted it so much, he couldn't resist asking for it.

That was as close to begging as a warrior such as he might get.

Opening her jaw, she sucked the head inside her mouth. The hand in her hair tightened, pulling the strands. The little nips of pain encouraged her. Lifting her head, she moved close between his thighs so that she might take more of his length on her next dive. Her own hunger was still burning. Her passage hot and needy for the hard flesh in her grasp. His hips lifted slightly, and when she took him deep, harsh growls drifted over her bent head.

"Enough."

Harsh and ragged, his voice told her that he was as needy as she. Raising her head, she teased the slick length of his cock with her fingers while their eyes met. His were narrowed to slits, his lips a hard line.

"Enough toying, Bronwyn."

"Aye. Enough." She spoke softly, agreeing. For that moment they both craved each other. There was no captor, no captive. Only a man and woman.

"Stand." He was commanding her but at the same time hypnotized by her when she complied. His eyes roamed over her body, making her feel pretty. It wasn't something conveyed in polished words, it was in his expression and the way his jaw was clenched.

He liked what he saw.

"Enough playing." He leaned forward and grasped her hips.

He lifted her off her feet and set her in his lap. She grasped his wide shoulders for balance, gasping as his cock pressed along her slit. The seat of the chair was wide enough for her knees to rest on the padded seat on either side of his hips.

"Have ye ever ridden astride, wife?"

The picture that blossomed in her mind stole her breath. Heat surged through her passage. His hands stroked her bare bottom, cupping each side.

"Aye, ye understand my meaning don't ye?"

"But—"

"No buts, lass." He lifted her up with his hands under her bottom, and his cock straightened once she was high enough above him, the head pressing against the opening to her passage. He began to lower her onto it, a soft growl leaving his lips as she sheathed him.

She shivered. Her hands curled on his shoulders. Pleasure engulfed her as her body took him. But she craved friction. She rose off his cock on her own. All the way up until only the head was still clasped inside her passage.

"Yes, Bronwyn . . . *yes.*" He captured her hips and pushed her back down.

She gasped, delight spearing into her along with his cock. She was rising off it in a swift motion before he had time to lift her, the hard length rubbing against her clit when she leaned toward him. Completely in control, she increased the pace.

"That's it, ride me."

"Aye, husband."

Her voice had turned husky and he chuckled, the hands on her hips tightening. He lifted his hips with each downward plunge from her, sending his cock up to meet her. Pleasure tightened more and more until it burst through her. She lost the rhythm when it flooded her belly, the muscles contracting around his cock. He took command in that instant, lifting his hips beneath her and guiding her up and down with his hands. His sharp cry echoed off the back wall and he slammed her down on to his length, holding her tightly in place while his seed filled her. Hot pulses of it hit her womb while she was held in the grip of the pleasure still shaking her body.

A soft kiss was pressed against her neck and then another. Then hands on her hips released, smoothing over her curves before sliding up her back. It was a sweet touch that unleashed tender emotions. He didn't have to be kind to her and still he was even after having her. Maybe she was a fool to think such things, but at the moment she was powerless to prevent her emotions from going soft.

He cupped both sides of her head, lifting her face so that he could press a kiss against her mouth. His lips teased hers, his tongue tracing along her lower lip in a lazy motion that sent little ripples of enjoyment through her.

A soft ringing intruded on the moment. Cullen raised his head, breaking their kiss quickly. One bell was joined by two others and then more until the sound echoed up and down the long walls.

Cullen was on his feet in a second. He spared a moment to make sure she had her balance before striding to where he'd left his clothing. Bronwyn followed him without thinking. The bells meant trouble and a castle's defense was her men. It didn't matter that she was newly arrived at Sterling; if it was set upon, she would suffer the same fate as the other inhabitants.

She made quick work of pleating Cullen's kilt without stopping to put any clothing on herself. In a battle, his colors would keep his own men from mistaking him for the enemy.

"That's something I no expected to see ye doing."

His voice startled her because she'd been so intent on her task. The length of McJames wool was neatly folded over the wide belt that would hold it secure around his waist.

"I know that the bells mean ye need to hurry."

He was in his shirt and had his boots laced up to his knees. He cupped her face and pressed a hard kiss against her mouth.

"Aye, but no in so much of a hurry that I won't tell ye that it warms my heart to see yer hands folding my kilt."

Behind the shutters they heard a commotion in the yard below. Cullen leaned over the table and grasped the ends of the belt. With a hard motion he buckled it, the McJames plaid secure.

"Get dressed, Bronwyn. Hurry, lass, ye dinna know where to go. I should have shown ye."

"Go on, I'll find my way. I'm nae a child."

And hiding wouldn't be worth anything if the enemy found the walls easy to breach because they weren't manned. Instead of reaching for her clothing, she grasped his sword from where it had been leaning against the wall behind the chair. Turning around, she held it out to him.

Uncertainty flickered in his eyes because he was ready to go and she still completely bare. Every man would be on the wall in response to the bells, leaving her unguarded.

"Go on, Cullen. I'll find my way to the other women."

"I don't doubt that ye can."

But what he truly doubted was that she would join the McJames women.

Bronwyn saw that truth in his eyes. He hesitated but the ringing persisted, pulling on the years of training he'd had to become the warrior he was. The castle had to have priority.

"All right, lass, we'll see where ye go."

He turned and pulled the door wide. Bronwyn hurried to find her chemise and cover herself.

She was torn.

The desire to run home was nowhere to be found. It had

somehow dried up and blown away. It shouldn't have, shouldn't have been so swiftly gone from her heart. But all she found instead of the need to escape was the need to remain with Cullen.

Oh, the man was stubborn and arrogant, to be sure, but there was part of him that was tender. Only Keir came close to holding such regard for her. Confusion gripped her hard while she dressed.

Run back to a father who called her slut, or remain with a husband who distrusted her?

Well, that dinna take much thinking. No much at all.

The most surprising thing was that it hurt to think of leaving Cullen. The shock of that emotion held her still in the chamber for long moments she should have been seeking shelter with the other women. The soft kiss he'd given her after sating his lust still lingered on her lips.

She hugged the feeling tight to her heart, feeling it fill that empty place that had ached so badly when her life crumbled in the face of her father's accusations. She was a McQuade but she was also a McJames wife.

She would join the McJames women.

"McKorey riders!"

Cullen gained the upper wall and stared at the group of horses approaching. They were riding hard, pushing their animals. It wasn't like Alarik to arrive in such a fashion even if it was past sundown. The man was no afraid of the dark.

"Hold the gate fast!" Cullen gave the order. The men wore the plaid of the McKorey but he could not see their faces yet. He'd be a fool to trust in just the kilts. The group leader raised a hand and the last man raised a banner, flying Alarik's shield on a flag. No honor-respecting Scot would fly the shield of another, and Jamie had tossed a few into chains for doing it to invade their neighbors.

That wouldna stop the McQuades from attempting it, and he'd bet his sword on it. Erik McQuade would wager a few months in prison against the chance to strike at Sterling.

"Archers ready."

Brodick's deep voice bounced off the walls. He gained the wall and peered at their company.

"Do ye think yer new father-in-law is paying us a visit under false colors?"

Cullen lifted a spy glass and angled it toward the riders. They had slowed now, their horses at a walk.

"I wouldna dismiss the idea, but I count only fifty retainers."

"Not enough for an invasion." Brodick took the spy glass to take a look at the riders. In the dark it was hard to make out features.

"But enough to lay plenty of men in their graves if we open the gate."

Brodick grunted. "Aye, that's a truth."

Tension held every man on the wall in its grip until the riders closed the gap enough to be recognized. Cullen breathed a sigh of relief as he got a look at Alarik McKorey through the spy glass. Seeing the man was more relieving than he'd anticipated.

"What's that frown for?" Brodick held his hand up to keep the gate closed. "Is there a reason I should still be worried about our visitors?"

Cullen shook his head. "None that I know of, but Alarik is running his horses rather fast in my opinion."

"I noticed that meself." Brodick signaled the captain of his guard to raise the heavy gate. "But that doesna explain the look on yer face, brother."

"I just dinna want to spill McQuade blood."

Brodick raised a dark eyebrow. "It's more likely they will begin raiding again than not."

Cullen snorted. "I know it, but can still hope for a peace now that we're joined by marriage."

The gate lifted with a groan, the thick chains making a metallic sound that echoed through the castle. Brodick moved toward the stairs, eager to assure his people that all was safe.

"We can hope, but it will most likely take Jamie laying down his fist to get McQuade to end his raids."

It was a truth that Cullen didn't enjoy. But his marriage would give them the leverage they needed to force the king to involve himself. Yet that wasn't the reason behind his reluctance to engage the McQuades.

Bronwyn was.

They were her kin, and for the first time in his life he saw them as men who had lives the same as he did. Over the years they had become a faceless enemy that he felt no remorse for. Now he saw Bronwyn with tears in her eyes for her kin. It was a pain he'd like to spare her.

McKorey rode through the gate and into the yard.

"McJames, I've news!"

Brodick stood on the steps leading to the hall. "As if I dinna already guess that, man. It had better be something good because I've a pretty, warm wife that I left to greet ye."

Alarik McKorey swung his leg over the head of his horse and dismounted. A stable boy came forward to take the stallion. Alarik took a silver piece from his doublet and tossed it to the boy.

"For yer loss of sleep, lad."

"Thank ye, sir!" The boy grinned, showing off a missing tooth. Several of his comrades from the stables eagerly approached the other horses in spite of the hour, hoping for a similar reward. Sterling offered hospitality to all its guests, but sometimes, when you arrived with fifty men in the middle of a freezing winter night, it was wise to add a little something to sweeten the servants' mood.

McKorey pegged Cullen with a hard stare. "I've news for yer wife."

"Depends on the news." Cullen shot a harder look back at the man. Friend or not, he'd be the one who decided what manner of news was delivered to his bride. "There's no need to tell her something her father said in court that is only going to upset her. I'm the one who stole her."

Alarik joined them on the steps. "Aye, given the last thing her father said about her at court, I canna blame ye for thinking like that."

They entered the lower floor of the main tower. It was connected to the other towers by long hallways that ran behind the curtain wall of the castle. Above them were the chambers used by Brodick and his family. There was meager light, only a few tin lanterns set onto large iron hooks set into the wall.

"I pushed me men hard to get here."

Cullen paused along with Brodick. There was a note in McKorey's voice that promised trouble.

"Erik McQuade is dead by the hand of the king's guard."

"How, man?" Cullen demanded.

Alarik clenched his hands into fists. "It's the truth that I was trying to break his neck with my own hands. The bastard wanted my sister for his bride." He paused and snarled softly. "McQuade drew a dirk . . ." He pulled the collar of his shirt down exposing the fresh cut on his throat.

"When I turned aside, he fell toward Jamie."

"Christ, man, that's enough to get ye hung." Cullen swore softly in Gaelic.

"I'm a lucky man to be standing here. His guards ran Mc-

Quade through with their pikes, and it crossed me mind that I would follow him."

"But ye dinna, so I'm guessing that Jamie sorted the mess out."

"Aye, but the McQuade are no hearing any of it. They blame my sister, Raelin, and have labeled her a witch. I rode hard enough to kill my horse because that clan rode home with vengeance burning in their bellies." Alarik pointed at Brodick. "If ye are planning on getting any dowry for Bronwyn, ye'd best take yer case to Jamie before McQuade's son takes over the title."

The men walked off toward the great hall to find food for Alarik McKorey. Bronwyn stood in the opposite hallway, hidden in the shadows. The stone wall held her up as she sagged against it.

Dead.

It was such a final word. She didn't know what to feel or even how to feel about the man who had detested her. In spite of his frustration with her gender he was still the only father she would ever have. To loathe him was to hate a portion of herself.

She turned and began walking. The dark corridors suited her mood. Too many things had happened in so short a period of time. Two months past, her life was neatly predictable, now it was nothing like it had been.

She passed the stairs that led to Cullen's chamber. Another length of hallway and she found herself in the work room that held the loom she'd spent the day at. No one slept here and it must have been to conserve firewood. At Red Stone, several maids laid their pallets on the floor between the looms because no indoor space was wasted.

The empty room felt like a haven once again. She moved through it slowly with only the light shining in through the glass windows to guide her. Sitting down on the stool, she ran her hands over the cloth she'd woven.

Here was a part of her that had come from her father, born of the demand that she earn her keep like the other female servants. Her fingers glided over the soft wool, finding it smooth and even.

No tears wet her cheeks.

She sat waiting for them, but her heart did not ache for her sire. Guilt needled at her but it never grew into shame or anything that hurt her enough to weep.

The only thing that truly saddened her was that she did not grieve for him because he had never been a kind father to her. That was lamentable. She still missed her mother, still ached at times for the woman who had been her sweet parent. That was the wealth of a family—their love for each other.

All her father left her was the talent for making the cloth beneath her fingertips. She leaned down and placed her cheek against it. Her soul was weary. She was tired of the constant struggle her life had become recently. So tired of the uncertainty.

Tears eased from her closed eyes. Not for her father, but for the affection they had never shared. She slipped off into slumber, with the fabric beneath her cheek. For the moment it was the only thing that she might call her own.

The McJames retainers returned to their pallets on the great hall floor. Cullen sat with Alarik and Brodick while their guest ate a hastily gathered meal of bread and cheese along with cold meats left from supper. Alarik didn't mind, nor did any of his men. They ate with the hunger that all day in the saddle gave to a man. A few of the maids had risen to the chore of serving, many of them still wearing their sleeping caps. But the inhabitants began to settle back down to sleep while they might.

Sybil appeared. She wore only her long stays over her chemise with a length of wool held tightly around her body to keep her warm. She approached the table softly, but with a determined look on her face. Cullen lifted his face and stared at her, his stomach knotting with dread.

He'd trusted Bronwyn.

"I beg yer pardon, but I canna find my mistress."

Cullen felt his temper ignite but he held it in check. "She dinna join the women?"

Brodick looked at him because his brother knew that the tone of his voice promised retribution to whoever had enraged him.

Sybil shook her head. "And I checked yer chamber. She is no there, either."

He'd trusted her.

Brodick gripped his arm. "She has to be here, brother. The gate was lowered behind our guests."

"That is no the issue." He stood up. "I trusted her." His anger bled into his words so clearly Sybil flinched. Her eyes widened before she backed away.

"Perhaps the mistress is lost."

"And perhaps I should have had the foresight to suspect her of lying to me."

Brodick stood up. "Easy, Cullen. Dinna condemn the lass afore we discover why she's nowhere to be found."

"I'll help ye search for her." Alarik wiped his mouth on linen and stood up. "Since it appears that I helped ye lose her with my arrival."

"Oh, I shall find her and that's a promise." One that he was going to enjoy teaching his wife that he would keep for the rest of their lives. Hurt slashed through him but he shoved it aside. He refused to feel anything but anger over her deception. He would not go soft for Bronwyn McQuade.

He would not.

The retainers who had just lain down were roused. They grumbled quietly when told who they were searching for. It was not the first time a McQuade had kept them up all night, and that was precisely why they detested anyone born with that name.

Candles and lanterns were lit. Every hallway burned bright. The maids were awakened when light was shone on their faces to identify them. Every pallet was searched, no door left closed. Cullen gritted his teeth because every person at Sterling knew that his young bride had deserted him. His pride became bruised as the search continued.

It took another two hours to search the outer buildings. By the time the retainers discovered Bronwyn bent over her loom, their tempers were hot enough to melt iron.

She awoke to rough hands on her as she was dragged through the hallways, her feet trying to keep up as her mind attempted to understand what was happening now. They took her toward the great hall, refusing to unhand her.

"Let me go."

The burly retainers didn't pay her any mind. They stood with their hands locked around her forearms until Cullen arrived. His face was drawn tight with fury, his eyes already cold with judgment against her.

The men holding her released her abruptly, pushing her forward with their greater strength so that she stumbled.

"Enough. There's to be no rough handling of my wife." Cullen's voice didn't sound very friendly; in fact, the man was enraged if she didn't miss her guess. He studied her with hard eyes.

"Ye broke yer word to me." His voice dropped to a deadly

tone. Cullen pointed a finger at her. "Ye said ye would join the women."

"There was no reason to join them. I watched ye welcoming Alarik McKorey in the keep."

Her words stopped Cullen in mid-thought. He pressed his lips together, his change of expression showing her a glimpse of the side of him that she hadn't wanted to run away from. But not enough to soothe her anger away. But the hall was full of pallets and McJames people who were all listening to their quarrel. The two retainers still stood behind her, guarding her. She turned her back on Cullen and challenged them. But they didn't look at her. Their attention was on Cullen. His men waited for his permission before parting to allow her to leave.

But they followed her.

It was an insult that jabbed through her heart. Back in their chamber, she stood staring at the bed with tears in her eyes. The chair was less appealing. The self-pity she'd avoided descended on her in full force. Hopelessness strangled her spirit. Suspicion was such an ugly thing set with teeth that chewed on the tender emotions.

For the moment it felt as though the life in front of her was nothing but one struggle followed by another.

Bonnie stood silent, overlooked by everyone. She was used to it, in truth encouraged such. The argument made her flinch but she kept her eyes glued to it. There was a lesson to be learned and she forced herself to absorb it.

"Ye should leave. This is no something a young lass should witness."

Bonnie jumped but held her gasp behind her closed lips. Alarik McKorey slid up beside her, having emerged from the dark hallway behind her. His gaze traveled over her face in a motion that was too familiar for her comfort.

"I am married." Telling men that fact always sent them away from her. It was the only thing her husband was good for.

"Is that yer way of telling me to leave?" Alarik sounded amused.

"It is my way of reminding ye to not trespass against God's law."

The large Scot grunted. He was an entire head taller than herself, his shoulders twice the width of her own. His hair was dark as midnight, his eyes green. The argument in front of her drew her attention again. A firm hand on her arm made her jump. She turned on Alarik, scratching at the fingers that held her. He frowned but tugged her away from the hall before releasing her.

"As I said, lass, there's no need for ye to witness what is being said."

Bonnie glared at him, but he stood in the middle of the hallway with his hands braced on his hips. There was no way to go around him.

"I expect a man to advise me so."

"And why is that?"

She drew herself up straight and proud. "Because you lure women into contentment so that they will not fuss over wedding. But once you have your way, you turn cruel."

"Cullen is no cruel. 'Tis naught but temper. That lass has as much spirit as Cullen does."

"You are a man. You shall defend him no matter what he does." Bonnie cast a last look at the hall but she could no longer tell what was being said. No matter, she understood well enough. The Scot standing in her way only added confirmation to her belief that all men used women regardless of how the woman felt. They bent them to their whims ruthlessly.

"I defend him because I understand that this union would no be a simple one but that it will bring better days to a great many people."

"Exactly."

He stepped toward her but Bonnie backed away. She turned around and left. There was no point in remaining. He was a man and would always side with his brethren. Just another example of why a woman was wise to avoid them. She had no desire to become a submissive wife. Bronwyn McQuade had her pity.

Cullen sat back in his chair, a glass of whiskey in his hand.

"That won't help, lad." Alarik sat down beside him, keeping his voice low as the men settled in for a few hours of sleep.

"And yer an expert on marriage, are ye?" Cullen offered him a disgruntled look. "I must have missed hearing that ye took a bride."

Alarik scoffed at him but shook his head. "I dinna understand women any better than ye appear to."

Something crossed his friend's face that looked like frustration. Cullen offered him the pottery jug of whiskey. He took it and reached for a small pottery cup.

They sat in silence. It suited his mood. Bronwyn weighed on his mind. Settling her into his house was a far greater challenge than he'd anticipated.

But that was not what bothered him.

What captured his attention was the fact that it hurt to see her unhappy. He expected to be emotionally attached to his brother and sister. Even watching love grow between Brodick and Anne had not prepared him to find something tender in his own heart for a woman. Yet it was there, tangled around all of his motivations. He'd hurt her with his suspicions and it tore a hole in his gut.

"Yer right, this whiskey isna helping. I spoke too harshly to her."

Cullen stood up and left. Alarik watched him, baffled by the determined stride his friend was using.

"Yer wrong, my friend, this whiskey is helping . . . me." Alarik dumped what was left of Cullen's whiskey into his own cup and leaned back in his chair. Aye, it was helping—helping to keep him from touching a lass who was too tender for what he wanted from her. He raised his glass in a silent salute to young Bonnie. With her blond hair and blue eyes, she was an angel not meant for his hands to touch.

His cock dinna care . . .

The bed rocked and Bronwyn stirred. Her head ached and her eyes burned. It was dark in the room, but she could feel Cullen near. Actually smell the scent of his skin. A tiny shiver rippled over her skin. The response made her angry because she could not even control her own body. She turned away from him.

He followed her, gripping her in his arms and even laying one leg over the top of her thighs.

"Have done, Cullen, I've had enough fighting for one day."

He pressed a warm kiss against her neck instead. She'd gone to bed in her chemise but he was wearing nothing but his warm skin.

"I will never have done with ye, lass. But ye're correct that we have spent too many hours fighting. I'm sorry I spoke harshly to ye in the hall. Ye dinna deceive me, I understand that now." He smoothed his hands over her arms, unleashing another ripple of sensation. With exhaustion pulling at her, his warm embrace felt delightful.

"Leave me be. Ye've already had me tonight."

He sighed, pressing a warm kiss against her neck. "'Tis the truth that ye have more wisdom in ye than I do. Ye have my gratitude for leaving instead of blistering my ears as was yer right."

"Ye would have deserved it." Bronwyn sighed inwardly because her voice sounded too forgiving. The man was going to twist her around his finger if she didn't show more backbone.

"Aye, I know it."

There was true regret in his voice. She wriggled against his hold but he refused to allow her to place distance between them.

"I understand why ye dinna do as ye said ye would."

She jabbed her elbow backward and heard him grunt but his arms did not release her. "Ye dinna understand me. If ye did, we wouldna be fighting."

He suddenly rolled over onto his back, taking her with him. He kept rolling until her back was pressed into the bedding with his body pinning her down. One arm was trapped behind his back and he captured her wrist with the other hand, pressing it to the bed.

"Yer right. But ye are nae the only one that is recently married, Bronwyn. I've nae been a husband afore either. We are both bound to make mistakes."

In the dark he was only a shadow, but she felt him along her bare legs, every inch of her skin enjoying the warm contact. He kept enough of his weigh off her to keep her from being crushed, but she discovered that she enjoyed feeling the rest of it pressing down on her. As if there was some part of her that liked knowing he was stronger than she.

"I am sorry that I dinna trust ye, but I am no apologizing for wanting to keep ye." He leaned down until his breath touched her lips. She drew in a ragged breath. Even in the dark she saw his eyes glittering.

"I wanted ye when I stole ye away, but now I need ye, Bronwyn."

He kissed her, brushing a soft one against her mouth before deepening it. She pushed against him, trying to gain space but he insisted, kissing her with a passion that wasn't hard, but tender instead.

Her resolve buckled. Even her pride dissipated into the night around them. In the dark there was no one to judge her. There was only the hard body of her lover. His kiss soothed her. His hand tangling in her hair while his cock hardened against her thigh. Need built into a steady throb inside her passage this time. It was warm and steady and, in a way, comforting. He trailed his kisses along her neck and she arched to offer more of the smooth column to him.

But he didn't cover her immediately. One hand slid beneath her chemise, tugging the fabric up until he cupped a breast. Sweet sensation flowed through her as soft sounds passed her lips. She lifted her hands, seeking his skin. It was soft and hot beneath her fingertips but the muscle it covered was hard and full of strength. Every touch was slow this time, there was no rush. He stroked her with a sure hand that didn't miss any part of her. Over her ribs, lower toward her belly and across its soft surface to the curls at the apex of her thighs.

He teased them for a moment, pulling gently on the silken strands before slipping into the delicate folds that protected her clitoris. His lips claimed hers again in a kiss that was demanding, one fingertip plunging into her sex while his tongue speared deeply into her mouth. Her thighs parted for him, her hips lifting up in welcome.

He covered her then, cupping the sides of her face with his hands. He thrust slowly forward, easing his length back into her passage. Sweet delight filled her, building once more toward pleasure. The bed ropes groaned as he increased his speed, driving faster and harder into her. She shuddered as need tightened around the hard flesh. She lifted toward it, needing just a little more speed.

Her cry, soft and delicate, filled the bed curtains. Pleasure blossomed inside her belly. It didn't jerk her away from every thought, but instead grew warmer and warmer until her entire body was enveloped. Cullen shuddered and ground himself deep. The hot spurt of his seed hit her womb and the walls of her passage clenched tightly around him to pull every last drop from his length.

He caught his weight on his elbows on either side of her head. Both their breathing was rough as the bed slowly came to a stop. He placed a soft kiss against her cheek and then another on her temple.

"I promise ye, Bronwyn, I shall learn to be a better husband."

A soft whimper left her lips. She opened her eyes but couldn't see his expression in the dark. His voice was gruff and hard with emotion.

He kept his promises . . .

She trusted that. He rolled over onto his back and took her along with him. The bedding was shoved off to one side but he dragged it over them with a single hand, keeping the other around her.

"I canna say that I'm sorry about yer father, but I am sorry for yer pain."

His hand rubbed her back. It was tender and caring, bringing tears to her eyes. They dropped onto his chest before she lifted her head to hide the weakness. Cullen followed her, rolling onto his side while he allowed her to move. But he clamped a hand around her and pressed against her back, even tucking her head beneath his chin.

*   *   *

He was jealous.

Cullen was stunned, but amazed at the same time. Bronwyn shuddered in his embrace and he soothed her. Envy filled him, envy for the tears she spilled for another person. He wanted her to care that deeply for him. There was no way to deny it. He wouldn't be jealous of her tears if he didn't care for her deeply.

He could shove it off on the late hour or the stress of the long day, but that would be lying to himself.

Instead he held her, listening to the way her breathing deepened when sleep took her away. For the first time he understood why he'd often avoided his bed until exhaustion forced him to. The reason was clear.

His bed was a lonely place.

Now he realized it. Now that he had Bronwyn there to share sweet kisses with him, it wasn't the fucking, it was the intimacy. A word that he'd known but never felt before.

But it meant nothing without her returning the affection. Sleep pulled him away from his thoughts but not before he promised to win Bronwyn's heart.

It was a promise he would keep.

Laird Erik McQuade was laid to rest on his land with all his retainers in attendance. His three sons stood solemn while the pipes wailed out a last tribute. Keir McQuade watched frozen ground being filled in over his father and found it fitting. Maybe he was a poor son, but his father had always had a cold heart. He left the grave as soon as possible. His temper burned hot and it wasn't for the same reason his older brothers were cursing about.

He wanted his sister back. The fact that Bronwyn was only his half sibling didn't matter to him. It never had. She was the only member of his family who cared for him.

Liam and Sodac caught up with him.

"It's about time ye showed some courage, brother." Liam slapped him on the shoulder and snickered. "We've vengeance to extract on those bastards McKorey. I'm happy to see ye in such a hurry to begin."

Keir turned to face his siblings. The scent of whiskey was strong on both of them. With their father dead. Liam was making it clear that no one had say over his actions any longer. He drank any time and any place that he wanted to and fucked any woman that caught his eye.

"It's Bronwyn I'm intent on finding."

Liam looked confused for a moment. "Aye, the land. Father warned us about making sure she never breeds."

"What land?"

Liam shrugged. "Her mother came with a dowry that is willed to Bronwyn and her offspring. It's no McQuade property unless Bronwyn dies without issue."

Keir spat, rage turning his vision red. It was a good thing his father was dead or he might be tempted to do the deed himself. Greed had rotted the man long before a royal pike was pushed through his heart. He had treated his daughter little better than a servant her entire life because of land. He believed it because that fit with the greed-poisoned picture he had of his sire.

Liam and Sodac watched their younger brother stride away. Sodac pulled a leather flask from his doublet and took a nip. "I forgot about Bronwyn. What are we going to do about her? Cullen McJames will fill her belly for sure." He snickered. "I'd poke Raelin McKorey a few times before slitting her throat, too."

Liam smirked in agreement. "Raelin deserves to suffer before we choke the life out of her." He grabbed the flask and drank a long swallow. "But Cullen isna planning on killing

Bronwyn in spite of the fact that she's his enemy's daughter. We'll have to see to that ourselves."

"Do we have to kill her?"

Liam nodded. "I don't want to waste all my time making sure she's no fucking in the hay. Besides, her belly might already be full with a bastard who'll take our land."

Sodac stared at his brother. "Ye're laird now. Make the king give her back."

"And then what? She just dies after being returned?" Liam raised his hand, threatening to strike his brother for not thinking of a better solution. "Besides, Jamie is smitten by the McJames. He dinna even hang Raelin McKorey for causing our father's death. No, if we want to keep that land, we'll have to take care of Bronwyn ourselves."

Liam McQuade took another swig of whiskey. He was laird now. He'd think of something. It didn't matter that Bronwyn was his half sister; every McQuade served the laird. Even if it meant their lives. He expected it of his retainers, just as his father had. He wouldn't go soft over the fact that Bronwyn was a female.

He'd deal with the threat. Permanently.

Chapter Eleven

Dawn came too early.

Bronwyn rubbed her eyes and groaned when she sat up. The chamber was lighter, and with the bed curtains still open, the light roused her.

"I agree."

Her husband yawned before rolling over the edge of the bed. Her gaze followed him because she just couldn't help herself. She'd never noticed that men were attractive. Cullen was magnificent. Every ridge of hard muscle a delight for her eyes.

"Ye look like a siren sitting there tempting me back into bed."

A blush warmed her cheeks. She stood up, enjoying the grin playing across his lips. He didn't have to tease her, didn't have to be kind to her.

Yet he was.

"There are not enough hours of daylight to be wasting any."

Cullen pulled his shirt over his head. "Well now, if that's a promise that ye'll be welcoming to me once the sun sets, I'm content to endure the daylight."

"Stop yer teasing."

She walked across the room and picked up her surcoat. But

Cullen hooked her around the waist and pulled her back against his body.

"Why should I do that, lass? Yer cheeks are rosy from my teasing and yer eyes shining."

He nuzzled her neck, sending ripples of excitement down her. It was playful and sweet, drawing a soft laugh from her.

"Ye are an overgrown boy."

"Ah, but ye enjoy the fully grown man in the dark."

She giggled, and gasped when she heard the sound crossing her own lips. Cullen's wide chest rumbled with a deep chuckle against her back. He nipped her ear with a teasing bite.

"Ah, it's true, Bronwyn, ye cry out so sweetly when the man pleases ye in our bed." He cupped one breast and turned her slightly. "Or chair."

She slapped the arm holding her against him, but the blow lacked any real strength. "Enough."

He hugged her tight before releasing her. His kilt was already pleated and waiting for him on the table. He leaned over it and pulled the ends of his belt around his waist. When he straightened back up it took mere moments for him to buckle the belt and pull the loose end of his plaid up and over his right shoulder. His blue eyes sparkled with mischief but also determination.

"It is no enough, no nearly enough. I plan to tease ye much more."

"Why?" The chilly morning air made her shrug into the surcoat in spite of her distaste for the garment. She longed for a dress and that was a fact.

Cullen tugged a round Celtic bonnet down over one side of his head. He walked back toward her and she stood fast, watching him in fascination. This was not her captor and yet he was.

What mesmerized her was the fact that she was enjoying being the target of his teasing.

He cupped her chin in a warm hand. "Maybe because I like the way ye laugh when I tease ye. 'Tis a sound I want to hear more of."

She looked away, unsure of what to feel. He hooked her around her waist and pulled her against his body. He threaded his fingers through her hair and pulled gently to raise her eyes back to his.

"I plan to give ye more reasons to be happy, Bronwyn."

She was tempted to believe in his words. So tempted.

"Ye have had what ye want of me."

"And ye think I'm callous enough to believe that is the extent of what we should hope for from our marriage?"

"It is what most couples are content with."

He placed a soft kiss on her lips but didn't linger. "Ah well, it isn't enough for me."

He released her and turned, walking toward the door. He stopped when he reached it, looking back at her.

"Ye puzzle me, Cullen McJames."

"No more than ye did by folding my plaid last night. My McJames plaid." He winked at her and pulled the door wide. "But we'll have to wait until later to discover what our hearts are trying to tell us both."

She scoffed at him, but he left the room instead of taking issue with her.

What her heart was trying to say?

Nonsense.

Insanity.

The man had stolen her.

But from what?

Her life at Red Stone was not so nice. She saw the difference now. Her pride was still sore, making it impossible to simply let her feelings bleed away. But she was confused this morning. She didn't feel like a captive anymore. Somewhere in the dark hours as she'd enjoyed being held against him, the struggle that kept them from relaxing had vanished. Maybe it was her father's death. Feuds did sometimes go to the grave with the laird.

Their future was suddenly full of possibilities.

Sybil arrived with two girls in tow, saving her from her thoughts. They bustled about the chamber while Sybil insisted on braiding her hair once again.

"I'm so glad ye dinna try to run away last night, Mistress Bronwyn."

The two maids paused in their straightening of the bed. They were taking the sheets and replacing them with fresh ones.

Sybil continued, raising her voice enough so that the maids could not mistake her words.

"Now there will be no more talk about whether or no ye are trustworthy."

"I should think every person that was awoken from their rest will have far worse things to think of me now."

Sybil slid a final hairpin into her hair and smiled. "Och now, where do ye think ye are, England? A bit of determination in a woman is a fine thing. If ye gave that husband of yers too much obedience, he'd walk across ye like a carpet. Just where would that place the rest of us, I ask ye? Every McJames man would be expecting the same meek behavior."

One of the maids laughed while the other grinned. Sybil shrugged. "There are some things that women and men dinna understand about each other."

It was a peace offering from a McJames woman who hadn't had any more choice on what land she was born on than

Bronwyn had. The tension was missing from yesterday and it was a welcome relief.

"I am learning that, Sybil. Thank ye for braiding my hair. We should go before we are late to break our fast."

A soft expression of approval shone on Sybil's face. It was a fragile truce but one that made it much easier to walk toward the hall. The walls didn't seem so cold today in spite of the ice edging the windows.

Cullen sat at the table with his brother and family. Alarik McKorey looked as though his head ached, while Bonnie frowned at him from where she sat beside her sister. But what captured her attention was the way her husband watched her. His eyes were glued to her, with a playful grin on his lips, like the one he'd shown her the day they first met. She suddenly felt the warmth of that afternoon and the chill of winter couldn't melt it.

Perhaps affection was not as horrible as Shakespeare wrote it to be.

But then again, maybe her mind was simply broken.

Bronwyn's shoulders ached by the end of the day. But her cloth was rolled neatly into a length that would be cut and sewn into a dress on the morrow. Sybil and the other maids had worked diligently plying their needles on her behalf to produce undergarments. A pair of soft drawers restored some of her modesty. They came none too soon as her monthly courses arrived.

She would not share Cullen's bed tonight . . .

The thought should have filled her with delight. Instead her heart became heavy with disappointment. The supper bells rang and she sighed.

Her mind must truly be broken. There was no other explanation for her melancholy mood. It should have delighted her to discover that she did not carry a babe that would further cement her union.

Instead she dreaded sleeping alone.

Which was absurd since she had so newly begun sampling what it was like to share a bed. She was too quiet over her meal and more than one person at the high table considered her from under lowered eyebrows. She tried to shake her mood but it stuck to her as she felt the night looming over her like an empty cavern.

With a sigh she departed, leaving Sybil to inform her laird that he would be sleeping alone. It was a common thing for the maid to convey such information, but Bronwyn still felt her cheek color slightly. Her body had always been her own and it was unnerving to have her personal details discussed with others.

It was harder still to enter the chamber she shared with Cullen. But she didn't know where else to go. Would he sleep elsewhere? Or would he send her away until she was clean again? Her mother had never shared a chamber with her father. Erik McQuade had sent his man to inquire from her maid if she was clean any time he was of the mind to mount her. Bronwyn had always known when her father came to her mother's bed because she was sent away with a maid to sleep in the kitchen.

The door opened and she turned to face it, her face set against exposing her lament.

"Och now, dinna frown so. I swear I've seen kinder faces across the battlefield." Cullen held the door wide for Sybil, who was grasping a tray. She set it down on the table and curtsied.

"Good night, Mistress Bronwyn."

Cullen chuckled as soon as the door was closed. "I see Sybil found a way around ye asking her to no call ye mistress."

"She is a fine maid." Bronwyn fingered the wool of her sur-coat. "Do ye want me to sleep in the kitchens?"

"Ye sleep here with me." There was nothing teasing about his tone now. It was edged with hard authority.

"Did Sybil tell ye . . ."

He tossed his bonnet onto a hook set into the wall. "Aye, she did." His tone softened a bit. But his eyes flickered with the hard determination she'd seen in her captor. "I keep what I steal near."

"Is that so?" Her temper rose along with her chin.

But Cullen flashed her a smile. "Well now, ye are the first thing I've ever stolen so I think that be the way of it."

He was toying with her. She glared at him, frustrated and amused at the same time.

"Did yer father send yer mother to the kitchen?"

"He did not share a chamber with my mother. He only came when he was of a mind to . . ." Her voice trailed off as she realized how much information she was spilling to a man her sire called his enemy. A few days ago, she would have been horrified. Tonight she was simply weary of the need for walls. Where did their clans stop and each of them begin?

"Whenever he wanted to use her?"

Her cheeks colored slightly at the bluntness of the words. "Aye."

Cullen frowned. "I'll hold my tongue since the man has departed this world."

"Ye sound as if it is commonplace for couples to share a chamber."

He shrugged and pulled one of the X chairs around next to the table. "My parents did as my brother and Anne do now." A glimmer of playfulness returned to his face. "They seem to be very happy with the arrangement."

"I see." She didn't, but the tension knotting her shoulders suddenly released its grip on her.

"Sit down, wife. Alarik brought us a wedding gift."

Cullen reached for a pottery bottle sitting on the tray. He removed the costly cork stopper in it and poured a measure of whatever was inside it into a small drinking cup.

"Honey mead to celebrate our marriage."

A smile lifted her lips. She couldn't help it. Honey mead was the traditional drink given by the friends of the bride and groom. You knew if you were popular if the entire first month of yer marriage ye had enough honey mead to drink. It was a sweet drink that made ye think of spring even in the dead of winter.

"That was kind of him." Sniffing the cup, Bronwyn took a sip and grinned. Sweet as May Day.

"More likely he's trying to soothe yer ruffled feathers for helping to steal ye."

"That is no a topic to jest about." She glared at Cullen while he poured himself a measure of the honey mead.

"Now dinna be trying to tell me that McQuade men are so different from McJames men in that they don't tease about stealing brides." He opened his hands wide. "Admit it."

Her eyes narrowed but she couldn't remain vexed. He was correct. "Men jest about it, but nae women."

"Ah, but I am a man."

"I have noticed that."

His face brightened with victory. It went into his eyes and they glittered with male satisfaction. "'Tis glad I am to hear it. 'Course I'll be happy to remind ye as often as necessary."

He reached onto the tray and produced a set of dice. Challenge flickered in his eyes as he rolled them in the palm of his hand.

"What do ye plan to do with those?"

One golden eyebrow rose arrogantly. "I was thinking to get to know ye better, Bronwyn McQuade."

She laughed at him, but the way he rolled the dice intrigued her. "With dice?"

"Aye, ye and I thrive on challenge. So we'll play for the right of one honest answer for each win."

Her breath froze in her lungs as she contemplated his offer. It was a challenge and one that came with plenty of risk. The risk of laying out her most intimate secrets if the dice favored him instead of her. But the chance to discover what sort of man he was with her own questions was hard to resist.

He grinned at her, arrogant and mischievous at the same time. "Unless yer too timid to try me at a few rounds of chance."

She pulled the other chair closer to his and slapped the table with her hand. "Hardly. Ye dinna frighten me."

And she realized that he never had. That was truly surprising because she should have been scared of him. But something had always kept her from fearing him. It was rooted deep inside her, in that place where you didn't decide what you felt; the emotion was simply there like a living breathing thing. There was no decision making, only feeling it when it rose up to engulf you.

"I am not afraid of ye."

His face went serious. "Ye had every reason to be."

"But I wasn't."

She was suddenly conscious of how open she was being with him. His keen stare missed nothing. Her eyelashes fluttered, veiling her feelings.

"I believe I am tired."

His eyebrows rose in mocking judgment but he laid the dice down. "I suppose that's true."

She stood up and hung her coat up. Sybil had found her several chemises to wear, so at least she did not have to suffer with wearing a soiled one day in and out. The undergarment was loose enough to allow them to be worn without fitting issues making her uncomfortable.

The bed was warm and welcoming. Cullen blew out the candle that was burning in its holder on the table before he joined her. The mattress rocked as he climbed up onto it, the bed ropes creaking a tiny bit.

A startled gasp escaped her when he pulled her against his body. Her head cracked against his chin and she heard him growl. His arms tightened instantly, the hard strength in his larger body trapping her. But he controlled it expertly, never really hurting her. He adjusted her against him before easing his embrace.

"Cullen . . ."

"Enough talking, Bronwyn."

"But . . ."

He rolled over, pushing her onto her side. His arms held her in place as his warm body pressed up against her from the top of her head to her toes.

"Ye sleep in my bed, Bronwyn, and in my embrace. Always."

His voice was edged in steel once more. But instead of her captor she heard a warrior tonight, one who was worthy of her respect. He was a man of honor.

"I want more from a wife than the comfort I take between yer thighs." He sighed against her hair, a soft kiss landing on her temple. "I hope in time ye'll desire the same."

His voice was full of doubt and emotion that touched her heart. There was no ignoring it, no missing it. But the truth was she didn't want to. She was warm and secure for the first time in what felt like an eternity. Not since the days that she'd had a loving mother who had soothed the harsher details of life with her love.

The male scent of his skin surrounded her. She relaxed

against him, her hands smoothing over his forearm. He was strong and sturdy and it felt perfect. Sleep claimed her and she went willingly. Contentment wrapped around her, killing every need to struggle.

Sybil placed a set of long stays on the work table and stood up. "They are finished, Mistress Bronwyn."

Fingering the corset, Bronwyn smiled. "Yer stitches are very even."

"Sybil has always had a steady hand with a needle." Gerty's voice cracked but it didn't cut the way it had before. The older woman paused to inspect the new cloth Bronwyn had woven. She inclined her head slightly, acknowledging her skill.

"Ye turn a fair length of cloth."

Bronwyn smiled. She turned in a circle and her new skirts flared out around her ankles. A new hip roll was sitting just perfectly around her hips and the cartridge pleated skirt sat on it nicely.

Clothing. She would never take it for granted again.

Two sleeves were already finished, and a doublet was being worked on as well. Sybil had managed to keep two other girls with her the entire week to sew on her clothing. Tomorrow morning she would have a dress to wear once again. She felt like a child receiving a present. Anticipation made her happy enough to twirl across the floor. No silk damask court dress could have made her happier.

The reason was simple. This dress was hers. She had woven the cloth and helped to construct it. The women in the work-room were now women she knew things about instead of strangers. The dress represented far more than just a return to modesty. It was a beginning of life at Sterling as more than just a captive.

Sybil followed her with the corset. Bronwyn eagerly laced

into them. Happiness seemed to surround her. The corset was tightened and her doublet buttoned. The other girls brought the sleeves forward to be tied into the shoulders.

"I never thought a dress could feel so good."

"Wait until ye have to wear a surcoat for an entire year while growing a babe inside your womb."

Bronwyn turned to look at Gerty. The older woman cast her a knowing look full of her years of wisdom.

"With the way young McJames looks at ye, I doubt that dress will fit come the spring."

She wasn't being unkind, but Bronwyn felt her sunny mood darken. Uncertainty sat on her shoulders every day; only leaving her once she was held against Cullen in their bed. While the bed curtains were drawn it was so simple to allow herself to be content, but once the sun rose her doubts returned.

Was he attentive only because he wanted to breed her?

Would he have done with her once she bore him a child that would make their marriage impossible to dissolve?

Such doubts crowded her mind.

Her mother had lived such a life. Existing in a place where she was housed because of her dowry and the connection she brought to her husband. The McQuade clan had never truly accepted her as one of their own, her husband only using her as he pleased but never remaining faithful. Erik McQuade had enjoyed any woman in the clan he desired. He'd used his title as laird to take what he wanted.

The world would not think harshly of Cullen for doing the same. In truth, her father had sowed the seeds for his enemy to take her. It was a depressing idea, one that punctured the joy she'd sampled so recently. Now that her courses were finished, she faced the possibility that she might conceive. Her choice to follow her heart into Cullen's embrace might well affect more than just herself.

But doubt was a cruel thing, nipping at her joy. The passion between them might very well grow cold, leaving her a forgotten wife like her mother had been.

"Yer husband will enjoy the way that blue sets off yer hair."

Sybil carried a costly mirror over and held it up for Bronwyn to study her reflection. Her cheeks were full of color just like in the spring, and her blond hair did look nice against the blue of the wool. She had never been a vain girl, but she suddenly smiled because she felt pretty. And the idea that Cullen might agree with her was intoxicating.

Bronwyn allowed it to take her melancholy mood away. After all, there was no point in worrying about what could not be changed. If she was destined to become a forgotten wife, she should enjoy today all that much more.

The memory would become one of her dearest possessions.

Anne looked at her sister, Bonnie, and cautioned the younger girl to remain poised with her features pleasant and unjudging.

It was quite the effort, but Anne remained sweetly helpful while searching for the single book of sonnets she owned.

"Ah yes. Here it is. I do hope ye enjoy it."

Cullen glared at her. The sternness of the look cracked through her composure. Her brother-in-law scowled.

"Dinna ye laugh at me."

"Of course, Cullen, whatever do ye mean?"

Bonnie covered a giggle with a fake sneeze that allowed her to cup a hand over her face and hide her smile.

Cullen huffed but took the book of sonnets. He stared at it for a long moment, confusion on his face. He suddenly shook it off, noticing that both Anne and Bonnie where watching him.

"Thank ye."

He stomped through the doorway and Anne held her breath until she heard his steps fade near the end of the hallway.

Bonnie collapsed against the back of her chair in giggles. She wrapped her arms around herself as she shook with amusement. Anne wasn't far behind. The image of her stern brother-in-law reading love sonnets was enough to make her wet herself.

But it was also sweet. So sweet that she sobered.

"It looks like I may have misjudged Cullen in the matter of his marriage."

Bonnie sat up, all traces of humor washing off her face. "He stole her."

"Yes, but I had never thought to ever see Cullen McJames asking for sonnets." Anne sent a gentle smile toward her sister. "It proves that he is not intent on merely breaking his new bride's spirit. He intends to woo her."

"He still kidnapped her." Bonnie's voice rose in her passion to champion Bronwyn's cause. "Stole her without any regard for her feelings."

Anne sighed. She and her family had spoiled Bonnie. As the youngest child, they had all allowed Bonnie to remain whimsical when the world was anything but. Bonnie believed in gallant knights who protected the honor of their lady fair. Such was fine for bedtime stories and winter nights when everyone needed diversion, but it was not a way of life. Anne stiffened her spine. The look of righteous anger on her sister's face was bound to end with young Bonnie in trouble if someone did not crack the shell sheltering her. With their mother in England, the task fell to her.

"Bonnie, you will have to begin growing up now." Anne kept her voice low but firm. "It is a good match between Cullen and Bronwyn. Even blessed by the king. Marriage is a union best forged for reasons other than affection."

"But you love Brodick." Hurt edged Bonnie's voice. "He rode into Warwickshire to rescue you and—"

"And we are truly blessed, but he courted our marriage because of the gain it would bring him and his clan."

Bonnie frowned. She stood up, her body quivering with anger. "Well, I shall never allow a man to touch me that I do not love with all my heart. *I swear it*."

"Bonnie." Anne's reprimand was lost on her sister because Bonnie ran out of the chamber before it passed her lips. Anne sighed. Dear sweet Bonnie. What was she going to do with her sister? At sixteen, the time for maturity was at hand. Anne might wish otherwise, but it was going to be a crushing blow for her sister. Brodick had sent his own sister to Warwickshire for the winter to begin the process of learning to manage a large house. More importantly, to grow confident in herself and learn to live outside her family's embrace. Such was the expectation of a noble daughter.

Bonnie would have to go next season to some place where she had no family to indulge her whims. It might sound harsh, but it was what made girls into women.

Cullen didn't arrive at the evening meal. The seat beside her remained empty. She found herself keenly aware of his absence, actually missing him. The others made light attempts to include her in their conversation, but her appetite died anyway.

She tried to finish her meal, actually ordered herself to continue eating. But her stomach refused to obey, the food looking unappetizing.

"Excuse me, please." With a nod to her host, she left the table. There was an odd pulse of anticipation moving through her that made sitting still difficult.

Would Cullen want her tonight?

She wanted him . . .

Her cheeks colored, but she could not deny her own thoughts. The little quiver of excitement was moving through her blood like fine wine. She began walking without a destination and ended up at the bath house.

A shudder shook her when she realized how much her body wanted Cullen to have her tonight. Subconsciously she was thinking about it, her instincts guiding her, undermining the things she thought she wanted with the things her body craved.

"A bath is a fine idea, Mistress Bronwyn." Sybil arrived a bit out of breath. Her hurry sent a shaft of guilt through Bronwyn for making the girl nervous.

"I'm sorry, Sybil, I wasn't thinking when I left the hall so quickly. I dinna mean to interrupt yer supper."

Sybil grinned as she began setting one of the tubs for bathing. There was a splash of cold water running into it, although since this was snow that had slid off the kitchen roofs and melted against the hearths that burned all day, it was already warm. The large rain barrels were frozen over and wouldn't be used until spring. Sterling was quite modern in its bathing facilities.

"Not to worry, Mistress Bronwyn. With such a handsome man awaiting ye, I believe I would be anxious to join him myself."

"What do ye mean?"

Sybil took a piece of soap from where it was stored. She looked perplexed for a moment. "I told yer husband that yer courses were finished this morning."

Of course she had.

That was a personal maid's responsibility, especially considering that Cullen also used Sybil to keep an eye on her when he wasn't with her.

Her temper surged forward but it collided with the excitement pulsing through her. If she wanted to be angry then she had to aim part of that temper at herself. Cullen was not the only one interested in resuming their marriage bed activities.

She sighed as she sat down in the tub, her new dress set carefully aside. Confusion held her in its grip. Why was it so wrong to crave her husband anyway? Because her father called him enemy? She scoffed at that idea, completely dismissing it.

He'd stolen her . . .

That was true enough, but she'd been foolishly naïve to think that she would never marry. She was the laird's daughter. In spite of her father's determination to hold on to every silver penny he had, it was not beyond the power of the king to see her wed.

Cullen was not a brute, her father had pushed him too far and that was the truth.

She sighed as Sybil rinsed her hair. Cullen would be a fool to not keep track of when her courses ended. Planting a child in her would make their marriage solid.

"Sit by the fire and I'll brush yer hair out. Won't ye look lovely with it all flowing down yer back."

Bronwyn sat down. She lifted her chin and enjoyed the heat of the fire on her back. Sybil drew the brush in long, even strokes down her hair. It was soon a cloud of golden silk, the ends curling gently in the heat from the fire. Each stroke had set her heart rate going a tiny bit faster. Anticipation tightened every muscle. Her dress felt constricting, her breasts slightly swollen behind the new long stays. Remaining still for her hair to dry took more and more self-discipline. The battle was mesmerizing in a way because the more she resisted the urge to go to Cullen, the deeper the longing burrowed into her belly. Her body began to throb gently and she stood up.

"Thank ye, Sybil."

There was too much light in the outer hall. Darkness seemed to suit her mood. Most of the supper had been cleared away, but with snow on the ground, a good number of retainers sat at the tables passing the time. Some with cards or dice. Several women were playing music at one end of the hall. Even with a few missed notes, it was delightful to hear.

Bronwyn passed through them and conversation died. She captured their attention but this time genuine smiles appeared on their lips. Hands tugged on bonnets while several of the women blew her kisses for good luck.

She suddenly felt like a bride, with all of the happy looks and enjoyment that went along with weddings.

Most importantly, she wanted to go to her bride groom. Joy filled her, urging her forward. Her cheeks flushed, but not because she was horrified by the fact that everyone knew she was going to bed with a man, but instead because she wanted to join him in that bed.

It was sinfully luring, drawing her toward the chamber where she'd known her captor's touch. Tonight she would enjoy her husband's.

Cullen was indeed waiting for her, the chamber lit by beeswax candles, the sweet scent of summer honey drifting lightly in the air. There was also rosemary in the air. A very small ceramic pot sat carefully on the table with the dried herb boiling over a candle flame. It was the traditional herb for bridal nights, one that midwives swore increased fertility and passion.

Sybil and the maids following her did not enter the chamber. They remained in the hallway.

"Good night, Mistress Bronwyn."

Bronwyn didn't really hear Sybil. She was too distracted by the man waiting for her.

And Cullen was waiting for her.

He was magnificent. Her gaze being drawn to the wide shoulders and his towering height. He wore only his kilt and shirt, the doublet he'd taken to wearing in the cold weather hung up behind him. His bonnet was missing, too, leaving his hair free to softly curl. What drew her attention the most was the way he looked at her. The door closed softly behind her. The moment it thumped against the door frame, he came toward her. His body moving like the powerful animal he was. She'd never considered that watching a man might be as awe inspiring as watching a stallion, but it was.

His gaze roamed over her, lingering on her unbound hair. Reaching out, he fingered it, a soft smile decorating his lips. Without a word he'd managed to make her feel pretty. More beautiful than she ever had in her life. The expression on his face worth far more than her reflection in the mirror.

"Yer beautiful, Bronwyn, so much so, I'm afraid to touch ye for fear ye'll disappear like a dream."

Reaching up, she touched his forearm. He had his sleeves caught up near the shoulder. Her fingertips slid lightly along his warm skin, a tiny shiver racing up her arm from the contact.

He drew in a stiff breath.

"The chamber is very lovely." And he had gone to some trouble on her behalf. That knowledge warmed her heart.

"Aye." He frowned. "I planned to woo ye properly for a change but I dinna understand these sonnets."

He picked up a small book from the tabletop, clearly vexed by the verse on the page. "One is lively and the next depressing."

"Poets are often melancholy. Or so I have heard." She reached for the book. Taking it from his hand, she closed it gently. "But it was very sweet of ye to fetch this here."

His eyes narrowed suspiciously. Bronwyn looked down at the table and laid the book on its polished top while trying to hide her amusement.

"Yer laughing at me."

"Nay. I am not." She walked away from him, but he followed. It was a teasing chase. She shied backward and he closed the gap every time.

"Aye, ye are. Yer eyes are sparkling."

Bronwyn shrugged. "I am no laughing *at* ye."

"But ye are laughing." He said it triumphantly and hooked an arm around her. With one more step he closed the remaining distance between them. She gasped when their bodies connected. Sensation rippled down her length, unleashing every urge she'd restrained.

"It's nae very kind of ye to be amused by my attempts to seduce ye."

She reached up to stroke his cheek. He narrowed his eyes, enjoyment showing on his face. "I dinna mean to be unkind, but ye have never struck me as the sort of man who uses poetry."

He snorted, a wicked gleam twinkling in his eyes. "Aye, that is correct, lass."

He hefted her up and tossed her over his shoulder.

"I'm more of a hands-on sort of man. I love to wrap my fingers around the lass I'm trying to catch." A soft smack landed on her bottom before he turned in a circle. A dizzy wave of excitement went through her while she grabbed his waist to steady herself.

"Put me down, ye brute."

"Ah now, I'm getting to that part. But I do enjoy knowing that yer eager for me to place ye on yer back." He crossed to the bed and tossed her onto it. Bronwyn came up in a tangle of skirts and hair. She scowled at him, her face turning scarlet because she was indeed on her back. It was infuriating but exciting at the same time. Cullen looked too pleased by far.

"Ye'll ruin my new dress."

"Not so." He pushed the blue wool right up to her waist, baring her thighs in one swift motion. "I heard the women complimenting ye on the fine cloth ye wove. Trust me when I say that Sterling wool will hold up to a bit of rolling in the hay."

"Ye'll be the one ending up in the stocks if ye keep talking like that." She had never heard such talk from a man. It was wicked, to be sure, but her clitoris began throbbing again, betraying how much she enjoyed his shocking behavior.

He chuckled at her, a wicked sound of intention that sent a shiver through her.

"It might be worth a bit of time in the stocks if I get to lay down with ye." He pressed her thighs apart until they were spread wide. "Yer flesh is tempting me to indulge my lust."

A shiver raced down her spine as the night air brushed against the folds of her flesh. With her skirts raised, she was completely exposed. Cullen hovered over her, using gentle strength to keep her thighs apart when she would have closed them. His attention lowered to her sex, hunger replacing the playful glint in his eyes.

"But I dinna think I'm alone in my desires."

His fingers slid all the way along the inside of her thighs until they found her tender folds. A whimper crossed her lips when he stroked one fingertip across her clitoris. Pleasure speared up into her passage, her heart increasing its rate. He fingered her again, this time stroking her from clitoris to the opening of her passage. A soft cry left her lips as pleasure erupted inside her. Her eyes closed and her hands fisted in the bedding beneath her.

"Am I, sweet, passionate wife?"

She jerked back up when his mouth touched her sex. Her thighs closed around his head and she tried to push him away. *"Cullen!"*

He raised his head to stare into her shocked eyes. Hard determination glittered in his. He pushed her legs wide once more.

He grinned at her. "Ah . . . have I discovered the way to tame ye, lass?" He pressed his thumb on her clitoris, rubbing it gently. Her breathing became hard, bolts of white-hot delight spearing through her.

"Ye like that, don't ye?"

There was no way to hide that she did. A moan surfaced from her chest when he lowered his gaze to her spread body. Her eyes went wide but she couldn't stop herself from watching. She felt his breath on her before the first touch of his lips.

She collapsed back onto the bed, incapable of controlling anything. Her body twitched, jerking in small motions while Cullen sucked her. Never had she even considered that her body could feel such intense pleasure. It burned through her, the flames eagerly licking every inch of her body. Need clawed at her and her passage ached to be filled. Cullen toyed with her clitoris, flicking his tongue across it over and over until sweat dotted her skin. Tension knotted tighter and tighter beneath his lips. She lifted her hips toward him, eager for more.

Abruptly, he raised his head. Bronwyn moaned. The sound wasn't anything she recognized. It was deep and husky and completely wanton. She wanted him, and lying so submissively made her angry. Pushing up off the bed, she reached for him. He caught her, pulling her into a hard embrace.

She kissed him.

Holding onto the sides of his head, she angled hers so that their lips might meet. He didn't claim her mouth but followed her, mimicking her motions, allowing her to lead the kiss. She licked his lower lip, urging him to open his mouth. He took command of the kiss the moment her tongue slipped inside his mouth. One hand cupping the back of her head, his fingers gently pulling her hair. Little twinges of pain moved over her scalp but somehow it only added to the heat of the moment. Part of her enjoyed feeling his strength.

But the fabric of his kilt and her skirts prevented her from gaining what she really craved. She groaned, trying to pull at the layers of clothing between them. Cullen chuckled at her frustration.

"Well now, rolling in the hay does take a wee bit of skill. It's a bit awkward the first time. But I'm rather happy knowing that ye never learned the art of lifting yer skirt for a bit of afternoon pleasure." He laid her back down on her back and raised his kilt. His cock stood at attention, stiff and swollen.

"Are ye now?" Wasn't that just like a man to say. "Ye know the art rather well, telling me that ye have done some rolling, but wanted a pure bride."

He shot her a hard look. "I wanted ye and it dinna stay my course to hear that ye were considered impure. Besides, I dinna know what is wrong with a few spring trysts. It's a way to know if they will be able to enjoy the winter as man and wife."

"I dinna want to know how ye know anything about rolling in the hay." She sounded jealous and realized that she was. "And ye can just tell any woman that ye trysted with last spring that ye are wed now."

He laughed at her, but reached for her hips and pulled her back onto his lap. This time his cock nudged the slippery folds of her sex, the round head pushing into her passage with ease. He gripped her hips, pulling her toward him until his length was buried inside her.

"Now, why is that, Bronwyn? Are ye jealous?"

"Maybe. I am yer wife." She clasped her hands around his

neck for balance. He lifted her until only the head of his cock was still stretching her passage. It was a sweet torment, waiting for him to lower her again.

He thrust upward at the same time that he lowered her. His cock penetrating in a smooth thrust that made her gasp. Pleasure filled her, the walls of her passage full and satisfied.

"Ah, well then, I suppose I shall have to do my rolling in the hay with ye from now on."

He tried to sound playful, but need made his voice raspy. His hips thrust harder and faster as his face became drawn.

"I may hope."

His eyes opened all the way and he stared at her. His hands held her in place, all motion stopping.

"Ye may depend upon it. I'm going to make sure ye yell loud enough with yer pleasure for half of Sterling to hear."

He lifted her free and sat her away from him. "Now, if yer going to be the lass I'm rolling in the hay, we need to practice a wee bit to make sure we have it right."

"Are ye daft?"

He winked at her. "I'm a lusty man that wants to dally with ye. Let us hope we don't get caught."

A giggle escaped her lips because she'd heard the maids talking about such things. Many a lass and lad rolled in the hay. And many a bride had a plump belly on her wedding day, too.

"What's the matter, husband? Do ye fear the stocks?"

"I'd stand in them proudly next to ye, lass."

She pouted at him. "Yer a brute. Aren't ye supposed to suffer the chastisement while protecting my name?"

He winked. "But it would be yer yelling that would get us caught." He reached out and fingered her sex, running his finger between the swollen folds to her clitoris. He rubbed the little nub and her breathing became rough. All hints of teasing left her. Need clawed at her, demanding she appease it.

Cullen slipped an arm beneath her hips and turned her over in one swift motion. She flopped onto her belly, pushing her hands against the bedding to rise. Cullen grasped her hips and lifted her bottom until she was poised on her knees.

"Ah, one of my favorite hay positions. Just right for keeping yer skirts out of the way." He tossed her skirts up to her waist again, making sure to raise the tail of her chemise as well. The cool night air brushed against her bare bottom, sending a shiver through her.

A warm hand cupped one side of her bottom, smoothing over it before delivering a soft slap.

"Cullen . . ."

He rubbed the spot again, removing the sting. "Ah, yer a hungry one, are ye? No patience for playing, ye want yer maypole dance right now."

"Cullen McJames."

He clasped her hips and the folds of his kilt covered her bottom. His cock slid into her again, drawing a moan from her lips.

"What? Isn't that what the maypole is about? Fertility?"

He thrust in a steady motion behind her, moving the bed with each steady forward thrust. She was losing track of the conversation, her body more than content to sink into the rising tide of pleasure.

"May Day is one of the best days to roll in the hay, Bronwyn. I can't wait to take ye out to the festival and sneak ye off into the shade to fuck."

"Um . . . yes . . ."

She didn't care what he said, only that he kept up the hard thrusting behind her. Each time he pushed his length deep, her passage tightened around him, trying to milk his seed from him. Every time he withdrew, she nearly cried for his return. She was too needy, too hungry for the release he'd given her before. She wanted it and she wanted it now.

"Aye, yes is right. I want to hear ye say yes to me over and over."

He flipped her back over, covering her before she finished bouncing. "Just as I want to see ye lying back with yer thighs open in welcome." He thrust hard, burying his length in one quick motion. A groan left her lips and then another. Her spine arched and her eyes shut. He moved on her with increasing speed, his cock harder and larger than she remembered. It filled her completely, satisfying her need to be stretched again.

"Aye, lass, let it out. Yell for me."

With her on her back, his cock slid along her clitoris with each stroke. There was no containing the pleasure inside her, there was too much. She sobbed with delight, clasping him with her thighs and lifting her hips to meet him. It took only a few more thrusts to burst the knot of tension he'd built deep in her belly. It sent intense pleasure racing through her. It drove the breath from her lungs but she dinna care. Cullen ground himself into her a few times more before his seed finally began to pump into her. He gripped her head, holding her in place while pleasure shook them both.

He rolled over onto his back, his breathing as labored as hers was. One hand clasped hers, their fingers interlacing while they panted.

"I meant to seduce ye."

He sat up, gently pulling her with him. A soft sigh left his lips before he stood up and turned to lift her onto her feet.

"Truly I did."

He reached for the buttons on her doublet, undoing each

one swiftly. "I planned to take yer clothing off, one piece at a time, and pausing to kiss each new patch of skin before I went any further."

He pulled her doublet down her arms and tossed it aside.

"That's my new dress yer throwing on the floor for the mice to nest in."

Bronwyn hurried after her clothing, rescuing it from the floor. A male groan made her turn around but she wasn't impressed with the look of frustration on Cullen's face.

"I can't go to any May Day festival without a dress, ye know."

He was frowning at her, but she could tell that he was thinking now. Their teasing dropped as his mind identified something he wanted to take issue with. This was the harder side of him, the one who had taken her captive, but she didn't find it so cold anymore. This was the man who was a warrior. He was only a boy when they played. That was a secret part of him he chose to share with her. It was a gift and one that she suddenly understood the value of.

"I always knew yer father was possessive of his land, but he treated ye poorly."

It wasn't a question. Bronwyn turned to hide her expression from him but he cupped her shoulder, making her face him. She raised her chin, refusing to lament who she was.

"My life molded me into who I am. Would ye truly prefer a delicate wife who needed looking after? Yer brother's wife seems very practical. I dinna see her snapping her fingers at the servants. She works beside them."

"Anne is that, true enough." His gaze turned hard. "Her stepmother had her serving in her father's home afore she was sent to my brother in the place of her noble half-sister. Anne's life was a poor one and ye are very much like her. Competent, self-reliant, and ye never think to ask for help with anything."

Her throat tightened just a tiny amount. "I dinna see why it matters. I am healthy and able to see to my own needs. There is no shame in that."

She turned around in a swish of skirts, moving fast enough to avoid his hand. Placing her doublet on a hook, she took care to hang it correctly, lest the fabric become pulled. Cullen's hands appeared in front of her, pulling gently on the laces that held her skirts closed. His hard body brushed against her back, surrounding her with security.

"It matters because I ken now that ye were not insulting Sybil when ye said ye dinna need a maid, and ye weren't trying to escape me."

Her waistband loosened and he reached into the opening to untie her hip roll.

"I told ye that I'd never had a maid before." And she didn't care for how hurt her words sounded.

"Aye, ye did. But it appears that I was nae listening to ye, only making assumptions on what I thought I knew of ye." The hip roll dropped down her legs and her skirts were simple to push over the curve of her hips.

"We both have to learn to trust one another."

Cullen didn't let her step out of her skirts on her own. He began unlacing her new corset from the front, his fingers dipping in to tease the swells of her breasts.

"I won't let ye go without, Bronwyn. Dinna fret about that. There are plenty of hands who can see to sewing clothes for ye with the snow drifting outside the walls."

"They have sewing of their own to do. I'll see to myself."

He sighed. Her long stays were open and he pulled them down her arms. They landed on a hook and one second later he'd pulled her chemise up her body and over her head. She felt the wool of his plaid against the back of her bare thighs and quivered, suddenly aware of the fact that she was nude.

"I will see to ye, Bronwyn, even if the person I need to convince most is ye. But there is something to be said for learning how to make the people around ye feel needed. Wear some cloth woven by a McJames woman's hand and there will be more smiles aimed yer way because they dinna think ye believe yerself too good for what they produce. Even if ye are a fine weaver." He scooped her up, cradling her against his wide chest. There was a solemn look on his face that made her shiver. He placed her in his bed, standing at the foot of it, watching her pull the covers up with his keen eyes.

"That is a good idea." She should have thought of it, too, but had never had the option to choose before. She did it herself or went without. Sewing her own dresses had become her duty since she was small, each winter spent in the work rooms of Red Stone along with the other women.

"Perhaps it's a good thing that it's winter. That gives us plenty of long cold nights to learn about one another."

He turned around and undressed. He laid his plaid on the table in even pleats with the belt beneath it so that it was ready in the event of the bells being rung. He snuffed out the candles before coming to bed.

In the dark, he was everything she needed. His hands warm and his kiss potent. She returned his embrace, stroking his warm skin. In the dark there was no suspicion. The clan plaids were not visible. Cullen rolled her beneath him, her thighs parting in welcome. This time their pace was slow and even, the pleasure building in a steady rise until it poured pleasure over them.

"I hope it's a long winter, lass."

"As do I."

His arm held her while the sound of his heart lured her off to sleep.

He would take care of her.

Cullen remained awake long after his bride surrendered to

slumber. He didn't want to miss the moments when she was content in his arms. He wanted to savor it, smell the sweet scent of her skin, and enjoy the way she clung to him.

Every reason he had for bending her to his will evaporated. There was only the knowledge that she had come to him with her hair flowing down her back.

Come to him as his bride . . .

It was a gift that humbled him. It also filled his heart with tenderness.

There was still much to do the next day. Bronwyn rose early and set to work on another dress. This time she chose a brick red that Gerty had woven. The older woman couldn't hide the pleased expression that crept across her face.

"Ye've got good taste."

"For a McQuade?"

A few gasps filled the workroom but they were followed by amused giggles when Bronwyn smiled at Gerty. The older woman grinned, and wrinkles appeared around her eyes.

"Well, I'm pleased to see ye have a sense of humor. I was a bit concerned about that. Indeed I was." She propped a hand on her hip. "Nothing worse than a winter spent working with a sullen girl nearby."

Many heads nodded. Everyone knew what it was like to suffer the sharp side of a tongue. When it was winter, no one wanted a shrew assigned to where they were spending the chilly days.

"Excuse me, Mistress Bronwyn."

Bronwyn turned around in a swish of blue wool to face one of Cullen's captains. She recognized the man now; he was often at Cullen's side. He inclined his head toward her, tugging quickly on the corner of his bonnet.

"Would ye come with me, ma'am? The earl and his brother would see ye in the armory."

It wasn't really a question, in spite of the cordial tone he used. Two more burly retainers stood behind the man, their eyes on her.

"Of course."

The captain looked beyond her at Sybil. "Ye may stay here."

Sybil looked torn for a moment, but sat back down and took up her work once more.

"I shall show ye the way, Mistress Bronwyn."

The captain turned and left the work room, but he waited in the hallway, watching her. Tension returned to her shoulders, knotting between them. The two retainers fell into step behind her. The captain led the way, the sword strapped to his back a blunt reminder of the harsh world outside Sterling's walls. Peace reigned inside, but it was enforced by the men who defended the McJames stronghold with their lives. Order was necessary or there would be suffering. Sterling was built to ensure safety of the clan. The members of it had helped raise the walls. Along the hallways there were archer cuts in the windows in case the yard was breached. Brass bells were hung from the stone every few hundred feet to be used if help was needed in a hurry.

It was a fine home, to be sure.

They took her to the great hall and past it to the next tower. Armor was stored on the floor level of this keep. Helmets lined the room, set up on wooden stands. There were also arming jerkins made of leather with small rings of metal sewn into them. Even full chain mail shirts were in view. The sound of the blacksmiths working made it through the windows here, a steady clang of metal against metal.

This was where the men held their meetings. It was a place

the women of Sterling didn't venture unless invited. Hard decisions were made here, many times ruthless ones. A plain wood table sat near the far wall with benches and chairs gathered around it. Brodick McJames sat there with Cullen and their cousin Druce. Bronwyn stared at the laird of White Tower. She hadn't seen the man since riding away toward Sterling on the day of her wedding.

All three men stopped talking when they saw her. Their attention lingered on her as the captain led her toward them. A tingle went down her neck and the final few paces felt excessively long.

"Yer brothers have proposed coming to visit ye." Brodick McJames spoke quietly, his tone betraying his apprehension.

Surprise held her silent. Cullen aimed a hard stare at her.

"They claim that yer father was the one who wanted to keep our clans fighting."

"That is true enough." She had listened to her father curse the name McJames her entire life.

Brodick frowned. "True that only yer father wanted strife?"

She suddenly felt stretched between the two clans. Born McQuade but wed to a McJames. Cullen didn't care for her silence.

"Are yer brothers honorable men, Bronwyn?"

The question hung over her. Cullen watched her with suspicion, once more rubbing her temper. Once again she was McQuade and he McJames. But there was still a hope burning in her heart that they didn't have to be separated by the names they were born with. It flickered deep inside her, refusing to die under the suspicious gazes slicing into her, last night's memory rising up to defend him in the face of her temper. Besides, they had faced her father over drawn swords. Truly, she could not blame them for being suspicious when those same men asked to enter their home.

"My brother Keir is an honorable man. That is all I can tell ye for sure. Liam and Sodac were ever my father's sons. I dinna know them well."

The three men relaxed slightly and looked at one another. The earl nodded toward her. "Thank ye."

It was a dismissal. Bronwyn lowered herself before leaving. Before she rose, Cullen aimed his attention at her. His expression was a stone mask, concealing his feelings from her. But there was a flicker of satisfaction in his eyes that sent a ripple of apprehension down her back. He would use her against her clan; she saw the truth of it reflected in his eyes.

Turning her back on him, she strode out of the room. The captain and his men stayed behind, conversation resuming as she left. She found herself alone for the first time in a week.

And clothed.

Temptation needled her but she was torn.

Liam and Sodac had never been kind to her. Their ugly accusations rose from her memory on that first day she had met Cullen. Returning to their judgment seemed a rather poor choice.

Staying just might be a poor idea as well. The clang of the blacksmiths told her where the stable was. She moved toward a doorway and caught sight of a man working glowing red iron on an anvil. A young stable lad held a horse nearby. The doors here were kept wide open during the day. It gave her a perfect opportunity to step into the yard. Plenty of people were moving around; she might slip away without notice.

But tears stung her eyes as she looked at the open gates. She actually backed away because it hurt to think of leaving.

She ran into a hard body.

A soft cry bounced off the wall, her body fighting against the arms that enclosed her.

"Shh, lass. Easy now."

A sob passed her lips. Relief surged through her thickly, so that she turned and hit him for frightening her so.

"Ye brute."

He hugged her close, trapping her arms against his chest. Raising her chin, she glared at him, but ended up feeling the tears ease from her eyes when she looked into his gaze. Approval shone there. So bright it sent more tears onto her cheeks. Cullen brushed them away with gentle hands.

"I had to follow ye, lass." His voice was rough with emotion. "But I dinna mean to frighten ye."

"I told ye before, Cullen McJames, I am no afraid of ye."

His expression softened. He stroked the side of her face with a warm hand, sending little prickles of delight through her. "Why aren't ye, Bronwyn? I've done more than enough to earn yer fear."

She pushed against his chest, but he didn't release her. "I just don't. My father hated ye enough, don't ye think? Do ye enjoy knowing there are people who dislike ye?"

"I enjoy knowing that ye do not dislike me. That ye are nae afraid of me in spite of having good reason to be."

"Ye have never hurt me . . ." Her words were soft and almost too quiet to hear.

A satisfied smile appeared on his lips. She stared at it because she had pleased him. Knowing it, sent a shaft of deep satisfaction through her. He reached out and stroked a hand across her cheek.

"Trust is nae something I could ever take from ye, Bronwyn. It's a gift and one I truly value."

He'd earned it . . .

Her trust. There had been plenty of times when he could have used his strength to force her into yielding. That was the truest test of honor. Cullen had prevailed, proving himself a man worthy of respect.

"Even with my father dead, I doubt this marriage will bring ye much gain." Bronwyn heard the disappointment in her own voice. "I am sorry for that."

"I'm not." Firm conviction coated his voice. "I wanted ye the first time I met ye."

"But that is no what ye should marry for."

His lips curled up into a broader smile. "Is that sweet affection I hear in yer words?"

"No. I just understand that ye will be disappointed. My elder brothers are very much like my father."

Cullen raised a single finger. "But why do ye care if I'm nae happy?"

Uncertainty held her silent.

She wasn't sure.

Wasn't sure why it pleased her to know that he thought she harbored affection for him. Only that her heart was full of happiness for the first time in what felt like years.

There was activity outside in the yard. The blacksmith halted his work and she heard men running. Cullen sighed, his arms tightening momentarily.

"We'll have to discuss our trust issues later. Yer brothers are here."

"Now?" He held her in spite of her squirming. His keen eyes watching her.

"Aye, they sent the message from outside the gates. I must admit it was surprising to see McQuade retainers in the light of day on McJames land."

"As am I . . ." She spoke without thinking. But his eyes brightened and it was a sight that warmed her heart. She couldn't say just why, only that earning his approval made her happy. He was not a man who gave it out; it had to be earned.

But as soon as it appeared, it vanished. Cullen frowned, his expression becoming guarded once more. His arms opened.

"I suppose I'd be a true blackguard to be angry over your joy at knowing yer family is here."

But he was, there was no mistaking it in his voice. She chewed on her lower lip debating her next words. It was the truth that she did not trust Liam or Sodac. Cullen was allowing them into Sterling because of her. Responsibility weighed her shoulders down. A captive wouldn't have cared about what befell those who imprisoned her.

The weight bearing down on her shoulders was unmistakable.

"Keir." Her voice was choppy. "I only miss Keir. He is a good man, Cullen. I swear that."

Cullen's face tightened. "Only the one, ye say?"

Let her father haunt her, she would not lie just because Cullen was a McJames. He was a good man who deserved honesty.

"Keir will keep his word. If he gives it, he keeps it."

The bells began ringing, alerting every person at Sterling of the approaching threat. Cullen stiffened. In a swift motion he drew her back against his body, his mouth claiming hers in a searing kiss that was hot and needy. Her hands slipped up his chest to his neck to hold him, her lips moving in unison with his. She forgot about everything except the man holding her. In his embrace there was pleasure and security without the harsh, cutting edge of reality.

Someone cleared their throat loudly. Cullen lifted his head, a scowl on his face.

"So sorry to interrupt ye."

Brodick McJames didn't sound repentant. Not a bit. He smirked at his brother but offered her a kind smile. "Sorry, lass, I'm just repaying me brother for a bit of teasing he put me through with my own bride."

"Damn poor time for ye to recall that."

"I'm thinking it's a fine time considering we've got Mc-Quades riding through our gate. We'd best get out there and set an example for the men or we'll find our wives needing permission to visit us in prison when Jamie clamps us in irons for allowing a melee."

Bronwyn turned to look out the doorway. Liam, Sodac, and Keir sat atop their horses in the middle of the yard. It felt almost like a dream but they were there as sure as she was in Cullen's arms.

Her siblings stared at her, the open doorway making it simple for them to see her. Liam and Sodac scowled at her. Keir's face was unreadable.

"I detest yer ruthlessness, Cullen, 'tis a fact I do."

He didn't release her quickly. The arms holding her against him remained firmly around her waist until she looked back into his eyes. Determination burned there, so bright it could have blinded her.

"Be that as it is, Bronwyn, but ye are my wife."

And he intended to make sure her clan knew it. She should have blushed. The few McQuade men with her brothers frowned deeply at her but her face didn't heat.

She pushed away from Cullen but couldn't escape the reason she wasn't blushing. It was simple, she wasn't ashamed. Her craving for him overwhelmed her sense of clan loyalty.

But he was her husband, too.

Keir swung off his horse first, giving up the position of height. It was a gesture of trust, one the McJames retainers watching him didn't miss. There was a ripple of approval from the Mc-James men as Keir walked through to reach her. Tension was thick between the men behind her and her brother. Keir paused at the bottom of the steps, sweeping her with his eyes. With a nod he climbed up until he was facing off with Cullen and Brodick.

A hard hand grasped her wrist, keeping her beside Cullen. Short of jerking against his hold, she was stuck in place.

"It looks like marriage agrees with ye." Keir sounded tired. More so than she could ever recall.

"It does." Cullen answered too quickly and far too boast-fully for her taste. Her brother frowned.

"I'll hear that from my sister if ye don't mind."

"I mind."

"Enough." She jerked on her arm and stumbled between the two men before they too got to quarreling. "This marriage is meant to end the fighting so don't ye two go picking at one another and quarrelling."

Keir stared at her, one dark eyebrow twitching up. He sud-denly smirked at Cullen. "Well now, it's good to know ye aren't cowering at his feet." Keir's face darkened. "I'd have to quarrel over that."

There was silence for a moment before Cullen spoke.

"Is that a fact, McQuade?"

"It is, McJames. My sister is a McQuade and I couldna have her acting like anything else."

Cullen nodded. "I can live with that."

Keir grunted. Brodick and Cullen both seemed to under-stand what the single sound meant. Bronwyn stared out at her other brothers. Liam and Sodac had still not given up their horses. Liam noticed her attention first and his lip curled in disgust. A tingle of foreboding went down her back.

She trusted Keir, only Keir.

Chapter Twelve

S omething wasn't right.

Cullen snorted at his own thoughts.

McQuade's sons sat at his father's high table and all he could think was that *something* wasn't right?

He'd watched McJames women mourning husbands and sons that his guests had run through. There was an uneasy quiet in the hall while supper was set out. Even the maids set their platters down carefully. He was gaining a new respect for his king. Dining with one's enemies was a task that took a lot more skill than he'd given it credit for.

But his wife had spoken truthfully about one thing. Her brother Keir was different than his older brothers. As the night progressed, he found himself thinking it was a pity that Keir wasn't the elder. The man was not like his father. That was not to say the man liked him. Keir sent him more than one hard glance.

"Enough." Keir pushed his chair back and stood. "I'm going to have a word with my sister. Alone."

He shot Cullen a look that dared him to refuse. Cullen stood up, but Bronwyn pushed away from the table.

"We can go to the chapel."

Cullen nodded but kept his attention on Keir. He couldn't deny her the chance to talk with her brother but dread twisted

through him. She brushed past him and he caught her hand.
She raised her eyes to stare at him.

"Ye shall have to trust me, Cullen."

He didn't want to.

Bronwyn saw it in his eyes. Anguish filled her. There would
always be a part of him that refused to trust her, trust her father's blood. It was so unfair, but at the same time the very
reason why he had stolen her.

Cullen followed her and Keir. The sounds of supper faded
behind them until the only thing she heard was her own steps
on the stone floor. Her heart accelerated, beating faster the
closer they drew to the chapel.

She would have to make a choice.

Keir was going to ask her if she wanted to stay with Cullen.
She knew it in her heart just as she knew that she was still
torn. Doubts twisted through her but an ache began to burn
in her chest. It increased with each step until all of the reasons
she had for leaving became trivial matters.

Every bride had to earn her husband's trust . . .

*Every bride had preconceived ideas to overcome in her
new home . . .*

Every bride longed for affection . . .

She froze for a moment, her feet still while her mind admitted the greatest betrayal of her father's ideals.

She loved Cullen McJames.

Oh, he infuriated her. He was a stubborn man who would
send her temper flaring a thousand times in the years ahead,
but she could not deny what she felt. It lived inside her. She
had only loved two other people in her life but she knew what
it felt like. She would never escape the emotion. She missed
her mother every day but didn't think of her father at all.

That was love.

She turned around, her skirts flaring up because she moved so quickly. Cullen and Keir jerked to a halt.

"I am his wife." She stared straight at her brother. "Make yer peace with him, Keir, he's a good man. Just as I told him ye are."

She couldn't decide which one was more shocked, Cullen or Keir. Their eyes widened and words failed both of them.

"I'll be in the chapel when ye two have finished." She shot a look at Cullen. "But I will have yer trust to speak to my brother alone."

Bronwyn didn't wait for Cullen to argue with her. She turned back around and entered the chapel. Candles lit the altar, even when everyone else was eating supper. The golden light was welcome. Walking toward it, she felt peace settle over her. She still worried, but resigned herself to her fate.

She could no more leave Cullen than stop breathing. He had stolen her completely now.

Even her heart.

"My sister is right. I've words to have with ye."

Keir looked like the walls were pressing in on him. Cullen found himself feeling the same way. This was the only man Bronwyn loved and he was good and jealous of it.

"By all means speak yer mind."

They moved through a door frame and into the yard. With the sun setting, no one took notice of them. Snow was piled up along the walls sending everyone inside for warmth.

"Did ye rape her?" Keir growled through his teeth. "I'm going to know, McJames. I swear to God I'll carve yer cock off if ye raised yer fist against my sister. It's nae her doing that my father was a greedy son of a bitch."

"And ye think I don't know that?"

"Ye stole her." Keir blew out a snarl. "If ye raped her . . ."

"I did not rape her. I did steal her against her will."

Keir shook, his body stiff with rage. Cullen stared at him without a hint of fear. "On my honor, I swear I seduced her, overwhelmed her, and took advantage of her innocence but I did not rape her." He raised a single finger and pointed it at Bronwyn's brother. "I also tried to marry her first."

"What do ye mean tried?"

Cullen shrugged. "She refused to wed with me."

A suspicious glint entered Keir's eyes. "Is that when ye overwhelmed her?"

Cullen just couldn't suppress the grin that curved his lips. He was too happy to know that Bronwyn was his to keep it hidden.

"Since me cousin and Bishop Shaman caught us in bed the next morning, yer sister ended up marrying me in spite of our rather strained introduction. I dinna rape her. And yer free to go ask her that yerself."

Keir growled.

His fist connected with Cullen's jaw a second later. Cullen stumbled backward, snarling in return.

"Since ye dinna rape her, I'm going to use my fists on ye instead of this." Keir untied his sword and tossed it aside. "For seducing my sister before she agreed to marry ye, I'm going to turn that pretty-boy face black."

Cullen untied his sword and placed it against the wall. His grin returned.

"That was a lucky shot, but now it's my turn to return the favor for allowing yer bastard father to treat my wife like the lowest maid."

They circled each other, their large bodies smashing into each other with muffled grunts. The fight raged on without interference.

Far from it. Liam watched for a moment from the doorway. Keir was falling into his plan perfectly. All he needed was a few minutes to deal with Bronwyn so that she might never threaten what was his. Sodac was keeping the earl busy, while he had made the clever excuse to use the privy. His father had been right. The McJames were idiots. Trusting fools.

But there was one thing he disagreed with his father on. Bronwyn should have been smothered years ago. Every threat to the McQuade clan had to be cut away without pity. She was a useless girl child; no laird needed daughters draining their gold away when they married. Alliances could be made through the marriage of sons to other lairds' daughters. That would bring money along with the connection. He was going to make sure no daughter of his own lived to see a single birthday, nor any niece either. Being laird came with responsibilities, after all.

He turned to look at the chapel. His duty stood there. Liam refused to think of her as his sister. She was nothing but the person who could steal his land. Reaching into his doublet, he pulled a small ball from an inside pocket. It was the size of a gooseberry, but the man he'd bought it from assured him it could kill three men once swallowed. It was a quick poison, one that was impossible to counteract once it was absorbed.

Exactly what he needed. A death that was suspicious enough for him to wage war on the McJames. His father would be avenged.

What were they talking about?

Bronwyn rubbed her eyes. Behind her forehead, tension made her head ache. She fingered the wool of her skirts, trying to remain in place. She didn't dare turn around or she would be tempted beyond her self-discipline to venture out to where Keir and Cullen were.

They were the only two people she loved in the world. She needed them to make peace, needed it more than she'd ever thought she needed anything before in her life. With a sigh, she resigned herself to waiting. Men often needed to make peace among themselves without women around.

A hard hand slapped across her mouth, pushing something inside. She bucked and fought but a brutal hand wrenched her hair down, stretching her neck to a painful angle.

"Swallow it, sister." Liam didn't wait for her to comply. He shoved two thick fingers into her mouth to push whatever he'd placed inside it across her tongue. She gagged on his fingers but he pulled his hand free and she swallowed out of reflex. Whatever it was, it rolled down her throat before she regained control of herself. So surprised by his attack, she sucked in a gulp of air that sent whatever it was toward her stomach.

Liam threw her away from him a second later. He did it with no care for her at all, his greater strength tossing her against the altar. Pain tore through her side when her hip knocked against the polished wood. Tears sprung into her eyes but she turned to face her sibling.

He wore a sneer that was chilling.

Hatred blazed in his eyes. It was a horrible sight, making him ugly beyond anything she had ever seen.

"What was that?"

He laughed softly. "A solution that is very much overdue in this family."

Icy dread crawled over her skin. "What do ye mean, Liam?" She moved along the altar, the need to flee roaring through her mind. She was suddenly frightened.

"Father should have dealt with ye when ye were a babe instead of leaving it for me to do." His eyes flickered with satisfaction. "But it doesna matter now. 'Tis done. As long as Sodac does his part and keeps the elder McJames talking at his supper table, I will have ye on the path to facing yer final judgment."

Liam looked at the altar behind her. "A fitting place, too. But I doubt God will forgive ye for turning traitor to yer kin." His gaze landed back on her. "I know I won't. I canna wait to tell Keir how much he helped me by keeping that husband of yers busy. Keir is soft on ye. Sodac and I dinna bother even trying to convince him of the need to poison ye."

Horror filled her. The hate aimed at her left little room for hope. The small ball in her belly began to burn. Raising her hand, she meant to stick her own fingers into her mouth to force herself to retch. Liam grabbed her before she touched her lips.

With brutal force he wrenched her hands behind her back. He shoved her forward into the altar, using his body to trap her against it. She strained against him but he held her fast, hurting her as he twisted her arms until the bones cracked. He clamped one hand around her neck, squeezing until her vision started going dark.

"Just a little longer, sweet sister. That poison cost me a lot of gold. But it will be worth it if it snuffs out yer life and gives me the right to blame the McJames for yer death. Be an obedient McQuade, and die by poison so that I can accuse the McJameses of murdering ye." His fingers tightened. "But make no mistake, I'll gladly crush yer throat with my own hands if there is no enough time."

He opened his hand enough to allow her one huge breath. A soft chuckle brushed past her ear.

"Liam . . . I am yer sister!"

"A fact that makes it necessary to end yer life. Yer bitch of a mother left ye land. It's willed to yer offspring. So ye must die. I am yer laird and that land is mine."

"Ye've got that wrong. Ye are the one who is going to die tonight."

Cullen's voice was deadly cold. Liam jerked but never got the chance to turn to face his death. Cullen pulled his head back by his hair and slipped his boot dirk between her brother and her. The blade sliced Liam's throat from ear to ear, spilling his blood down his chest while he still held her. His hand tightened around her throat in those last moments, compressing the fragile bones and cutting off her breath.

Keir grabbed his brother's fingers, pulling them away from her neck. In his death throes, Liam had more strength than normal, his hand compressing her throat mercilessly. Keir's fingers gouged into the soft skin on her neck as he pushed them beneath his brother's. Her vision darkened, dizziness beginning to spin her around.

A moment later and Liam's hand went limp. Keir dragged her up and over the altar in a hard motion that knocked her knees against the ornately carved edge of the table. Pain smashed into her brain but there was no time to express it. When she opened her mouth to drag a desperate breath into her burning lungs, Keir shoved his fingers deep into her mouth. There was no controlling the urge to retch. Her stomach heaved with Keir's fingers touching the back of her throat.

Two minutes later, humiliation turned her cheeks scarlet. Poised on all fours behind the altar, she shivered, quivering from the violence of losing her stomach contents. The metallic scent of blood filled her nose, making her belly roil once more. If she hadn't already vomited, she would have when she noticed the warm feeling along her shoulder blades.

She was drenched in her brother's blood.

It made her sick. She retched again unable to contain the horror. The moment she finished, Cullen scooped her up. He cradled her tightly against his body, his arms quivering slightly. She heard a brass bell being rung. The things were set throughout the hallways to be used to alert the rest of the inhabitants to danger.

"I'm fine."

"The hell ye are." Cullen roared loud enough to shake the glass mosaic window set into the wall. "I wish I could kill that bastard again."

"There's still one rat." Keir sounded deadly.

"Ye can't kill Sodac." Bronwyn wiggled, kicking against the hold on her, but Cullen refused to release her. "He's yer brother. Everyone will think ye did it to become laird."

"Good, that leaves the bastard for me." Cullen snarled and went to hand her to Keir. Bronwyn gripped his shirt, refusing to allow him to let her go.

"Ye must send him to the king for justice, Cullen."

The side of his jaw twitched, the muscles running along his throat tense and corded. Keir released her and she stood up, refusing to let her husband go. Rage burned in his eyes, and may God forgive her, she enjoyed the sight of it.

He cared. Cared enough about her to be enraged.

"Please, Cullen. If ye hang him here at Sterling, no one will believe any of this happened. Ye will be called worse than blackguard."

He growled softly, his hands framing her face. "I can see that ye are going to be nothing but trouble for me, now that ye know how soft me heart is for ye."

"No more so than ye are to me, since ye are in possession of mine."

He gently rubbed her head, tucking the hair that had been pulled loose in her struggle with Liam behind her ears. "I plan to keep it, lass, and that's a promise."

"I'm glad ye keep yer promises, Cullen."

A soft chuckle left his throat, but his eyes remained hard. There was the scuff of boot leather on the stone floor as the McJames retainers responded. They filled the chapel with their swords unsheathed. They surrounded Keir, suspicion evident on their faces. Cullen left her to protect her brother. Bronwyn stood and watched, silly happiness filling her.

If that was the insanity of love, she was a willing victim.

Sodac was gone.

Bronwyn hurried to keep up with her husband and brother. The men rushed toward the hall, only to discover that Sodac had cleared the gate. He must have fled the second the bells began ringing.

Such an action confirmed his guilt.

Keir cursed before heading toward the yard. "I've got to beat that bastard to Red Stone or I'll have to besiege me own home."

"I'm going with ye."

Cullen followed her brother, Brodick joining them, along with Druce.

The yard became a mass of activity, boys and men all running to get the horses out of the stable. Keir didn't bother with a saddle. He swung up onto the bare back of his stallion and headed toward the gate, the three McQuade retainers following him. Cullen was two paces behind. Bronwyn didn't know whose horse she took and didn't care if they swore she stole it. She was going with them.

The main body of the men Liam had brought with him was camped over the first rise. It was in pandemonium when they crested the hill, some of the men disappearing over the next rise. Keir reined in long enough to address the remaining men.

"Sodac is a murdering bastard who planned to poison our

sister. I saw it with me own eyes. Follow me if ye be honorable men."

Astonishment held the men in silence for a long moment. One noticed her and pointed at her. Suddenly every set of McQuade eyes was aimed at her.

"My marriage will bring peace to every McQuade."

The McQuade men sent up a cheer and swung into their saddles. Keir spurred his horse forward, riding as though the devil himself was on his heels after Sodac and the men following him. Cullen hesitated, reaching out to grab her reins.

"Ye dinna belong here, Bronwyn." Fury coated his features along with fear. She stared at that fear. Only she did that to him.

"This is my fight, too, Cullen. Our fight. We'll only win it side by side."

He cursed. He looked at Keir and the McQuade men following behind him. With a sharp command he took the McJames retainers after them. McJames men surrounded her, keeping her in their center.

But she never felt her temper rise. Instead she looked ahead of her to where Cullen was closing the distance between Keir and himself. Argyll stretched out his longer legs, using the powerful chest to fuel his charge up the rise. McJames and McQuade plaids mingled and merged into a single body of men all focused on one goal.

Sodac turned to face the force bearing down on him. A third of the men on his heels had stronger horses and he didn't have enough of a head start to outrun them. The moon cast a white glow all around them. No torches had been lit but the snow reflected the moonlight. In the silver light there was no telling McQuade from McJames. There were only the two forces facing each other.

"Hold!" Keir's voice echoed across the distance. Her brother rode out in front of the men to face his sibling, Cullen joining him. But the retainers surrounding her refused to allow her any closer, one of them yanking the reins from her grasp.

"Forgive me, mistress, but I canna allow ye into harm's way."

She didn't have time to quarrel with him. Keir raised his sword and pointed it toward his brother.

"Sodac! Ye plotted murder of our sister. I heard it with my own ears."

"Ye're a traitor to every McQuade, Keir." Sodac unsheathed his own sword. "She bedded a McJames, making her a McJames. Killing her is our duty before the king demands her dowry. This marriage will take McQuade land and make it McJames land."

Some of the men behind Sodac looked confused. A few shook their heads, clearly disagreeing with the man they rode with. Keir moved closer.

"Bronwyn's marriage will end decades of strife that drains McQuade resources. She has honored her position as the laird's daughter by embracing a union that puts everyone's welfare first. It will end the fighting that lays our comrades in early graves."

There was a murmur of agreement from the men behind Keir as well as many in front of him.

Keir pointed at Cullen. "Cullen McJames is now my brother by marriage."

"*Bastard!*"

Sodac charged toward Keir, screaming obscenities. Few men followed him. There was the sound of metal hitting metal, and screams of men who were run through. In the space of two minutes, Sodac and his followers lay on the snow, their blood turning it dark. The retainers surrounding her released her once the night went quiet once again. Bronwyn kneed her horse

IN THE WARRIOR'S BED

forward, guiding it around the fallen bodies of her brother's supporters. A lump lodged in her throat when she looked at the waste. It was her father's final legacy.

She swore that it would be. For the first time in her life, being Erik McQuade's daughter meant something good. She rode up until she was beside her husband. Keir's blade was darkened with blood, but so was Cullen's. The two men blew white puffs of breath into the winter night, their breathing harsh from the battle.

All eyes turned to her. Bronwyn sat proudly in the saddle next to her husband. Some things were better seen than heard.

Keir turned to face them. "I'll ride for court in the morning. Jamie will need to hear of this from my own lips."

"Aye, ye've the right of that . . . brother." Cullen reached up and tugged on the corner of his bonnet. The respectful gesture gained him a cheer from the watching McQuades. Keir returned it to the delight of the McJames.

Cullen reached across the space between them and pulled her onto Argyll. Male amusement surrounded her, including her husband's. He clamped her tightly against his body before turning around toward Sterling.

He could have let her ride her own horse.

Bronwyn laughed at her own pride. Aye, he could have, but it was so much better that he didn't.

Later that night she cried. Actual tears eased down her cheeks.

"Now dinna look like that. I canna bear it. 'Tis only a dress." Cullen sounded tired. He leaned against the back of a chair, a faint paleness to his face. Brodick McJames hadn't been willing to take any chances on there being more poison. He'd sent to the kitchen for purgatives for everyone at the high table. In spite of already losing the contents of her stomach, she'd been fed the noxious concoction the cook had produced.

There wasn't a shred of strength left in her now. The tears flowed from her eyes because her new dress was destroyed, blood staining the doublet and skirt. Even soaking would not save it—there was too much, and blood stained like nothing else.

"It was my only dress."

Cullen sighed, clearly frustrated.

Two more fat tears eased from the corners of her eyes. "I shall have to go to court in that surcoat. There is no time to make another dress."

"Dinna cry, lass. It breaks my heart."

He stood up and walked into the small antechamber attached to the main one they slept in. He reappeared with a chest. It was a large wooden one that had a lock on it. Cullen fit a key into it. He raised the lid and pulled the green dress that she'd been loaned at White Tower from it.

"Ye brought it with ye?"

Bronwyn hugged the skirt and bodice to her chest for a long moment, slightly amazed that she could love something that she had once despised.

"It wounded my pride the way ye married me in yer chemise. It's the truth that I wanted to see ye dependent on me for everything after that." Cullen smiled at her. "I was even jealous of me own cousin for getting ye a dress."

He grinned at her. "I'll be happy to shower ye with dresses once we reach Edinburgh."

He gently pulled the skirts away from her and hung them over the back of the chair. Turning back, he offered his hand to her. It was a beautiful thing, that offer. The power of choice made her bold and she laid her hand into his with a flirtatious smile. Cullen winked at her before leaning over and tossing her right over his shoulder.

She bounced in a jumble of arms and legs when he dumped her into the center of their bed. He followed her, his large body warm and hard against her own. His lips seeking hers in a kiss that drove away everything but the delight their skin made when it connected.

Chapter Thirteen

1603

The court of James of Scotland was pensive. As winter held the country in its grip, rumors of the impending death of the English queen circulated. Elizabeth Tudor was ill and every rider who approached the court was cause for attention. She had ruled longer than any other monarch—both English and Scot—but her time was near. She would do one last thing with her death, and that was to unite two countries that had warred with one another for centuries. James Stuart would wear the crown of both countries, making it one.

Bronwyn set up house in the McJames city house while her husband awaited permission to attend court.

"Mistress Bronwyn, the tailor is come to see ye." Sybil lowered herself before shepherding in a party of men all intent on staring at her. Assistants followed them, their arms heavy with bolts of fabric. There were French silks and damasks, rare velvet, and costly brocades. Bobbin lace and trims that must have taken months of work to make were laid out for her inspection.

"I dinna need such things." But her voice lacked conviction. She reached out to touch one silk, too tempted by its luxury to resist feeling it at least once.

"I need them." Cullen spoke from the doorway, drawing a sigh from the tailor and his entourage. His blue eyes met hers across the space of the dining room. "I've a great need to escort ye into court dressed as finely as a lady of Sterling should be." He closed the distance and grasped her hand. Rising it to his lips, he placed a soft kiss on the back of it that sent heat into her cheeks. His keen stare focused on the crimson stain for a moment. "We've a history to repeat."

"And what do ye mean by that?"

Her husband winked before turning to toss a small bag onto the table. It landed in the middle of the fabric with a clink that was unmistakable. The tailor's eyes lit up at the sound of gold.

"Why, to promote gossip, dear wife. We must give the wagging tongues something new to report about us. Think of the commotion we shall cause if ye stroll by my side with a smile on yer lips."

"Ye are being naughty."

He reached out and tugged some of her hair. A frown appeared on his face when Sybil's braiding kept his hand from gaining anything but a few wisps. His gaze returned to hers. "Hmm, I'll have to finish this tonight." There was a twinkle in his eye that sent a shiver down her spine.

She did enjoy the way the man kept his word . . .

He paused in the doorway and shot the tailor a stern look. "Something befitting a new bride. We are summoned in two days."

Brute . . .

Her lips curved into a smile as she thought the word. Aye, Cullen McJames was indeed an arrogant brute. But he was much more than that, too. He was a caring husband who provided well for her and his people. There was honor in him and she found that more attractive than anything else. Honor would never age, it would shine forever.

She followed her husband into the great receiving hall of the Scottish court two days later. Her gown shimmered in the candlelight, the silk rustling with every step. Lace fans snapped open as they passed, the whispers rising in volume.

James Stuart awaited them with his queen. Princess Elizabeth stood near her mother, smiling with the contentment of childhood. But Bronwyn hesitated in the aisle before they made it to the end where her king was receiving. A familiar face caught her attention. Bishop Shaman nodded his head toward her from across the way.

"So yer bishop is here as well, I see."

Cullen's face flushed a tiny bit. "Jamie made me promise that ye'd wed me willingly. He'll want a witness for that."

"Is that so?" She narrowed her eyes.

Cullen grinned like a boy once more. "Are ye no even impressed with my cunning?"

"Yer a brute."

"Aye, but I keep my promises." He pulled her closer, uncaring for the rise in conversation as he placed a soft kiss on her lips right in public. "And I promise to love ye, Bronwyn McQuade. Until the day I die."

"Now that is something I plan to hold ye to."

"I hope so, lass. I truly do."

Love . . . insanity or not, it was perfection.

Here's a sneak peek at Donna Kauffman's
HERE COMES TROUBLE, out now from Brava!

The hot, steamy shower felt like heaven on earth as it pounded his back and neck. He should have done this earlier. It was almost better than sleep. Almost. He'd realized after Kirby had left that he'd probably only grabbed a few hours after arriving, and he'd fully expected to be out the instant his head hit the pillow again. But that hadn't been the case. This time it hadn't been because he was worried about Dan, or Vanetta, or anyone else back home, or even wondering what in the hell he thought he was doing this far from the desert. In New England, for God's sake. During the winter. Although it didn't appear to be much of one out here.

No, that blame lay right on the lovely, slender shoulders of Kirby Farrell, innkeeper, and rescuer of trapped kittens. Granted, after the adrenaline rush of finding her hanging more than twenty feet off the ground by her fingertips, it shouldn't be surprising that sleep eluded him, but that wasn't entirely the cause. Maybe he'd simply spent too long around women who were generally over-processed, over-enhanced, and overly made up, so that meeting a regular, everyday ordinary woman seemed to stand out more.

It was a safe theory, anyway.

And yet, after only a few hours under her roof, he'd already become a foster dad to a wild kitten and had spent far more time thinking about said kitten's savior than he had his own host of problems.

Maybe it was simply easier to think about someone else's situation. Which would explain why he was wondering about things like whether or not Kirby could make a go of things with her new enterprise here, what with the complete lack of winter weather they were having. And what her story was before opening the inn. Was this place a lifelong dream? For all he knew, she was some New England trust fund baby just playing at running her own place. Except that didn't jibe with what he'd seen of her so far.

He'd been so lost in his thoughts while enjoying the rejuvenation of the hot shower, that he clearly hadn't heard his foster child's entrance into the bathroom. Which was why he almost had a heart attack when he turned around to find the little demon hanging from the outside of the clear shower curtain by its tiny, sharp nails, eyes wide in panic.

After his heart resumed a steady pace, he bent down to look at her, eye-to-wild-eye. "You keep climbing things you shouldn't and one day there will be no one to rescue you."

He was sure the responding hiss was meant to be ferocious and intimidating, but given the pink-nosed, tiny, whiskered face it came out of, not so much. She hissed again when he just grinned, and started grappling with the curtain when he outright laughed, mangling it in the process.

He swore under his breath. "So, I'm already down one sweater, a shower curtain, and God knows what else you've dragged under the bed. I should just let you hang there all tangled up. At least I know where you are."

However, given that the tiny thing had already had one pretty big fright that day, he sighed, shut off the hot, life-giving spray, and very carefully reached out for a towel. After a quick rubdown, he wrapped the towel around his hips, eased out from the other end of the shower, and grabbed a hand towel. "We'll probably be adding this to my tab, as well." He doubted Kirby's guests would appreciate a bath towel that had doubled as a kitty straitjacket.

"Come on," he said, doing pretty much the same thing he'd done when the kitten had been attached to the front of Kirby. "I know you're not happy about it," he told the now squalling cat. "I'm not all that amped up, either." He looked at the shredded curtain once he'd de-pronged the demon from the front of it and shuddered to think of just how much damage it had done to the front of Kirby.

"Question is . . . what do I do with you now?"

Just then a light tap came on the door. "Mr. Hennessey?"

"Brett," he called back.

"I . . . Brett. Right. I called. But there was no answer, so—"

"Oh, shower. Sorry." He walked over to the door, juggled the kitty bundle, and cracked the door open.

Her gaze fixed on his chest and then scooted down to the squirming towel bundle, right back up to his chest, briefly to his face, then away all together. "I'm—sorry. I just, you said . . . and dinner is—anyway—" She frowned. "You didn't take the cat, you know, into—" She nodded toward the room behind him. "Did something happen?"

"I was in the shower. Shredder here decided to climb the curtain because apparently she's not happy unless she's trying to find new ways to terrify people."

He glanced from the kitten to Kirby's face in time to see her almost laugh and then compose herself. "I'm sorry, really. I shouldn't have let you keep her in the first place. I mean, not that you can't, but you obviously didn't come here to rescue a kitten. I should—we should—just leave you alone." She reached out to take the squirmy bundle from him.

"Does that mean I don't get dinner?"

"What?" She looked up, got caught somewhere about chest height, then finally looked at his face. "I mean, no, no, not at all. I just—I hope you didn't have your heart set on pot roast. There were a few . . . kitchen issues. Minor, really, but—"

"I'm not picky," he reassured her. What he was, he realized, was starving. And not just for dinner. If she kept looking at him like that . . . well, it was making him want to feed an entirely different kind of appetite. In fact . . . He shut that mental path down. His life, such as it was, didn't have room for further complications. And she'd be one. Hell, she already was. "I shouldn't have gotten you to cook anyway. You've had quite a day, and given what The Claw here did to your—*my*—shower curtain—I'll pay for a new one—I can only imagine that you must need more medical attention than I realized."

"Don't worry about that, I'm fine. Here," she said, reaching out for the wriggling towel bundle. "Why don't I go ahead and take her off your hands. I can put her out on the back porch for a bit, let you get, uh, dressed."

Really, she had to stop looking at him like that. Like he was a . . . a pot roast or something. With gravy. And potatoes. Damn he was really hungry. Voraciously so. Did she have any idea how long he'd been on the road? With only himself and the sound of the wind for company? Actually, it had been far longer than that, but he really didn't need to acknowledge that right about now.

Then she was reaching for him, and he was right at that point where he was going to say the hell with it and drag her into the room and the hell with dinner, too . . . only she wasn't reaching for him. She was reaching for the damn kitten. He sort of shoved it into her hands, then shifted so a little more of the door was between them . . . and a little less of a view of the front of his towel. Which was in a rather revealing situation at the moment.

"Thanks," he said. "I appreciate it. I'll go down—*be down*—in just a few minutes." He really needed to shut this door. Before he made her nervous. Or worse. I mean, sure, she was looking at him like he was her last supper, but that didn't mean she was open to being ogled in return by a paying guest. Especially when he was the only paying guest in residence. Even if that did mean they had the house to themselves. And privacy. Lots and lots of privacy. "Five minutes," he blurted, and all but slammed the door in her face.

Crap, if Dan could see him at the moment, he'd be laughing his damn ass off. As would most of Vegas. Not only did Brett happen to play high stakes poker pretty well, but the supporters and promoters seemed to think he was also a draw because of his looks. And no, he wasn't blind, he knew he'd been relatively blessed, genetically speaking, for which he was grateful. No one would choose to be ugly. A least he wouldn't think so.

But while the looks had come naturally, that whole bad boy, cocky attitude vibe that was supposed to go with it had not. Not that he was shy. Exactly.

He was confident in his abilities, what they were, and what they weren't. But confidence was one thing. Arrogance another. And just because women threw themselves at him didn't mean he was comfortable catching them. Mostly due to the fact that he was well aware that women weren't throwing themselves at him because of who he was. But because of what he was. Some kind of quasi-poker rock star. They were batting eyelashes, thrusting cleavage, and passing phone numbers and room keys because of his fame, his fortune, his ability to score freebies from hotels and sponsors, and somewhere on that list, probably his looks weren't hurting him, either.

Nowhere on the list, however, did it appear that getting to know the guy behind the deck of cards and the stacks of chips was of any remote interest.

And there lay the irony.

Don't miss Kathy Love's latest, WHAT A DEMON WANTS, available now . . .

Jude stood in the doorway of a shotgun cottage that looked as if it had fallen out of the pages of a fairytale. He half-expected children in lederhosen to answer the door.

But instead of Hansel or Gretel, the door was jerked open by a tall man, fit and tough enough to be a bodyguard himself.

"Jude Anthony?"

Jude nodded. "Yes."

The man extended his hand. "Maksim Kostova. I'm the one who contacted you on behalf of my sister."

Jude guessed as much. He accepted the man's hand, giving a brief, firm shake. As he released it, he fought the urge to wipe his hand on his pants as if there was something thick and slimy clinging to his fingers.

Demon. That particular preternatural aura affected him more than some others. The energy from Maksim was strong and heavy, coating Jude's palm and fingers, creeping up his arm like a living thing. The Blob from horror movie legend.

Damn, he hated that sensation. He flexed his fingers, trying to subtly shake the sensation off.

Maksim raised an eyebrow, obviously aware that Jude had had some reaction to him, but he didn't inquire. Instead he stepped back, opening the door wider.

"Come in."

Jude moved past him, keeping a good distance between them. This male was clearly a powerful, high ranking demon. Jude could even feel his aura just in passing.

Jude steeled himself to the sensation, but was pleased to step into a fair-sized sitting room. More space was always better.

He could do this. Just a few more jobs, and he'd be done with this life. No more paranormal creatures. No more of this existence. He would reinvent himself.

With renewed determination, he turned his focus away from the demon and to the room they'd just entered. His impression again was that of being in a fairy tale world. Lavender walls, gold brocade furniture, and beaded lamps gave the room a feeling of a princess's private parlor.

But the woman who entered the room was no fairytale character. Not unless fairytales had changed greatly since he'd last read one. She was hugely pregnant, making her hard to miss. Her belly protruded, almost comically large when compared to her slight frame. Then his gaze moved to the tall, dark-haired woman followed the waddling pregnant one.

She was stunning. Definitely princess material here . . . except instead of a flowing gown she wore a faded concert t-shirt which clung to her small, pert breasts and slender midriff.

Dark washed jeans encased her long legs, accentuating the flare of her hips and cupping what he had no doubt was a great ass—not that he could see that, but he just knew. Pale bare feet with her toes painted cherry red peeped out from under the cuffs of her jeans.

Jude's body tensed at the sight of her, very aware—of her.

Just an observation, he told himself. What he was paid to do. Notice—things. But his body told him it was more than a detached opinion. He reacted. Instantly. Viscerally.

Don't let this be Ellina Kostova. Please don't let this be her.

He tried to ignore his response, relieved when Maksim

spoke. "Jude, this is my wife, Jo," Maksim said, gesturing to the very pregnant woman, drawing Jude's attention away from the beauty.

His wife stepped forward and offered her hand. The briefest touch revealed she was human. A welcome sensation after making contact with her husband. No supernatural residue there.

But of course, Maksim redirected him back to the other woman. "And this is Ellina, my sister. The one you will be protecting."

Shit. He'd been hoping this wasn't her. She certainly didn't fit his image of Ellina Kostova, the recluse, the eccentric author who preferred to stay in her world of demons, monsters and other things that went bump in the night.

He hadn't expected her to be so young . . . or so lovely. She had an almost ethereal quality to her features. Full lips, large pale eyes, creamy skin.

She moved closer and offered a hand to him. Her fingers were slender, elegant. A beautiful hand.

But she was paranormal, he reminded himself. So really, would she be anything less than perfection? On the outside, at least. That was the way of preternaturals.

He reached for her hand, waiting for the same clinging, distasteful aura to encompass him. The aura that would remind him that not all things were as beautiful on the inside as they were on the outside. He knew from the information her brother had given him that she was only half-demon, but half was all it would take for his preternatural awareness to kick in.

But instead of that sickening, clinging, creeping sensation, her touch sent tingles up his arm. Tangible, electric pulses. Pulses that were anything but unpleasant.

As if in utter synch, they released each other, both stepping back from one another.

But unlike him, Ellina didn't show any outward reaction to the touch. Her lovely face was as serene as a mannequin. Certainly she didn't show any indication she'd felt the same shockwaves passing between them. Instead her pale eyes roamed over him, taking very obvious inventory, although her expression revealed nothing of her thoughts. Just an assessment. Testing his musculature, his strength. Like appraising a horse about to be purchased.

Except he was no stoic equine. His body tightened further. His mind imaging what her fingers would feel like moving over him. Those tiny pulses radiating from her fingers into him.

His spine straightened, and he forced his attention, and his reaction, away from the woman who'd managed to affect him more with one fleeting brush of her fingers than hundreds of paranormals before her.

He turned to Maksim.

"I'm sorry. I'm not the right man for this job."

And be on the lookout for
INSTANT TEMPTATION by Jill Shalvis,
coming soon from Brava . . .

"I didn't invite you in, T.J."

He just smiled.

He was built as solid as the mountains that had shaped his life, and frankly had the attitude to go with it, the one that said he could take on whoever and whatever, and you could kiss his perfect ass while he did so. She'd seen him do it too, back in his hell-raising, misspent youth.

Not that she was going there, to the time when he could have given her a single look and she'd have melted into a puddle at his feet.

Had melted into a puddle at his feet. Not going there . . .

Unfortunately for Harley's senses, he smelled like the wild Sierras; pine and fresh air, and something even better, something so innately male that her nose twitched for more, seeking out the heat and raw male energy that surrounded him and always had. Since it made her want to lean into him, she shoved in another bite of ice cream instead.

He smiled. "I saw on Oprah once that women use ice cream as a substitute for sex."

She choked again, and he resumed gliding his big, warm hand up and down her back. "You watch Oprah?"

"No. Annie was, and I overheard her yelling at the TV that women should have plenty of both sex *and* ice cream."

That sounded exactly like his Aunt Annie. "Well, I don't need the substitute."

"No?" he murmured, looking amused at her again.

"No!"

He hadn't taken his hands off her, she couldn't help but notice. He still had one rubbing up and down her back, the other low on her belly, holding her upright, which was ridiculous, so she smacked it away, doing her best to ignore the fluttering he'd caused and the odd need she had to grab him by the shirt, haul him close and have her merry way with him.

This was what happened to a woman whose last orgasm had come from a battery operated device instead of a man, a fact she'd admit, oh *never.* "I was expecting your brother."

"Stone's working on Emma's 'honey do' list at the new medical clinic, so he sent me instead. Said to give you these." He pulled some maps from his back pocket, maps she needed for a field expedition for her research. When she took them out of his hands, he hooked his thumbs in the front pockets of his Levi's. He wore a T-shirt layered with an opened button-down that said *Wilder Adventures* on the pec. His jeans were faded nearly white in the stress spots, of which there were many, nicely encasing his long, powerful legs and lovingly cupping a rather impressive package that was emphasized by the way his fingers dangled on his thighs.

Not that she was looking.

Okay, she was looking, but she couldn't help it. The man oozed sexuality. Apparently some men were issued a handbook at birth on how to make a woman stupid with lust. And he'd had a lot of practice over the years.

She'd watched him do it.

Each of the three Wilder brothers had barely survived their youth, thanks in part to no mom and a mean, son-of-a-bitch father. But by some miracle, the three of them had come out of it alive and now channeled their energy into Wilder Adventures, where they guided clients on just about any outdoor adventure that could be imagined; heli-skiing, extreme mountain biking, kayaking, climbing, *anything*.

Though T.J. had matured and found success, he still gave off a don't-mess-with-me vibe. Even now, at four in the afternoon, he looked big and bad and tousled enough that he might have just gotten out of bed and wouldn't be averse to going back.

It irritated her. It confused her. And it turned her on, a fact that drove her bat-shit crazy because she was no longer interested in T.J. Wilder.

Nope.

It'd be suicide to still be interested. No one could sustain a crush for fifteen years.

No one.

Except, apparently, her. Because deep down, the unsettling truth was that if he so much as directed one of his sleepy, sexy looks her way, her clothes would fall right off.

Again.

And wasn't that just her problem, the fact that once upon a time, a very long time ago, at the tail end of T.J.'s out-of-control youth, the two of them had spent a single night together being just about as intimate as a man and woman could get. Her first night with a guy. Definiitely not his first. Neither of them had been exactly legal at the time, and only she'd been sober.

Which meant only she remembered.